Books by Margaret Allison

The Last Curve
Promise Me
Indiscretion

Published by POCKET BOOKS

MARGARET ALLISON

THE LAST CURVE

POCKET BOOKS

New York   London   Toronto   Sydney   Tokyo   Singapore

An *Original* Publication of POCKET BOOKS

POCKET BOOKS, a division of Simon & Schuster Inc.
1230 Avenue of the Americas, New York, NY 10020

ISBN: 0-671-56326-2

First Pocket Books printing May 1999

10 9 8 7 6 5 4 3 2 1

ihumw

POCKET and colophon are registered trademarks of Simon & Schuster Inc.

Front cover illustration by Greg Harlin—Wood Ronsaville Harlin, Inc.

Printed in the U.S.A.

QB/✗

For Brian, always

Acknowledgments

I'd like to thank my friend Cindy Haworth, Victim Advocate for the state's attorney's office, for the hours she spent answering questions, giving tours, and making introductions. Thanks also to Homicide Detective Richard Alban, who patiently explained the investigation process. (Any errors in this book are mine and mine alone.) A special thanks to my dad, Dr. Randall Guttridge, for taking me to the target range and teaching me how to shoot a gun. I'm also tremendously grateful to Pam Ronsaville and Greg Harlin at Wood Ronsaville Harlin, Inc. for the beautiful cover of this book. Finally, thanks to my husband, Brian, for patiently listening, editing, and breathing life into characters.

THE LAST CURVE

Prologue

Friday, May 10, 1988
Annapolis, Maryland

THE OLD ELM TREE STOOD INCHES AWAY FROM THE SMALL WOOD cottage, its branches towering over the roof and shadowing the porch. It was in these shadows he stood, waiting.

He leaned back against the house and reached under his wool mask, using his gloved finger to wipe away some of the sweat gathered on his brow. Annapolis had been suffering an unseasonable heat wave that had hit the entire East coast. Now, at midnight, it was eighty degrees but the humidity made it feel more like ninety.

He tensed and stood up straight as thunder sounded in the distance and a thick blanket of clouds slid over the moon, casting the world around him in complete darkness. A rain storm could sabotage his plan. Water

1

would create mud, which would mean footprints. He pulled back his long-sleeve black shirt and checked his watch. Almost one. *Relax*, he commanded. There might still be time.

He thought back to that very morning when, dressed only in a pair of shorts, he had sailed his small Catalina 22 on the Chesapeake Bay. Due to the unusually calm sea he had been able to do a trial run several times, each time maneuvering his boat with more skill. Practice made perfect. He had no trouble making it into the cove this evening—despite the dark.

The boat trip was just one of the many ways he had prepared. The time and effort he had put into his expedition had left him confident, though he had only hunted small game before.

He realized what he was about to attempt was still dangerous, of course; he wasn't insane. But he had analyzed the situation carefully and decided that the ultimate thrill was worth any risk.

If the anticipation creeping through his body was any indication, he had guessed right. He had experienced this euphoria once before, hunting fox with his father. Although he had been only nine years old, he remembered the excitement of the chase as though it was only yesterday: the look on his father's face as he fired at the already wounded animal, the moment of ultimate glory when the fox, still struggling for life, had lain helpless, whimpering at his father's feet. His father had handed him the rifle and given him the honor of stilling the creature. When the gun exploded and the fox stopped moving, he had been filled with a sense of power, a sense of glory unlike anything he had experienced since.

His father had clipped off a piece of the fox's tail for him to keep as a souvenir. In the years since, that tail had become one of his most beloved possessions. He spent hours admiring it, closing his eyes and holding the soft fur to his nose. But although he had done his best to recreate the exact sensation of the kill, he had been unsuccessful. In fact, a month after he shot the fox he attempted to reenact the same scene with his mother's cat. It had been a disappointing experience, mostly because the animal had not run from him, and had not shown any type of real fear. And of course, he had not had a gun, but had used his own hands. He had left the cat in his father's office chair—a surprise for him when he returned home from work. He knew his father would be pleased. After all, he had often complained about the irritating animal.

But his father had not been pleased—he had been furious. He had grabbed a shovel and ordered him to carry the lifeless cat into the woods. After they had walked for twenty minutes in silence, slowly making their way deep into the forest, his father handed him the shovel and commanded him to dig a hole. With every stroke of the shovel his father made him yell, "I'm sorry!" *I'm sorry, I'm sorry, I'm sorry.* . . .

The hole was at least three feet wide and two feet

deep when his father instructed him to lie down inside it. He had curled his sweaty, small, lanky form into a tight ball, tears running down his face as he quietly whispered for mercy. His father stood there a while, staring at him with a look of disgust. Finally, as if giving up, his father shook his head and offered him his hand. As he climbed out of the hole, his father had unceremoniously dumped the cat inside and covered it with the loose dirt.

Almost immediately he heard his mother calling for her beloved cat. His father glanced at him and shook his head as he said tiredly, *"Never, ever kill the things you or someone you care about love."*

He had remembered that commandment when planning this moment. He did not love this woman, in fact, he barely knew her. He knew her only from examining her habits, from watching her, following her. He knew her well enough to know that her roommate was gone tonight, that any moment her Ford Escort would pull into the driveway and she would step out, searching her purse for her keys.

He adjusted the black ski mask, a souvenir from a skiing trip last winter. The rough wool was scratching his face, but he didn't dare take it off. It would be foolish to give into a momentary feeling of weakness.

Frannie. . . .

He had grown infatuated with her. They were, after all, about to share an experience that would transform his life.

The sound of wheels hitting the gravel driveway alerted him to her arrival. He crouched down, holding his bag close to him as a surge of sexual energy tore through him. His lips tightened in anticipation as he ran through a mental checklist. *Boat:* hidden underneath some brush on the beach. *Utilities?* He obsessively pulled open his small black leather briefcase and checked its contents once more. A small gun. A large roll of silver duct tape. And a sharp, new pair of scissors. Satisfied, he shut his bag as he skipped to the next item: *Trap.* He had unscrewed the light bulb on the porch so when Frannie turned off her headlights, the entrance would be cloaked in darkness.

Frannie Garret's small, black car stopped in front of the house. The engine shut off and a second later she appeared from inside the car, petite and pretty as ever, with large brown eyes and short brown hair. She was wearing tight black jeans and a snug-fitting white T-shirt, her uniform at the local bar where she spent five nights a week. As if to tease him, she paused to rub her eyes. He had worried that the absence of the porch light might disturb her, but instead she was relaxed and comfortable, like a kitten stretching before her nap. He knew she had to be tired. She spent three days a week at Loyola Law School in Baltimore and on those days had just enough time to change her clothes before heading off to work.

She was humming softly to herself as she pulled her heavy handbag out of the car.

Come to me Frannie, he willed her. *Come closer.*

She stopped.

He felt his heart miss a beat. Had she heard him? Could she sense him?

She glanced around the front of the house suspiciously. And then with what appeared to be almost a shrug, she opened her purse and pulled out her house key.

She stepped up on the front porch and let her purse drop as she stuck the key in the lock.

Before she had a chance to turn it, he was behind her. He grabbed her by the neck and threw her down. She started to scream and a loud smack from his leather gloves resounded through the air as he hit her across the face.

He yanked her up and crushed her head in toward him. He whispered the words he had practiced saying in the mirror this morning: *Don't move or I'll kill you.*

He could feel her trembling in his arms. He ran his large, gloved hands over her soft hair. She seemed so fragile, so delicate. Then, still holding her up against him, almost as if he was comforting her, he pulled a piece of pre-cut duct tape out of his bag. Frannie kicked him as she pulled back. In an instinctual rage he threw her down on the ground once more, causing her head to whack against the cement block floor.

As she moaned he gently lifted up her head and stretched the duct tape over her mouth. He then took another piece and wrapped it around her wrists, tying them together. *I've caught you,* he whispered.

Grabbing her underneath her arms, he began to drag her toward the woods. Every time she struggled he would hit her, just to let her know that he was not the type of guy she could push around. Frannie Garret would not be a stubborn girl for long.

1

JAN'S CASE WAS EXPLODING IN FRONT OF HER EYES.

She took a step back and gave herself a moment to think as she muttered, "The court's indulgence," a standard phrase used when a lawyer needs to catch his or her breath in the middle of questioning. She scanned through her papers, stalling for time as she thought about her next question. Her witness, in fact, was also the victim—the woman whose rights Jan was trying to protect. Unfortunately, it was this frail woman, not more than a girl actually, who was responsible for the problem.

Jan's client was shaking not because she was frightened, but because she was a drug-addicted prostitute who was experiencing a withdrawal so intense, her

9

ability to testify was in question. Jan held herself responsible for the girl's pain. After all, Jan had told her that she would not prosecute the case unless she agreed to be stone-cold sober for the court date. Jan knew her case was in trouble. If the jurors felt that her client's testimony was unreliable, they might just side with the defendant, who had pled not guilty. He was claiming that he had promised her drugs for sex and when he refused to give her the entire bag of crack as promised, she, in a drug-induced haze, had gone crazy and called the police.

But, as usual, Jan knew things she couldn't tell the jury. Like the fact that the defendant, Walter Harbert, had a long and nasty record. He was suspected of brutally murdering at least two other prostitutes in Anne Arundel county alone.

Jan glanced at the jury. Her client had just finished telling them the story of how Harbert had abducted her and taken her to a desolate part of a Maryland state forest where he had brutally raped her. The jury looked bored, and more than one of them could be seen glancing at the clock as if worried their lunch hour might be infringed upon.

"Okay," Jan said softly. "After he was finished did he let you go?"

"He told me he was going to play Pin the Tail on the Donkey, only with a bullet—and I was the donkey. He said he'd give me a head start to run away, but told me he'd kill me for sure if I ran back toward the car. He said if I ran in the other direction, he might just let me go. So he shot his gun in the air and told me to run."

"And what did you do?"

"I grabbed my clothes and ran into the woods. I didn't even bother to get dressed until I was far away. Then I put them back on and started to head back toward the road."

Now for the climax. Jan paused as she leaned forward. "Do you see the man in the courtroom today that did this to you?"

She nodded.

"Will you point to him?"

The girl raised a short, slender finger and pointed to the tall, bearded man sitting next to his attorney. "That's him," she said. And then she proceeded to throw up.

"And then what happened?"

Jan glanced at Nick Fitzgerald as she put down her sandwich. Nick had interrupted her lunch, barging into the conference room just as she and Dave Newcombe, a fellow assistant state's attorney, pulled their deli sandwiches out of their white paper bags. It might have been bad timing, or a lack of consideration, but Nick was the state's attorney and that made him boss. He could ask questions wherever and whenever he wanted. She said, "The judge called a recess and everyone cleared out while it was being cleaned up."

Nick shook his head. "What a mess."

Just then Hank Nagimy entered, a homicide detective who was killing time before they were needed at the courthouse for testimony. Jan had known Hank for years and she liked him. He looked and sounded like a character from a gritty cop TV show: mid-fifties, short and balding with a big, friendly mouth and a thick Baltimore accent. "Hey," Hank said, holding back a chuckle. "Heard about what happened."

Jan rolled her eyes. She pulled a dry, shriveled pickle out of her bag. "Anyone want this?" she asked, waving it around.

"Who was the judge?" asked Hank.

"Peters."

Hank grinned. Peters was known as one of the toughest and fastest moving judges in the courts. He didn't like delays and once a case began, he often rushed through it for the sake of efficiency and out of respect for the jurors. Peters, more than any other judge, would be annoyed by an incident like that.

"What was the jury's reaction?" Nick asked.

"The old lady seemed sad for her. The rest were grossed out." She bit into her sandwich, still holding their attention. "Maybe even horrified."

"Poor GI," Hank said, referring to her by her nickname. He had christened Jan "GI" after an incident in which Jan had fought off a would-be purse snatcher in downtown Baltimore. Jan had been walking down the street with the deputy state's attorney when a burly seventeen-year-old boy had attempted to snatch her purse. She had fought him off with a swift kick to the side, knocked him down and held him there until the police arrived. Once the story started circulating around the office it became so twisted that one version even had Jan repeating lines from *Dirty Harry* as she wrestled the kid to the ground.

The truth of the matter was that Jan had studied karate in college, and although she was no blackbelt, she knew some basic moves. That, coupled with her aggressive nature in court, had earned her the nickname. Hank continued, "Did they think she was throwing up because of her dismay at having to face the rapist or because she was going through withdrawal?"

"I don't know," Jan quipped. "I thought the judge might frown on me taking a poll."

"Where's the girl now?" Nick asked.

"Angie took her back to the hospital," she said, referring to Angie Pantky, the victim advocate.

"Who're you calling next?" Dave asked, then swallowed nearly half of his tuna fish sandwich in one bite.

"Hank," she said, motioning toward her friend. "I'll ask him about Harbert's flight from the police and grill him on all the lies Harbert told when he was picked up."

She pushed her chair back and stood up. "I'm going to run. I'll see you over there, Hank. By the way," she said, hesitating, "I heard you were finally assigned a new partner."

"I heard they had to get one from Baltimore. No one here wanted the job," Dave teased.

"That's about it," Hank said. "All too smart."

"How's he working out?" Jan asked.

Hank shrugged. "Fine enough. I think you'll be happy."

"What?" Jan asked, confused.

"As my wife said, 'he's not bad on the eyes.'"

Jan blushed. "Why would I care—"

"Nice legs?" Dave asked, playing along.

"Better than my wife's," Hank said.

"Jan," Nick said impatiently. "Come into my office, would you? I want to go over some things."

So eager was she to escape the conversation, she practically jumped up. It seemed like nowadays everyone was trying to fix her up. It was as if they felt sorry for her—single, lonely Jan.

But she wasn't lonely, she thought defensively. She had her friends, her career, and besides, she wasn't going to date just anybody. Dating for the sake of dating was a waste of time. She hated it. Awkward chit-chat, the uncomfortable moment of staring at the bill as it lay open on the table, waiting to see if he called her afterwards. No, she thought, following Nick down the hall. Dating was for the birds. She wasn't going to go on another date unless she was already madly in love with the guy.

Nick led her into his office and shut the door. Jan smiled as she glanced at his outfit. He was decked out in white: white shirt, white tie, white linen pants. Nick liked his clothes. He reminded Jan of a movie star from the thirties, the type of guy who seduced women while wearing a smoking jacket and drinking a martini. He went through periods where he wore monochromatic outfits, and though he had begun to experiment with new combinations, he still liked to return to the blue suit with the blue shirt and the blue tie, or the creme colored suit with the creme shirt and the creme tie. On those days, he would make color-oriented puns and though the jokes would become tired, he would always enjoy them. Some days he would bring flowers, in that same color, and drop one on the desks of all the women in his office. Today every woman had arrived at work to find a white tulip on her desk.

Nick had been the state's attorney for eight years and had just announced this was to be his last term. Everyone knew why he was leaving. He was a rising star in the Democratic party and Senator Thurman's handpicked golden boy for his replacement. When the senator retired, he planned to transfer his powerful political base over to Nick.

Jan had met Nick ten years ago, when he was an assistant state's attorney responsible for prosecuting her sister's rapist, Curtis Custin. After her sister's death, Nick had rallied to her side, taking her under his wing and encouraging her to continue with her plans to attend law school. When she had needed a job, he had been there to offer her one.

Throughout the years they maintained an entirely platonic friendship, though Nick had made some discreet advances. Jan hadn't taken offense, in fact she had been flattered. She wished she returned his affection. But despite the fact that he was a wealthy, good-looking, forty-two-year-old bachelor, never married—she couldn't imagine dating him. She cared about him like a brother and the thought of kissing him was more ridiculous than anything else. He just seemed too, well, fussy for her, with his outfits and eccentricities. But still, women adored him. His easy charm and warm smile inspired women to slip him their business cards with their home phone numbers handwritten on top.

Nick said, "That was good thinking, bringing up her drug use before the defense. I'd also point out in your closing arguments that Harbert picked her for a reason. He picked her *because* she was a prostitute. That's why he didn't get rid of his weapon. He didn't think he had to. He never thought a drug-addicted prostitute would have the balls to go to the police."

Jan put her hand on the door as she glanced away from his deep green eyes. "Thanks, Nick," she said, anxious to get out of there. "But I already mentioned that."

He smiled. "I figured. How are you going to handle the jury?"

"What do you mean?"

"I mean regarding the way your client—what's her name?"

"Terry. Terry Turnbull."

16

"Regarding the dramatic way Ms. Turnbull left the courtroom."

Jan gave a little shrug and said, "What do you think?"

"I think you should apologize to the court and mention that she's been admitted to the hospital again. Try and work in some sympathy by letting the jurors know how physically difficult this was for her."

"Got it," Jan said. She liked the way Nick thought. "Anything else?" she asked politely.

"Yeah," he said, his voice softening. "How are you? Everything okay?" Nick had a way of connecting with a person that made them feel as if they were the only one in the world that mattered. She knew this was a habit of many successful politicians, yet she still felt embarrassed by the attention.

Blushing, she said, "Fine, Nick. Thanks. Just fine."

"I'm sorry we haven't had time to go to lunch lately."

She forced a smile. "Don't worry about it. I know you're busy."

He strummed his fingers on the desk. "Okay. Go get 'em. Bring me back Harbert's head."

She gave him a quick salute before marching out.

Jan sat in the courtroom watching the jury file in. Hank had been on the stand most of the afternoon, first as a witness for the prosecution, then as a witness for the defense. Harbert's attorney had presented a weak defense, basically trying to prove that when Harbert had initially denied ever having met Jan's client, much less had sex with her, he had done so simply because he had been frightened by the interrogation tactics of a mean and nasty police force.

Jan finished her closing statement a little after four. She strolled the short distance back to her office, taking her time as she imagined the jury settling in to weigh all the evidence in the lengthy police report. But at five o'clock she received a call from the courthouse that the verdict was in. She grabbed her suit jacket and scurried back.

The remarkably brief deliberation could mean one of two things: either she had done a better job than she thought, or she had done even worse than her opponent.

As she stood in front of the judge, she wondered if she too would lose her quickly eaten lunch all over Judge Peters' Lysol-disinfected room. She always fought nausea in the moments before a verdict was read. Nick had advised her to depersonalize herself from her cases, but she didn't seem able. In the seven years she had worked for the state, she had put her heart and soul into convicting these criminals and protecting their victims—past, present, and future. Each case was a quiet homage to her older sister, who had been a victim of a violent rape when she was only twenty-six years old. Frannie never recovered from the brutality of the attack, and on the day after her rapist's conviction, her naked body was found floating in the

Chesapeake Bay. The coroner had ruled her death a suicide, but Jan always had a tough time believing that her sister had intentionally taken her own life.

As the judge sat down behind his desk, Jan pushed these thoughts out of her mind so she could focus on the proceedings. She always thought of Frannie when the verdict came in.

"Ladies and gentlemen of the jury, have you reached a verdict?"

A small, elderly lady stood up and politely said, "Yes, Your Honor."

The bailiff took the paper out of her hand and handed it to the judge. The judge read the verdict and handed it back to the bailiff. "You may read the verdict," he said to the forewoman.

Jan paused, holding her breath.

"We find the defendant, Walter Harbert, on the charge of rape, not guilty."

Not guilty. After seven years of victories, she had finally lost a case. It felt even worse than she had imagined.

Almost instinctively she glanced toward the criminal—the rapist who had just been set free.

He caught her eyes. The corners of his mouth curled up into a smug grin. Still holding her captive in his gaze, he winked.

2

WHAT A DISGUSTING MAN, SHE THOUGHT, HEADING FOR THE parking structure. Just the fact that he had looked at her made her feel like she needed a shower.

Court had recessed two hours ago, yet she felt even worse than she had when the verdict was read. She knew that every attorney lost a case sooner or later, but that didn't make it any easier. She had done her best to distract herself with the mountain of paperwork on her desk, but her mind kept drifting back to the devastation in Terry's voice when Jan informed her they lost.

Jan entered the parking lot structure and headed toward the stairwell even though she was parked on the fourth floor. She never had the patience to wait for the elevator and tonight she was unusually rushed. She only had half an hour to get to the hospital before visiting hours were over.

Keeping this in mind, she practically ran up the steps, her briefcase swinging by her side.

She flew around the curve in the stairwell and crashed into a man headed down. As her briefcase went flying he grabbed her around the waist, catching her before she toppled down the stairs. "Whoa there," he said.

Jan glanced up at him. He was tall and muscular, with thick wavy brown hair and hazel eyes. "I'm sorry," she said, pulling away as she straightened her skirt self-consciously. "Are you all right?"

"Fine," he said, giving her a half-smile as he dodged down the steps, picking up the papers that had toppled out of her briefcase.

"Thanks but that's not necessary," she said. "I can get it." She checked her watch. Twenty-six minutes until visiting hours were over.

He didn't respond. Instead, he scooped up some papers and slipped them back into a folder. "Here you go, Counselor."

Counselor. He had obviously learned she was a lawyer by glancing at the papers he had helped her pick up. Papers which were confidential.

Jan took the folder from him and said coldly, "I'm sorry. Have we met?"

"As a matter of fact, no. But I couldn't help noticing your name," he said, motioning to the papers he had just handed her. "I've heard quite a bit about you."

She stopped stuffing papers back in her briefcase and glanced up at him, surprised. "You have?"

21

Hank's voice boomed behind her, "Holy crap, GI. What the hell happened here? Looks like you lost all your love notes."

Suddenly she realized who she was standing in front of. "I was just introducing myself to your new partner," she said. She shot him a professional smile and stuck out her hand. "I'm Jan Garret."

He gave her hand a squeeze and held on for a second too long. "I know," he said. "Max Hale."

Most men were intimidated by her, at least at first, but that did not seem to be the case here. She had to admit he was extremely attractive, so attractive that he probably thought he was pretty hot stuff. He also looked young, a big homicide detective before he cracked thirty. He was probably still flashing his badge in bars to impress women. Amused, she pulled her hand away. She picked up her briefcase and swung it back over her shoulder. "I have to run."

"Where to?"

"I've got to see a client," she said, continuing her run up the stairs. She called back down to them, "See ya later. Nice meeting you, Detective."

"That girl," Hank laughed, shaking his head in admiration. "She's like the Energizer Bunny." He glanced at his partner. Max was still staring after her, his lips pursed together as if thinking. "Oh boy," Hank said. "I know what that look means."

"What are you talking about?" he asked, jamming his hands back in his pockets as he continued up the stairs.

"Hey I may have been married for twenty years, mister, but I ain't dead—yet, at least."

Max shot him a little grin. "She's a lot younger than I expected."

"And better looking too, right?"

"Not that it matters," Max said quickly.

"Of course not."

"Is she—"

"Single? Yup. But almost every guy around here's made a play for her at one time or another and she's shot 'em all down. Fitzgerald took a shot at her and even he didn't get anywhere. Don't get me wrong though. She's not . . . well, you know," he said, nodding as he jerked his head.

"Gay?"

Hank winced. "For crissakes. I'm just trying to say that she's a tough nut to crack."

"I wasn't really asking about that. I just wanted to know if she was a good attorney."

"Yeah, sure," Hank said, huffing and puffing as they reached the ground floor. "Next time, we take the elevator, okay? Man, I can't take this shit," he said, pausing to pull out a cigarette. "She's the best. Aggressive and smart as a whip. Been here for years and never lost a case. Except for today," he said, taking a drag from his cigarette. "Except for today."

3

SIMPSON BROWN WALKED DOWN THE DESERTED BAY RIDGE Beach with his pail and shovel. It was nine o'clock Sunday morning and his mother, already overwhelmed with his younger brother and sister, had suggested Simpson look for shells. She had no qualms about him playing on the beach by himself. After all, their house overlooked the beach and besides that, this was Bay Ridge. Nothing bad ever happened here.

He focused his eyes on the pale yellow sand as he walked, half-talking to himself. Homer Simpson was what the kids at camp called him, if they called him anything at all. Tomorrow was show-and-tell and Simpson was hoping to find something cool to bring in, like maybe a dead crab or something. Something that would impress them.

He sat down in the sand and gazed out at the water. That's when he first saw it. It looked like a big fish or something, just bobbing up and down. He stood up and walked closer to the water's edge. It wasn't a fish, he realized. It was a person, somebody swimming in the water. They were right at the edge of the dock.

He stepped up on the dock and stopped halfway. Whoever it was sure knew how to hold their breath.

His mother opened up the sliding glass door and yelled down to him.

"Simpson! Get back on the beach," she said.

"Just a minute, Mom. I found something."

"Now," his mother commanded.

Ignoring his mother, Simpson walked to the end of the dock and peeked over. It looked like a lady floating in the water. The strange thing was, she wasn't wearing a top. And her eyes were open, too.

Cool, thought Simpson. *Let's see if the kids can top this.*

4

"HEY, GI," DAVE SAID, STOPPING AT JAN'S OFFICE. "DID YOU have a nice weekend?"

"I worked."

"That doesn't quite qualify." He stepped inside the office to let coworkers pass. It was almost nine and everyone was just getting to work, their light cotton suits already soaked in sweat. "Hot enough for you?" he asked. "I heard it hit a hundred and one yesterday."

"Wow," Jan said as if she hadn't even heard him.

Dave sat in the chair across from her, his damp shirt automatically sticking to the vinyl. He sneezed.

"God bless you."

"It's the damn air-conditioning," he said. "I hate this time of year. Hot as hell outside and freezing cold inside. I'm surprised we all don't have pneumonia."

26

"I hear you," she said, still staring blindly at the paper in front of her.

He leaned forward and grinned, giving his shirt room to breathe. "So no *hot* dates this weekend?"

"Hardly," she said, glancing toward him. "Why?"

"You seemed all agitated or something on Friday."

"Must have been the afterglow from losing that case."

"Oh yeah," he said, grimly. "How did she take it? The hooker?"

Jan winced. "Please don't call her that."

"All right. The victim—how'd she take it?"

"She's devastated. Worried that he's going to come back and kill her." She shook her head. "Quite frankly, I'm not so sure she's wrong."

"He'll leave her alone. He knows that if he did get her we'd be after him."

"Oh, yeah. I'm sure he's really scared of me." She glanced toward the window. "He had one of the worst attorneys I've ever worked with and he still got off."

Dave tried to think of something he could say to comfort her, but all he could come up with was, "You're a great attorney, Jan." When he first started working with Jan, he had a little bit of a crush on her. Although nothing ever materialized romantically, they did end up forming a close brother-sister type relationship. He would ask questions, share problems, and she would encourage him or offer advice. She had been a huge help to him, and now he was happy to try and do the same for her.

"I stink. I didn't persuade them that my client was a victim. I don't think they bought Harbert's defense. I think they thought since she was drug user and a prostitute she got what she deserved."

"Give yourself a break. Sometimes shit happens. There's absolutely nothing you could've done." He paused and said, "Sometimes the system just fails." He nodded to himself. Now *that* was a good thing to say.

She shrugged.

"Hey—you lost a case. It's not the end of the world."

"Maybe not for me. But for Terry . . ." Her voice trailed off. "You should've seen her yesterday."

"Back on drugs."

"Oh yeah," she said sadly.

"Jan," he said softly. "Even if you had won that case she'd still be doing drugs. Did you think you were going to save her?"

"She's had a tough life. I wanted to give her some hope, some . . . oh, cripes," she said, trying to shrug it off. "Bet you're glad you stopped in here this morning. I'm really cheery, aren't I?"

"Hey, you just lost your first case here. I knew you'd be bummed. Now, if you were used to losing cases like me, it wouldn't have fazed you." He laughed.

She smiled at him warmly. "So what about you— good weekend?"

He shrugged. "I went to that new seafood place in Eastport . . ."

"Morrow's?"

"Right. It was great."

"Sounds nice. Who'd you go there with?"

He shrugged.

"You had a date," she said, almost gleefully. Dave had moved to Annapolis earlier that year and she had felt bad that this quiet, good-natured guy seemed to spend most of his time by himself. He was a good enough looking man, handsome in an all-American football player sort of way; big and beefy with short blond hair and small blue eyes. He hadn't dated much because he was painfully infatuated with her closest friend and co-worker, Sheila Smith. Jan could understand why. Sheila was the type of woman who seemed to have it all together. She was gorgeous and tall, with a body any model would envy. She was smart and funny, dressed beautifully and seemed to radiate confidence. She was also a terrific flirt—a talent which years of cheerleading in high school and college had honed. But Sheila, who could've married any man she wanted, had chosen a handsome lothario who couldn't seem to keep his eyes and hands off other women. Jan had known they were having trouble for years, but Sheila wouldn't consider divorce.

So even though Dave was sweet and funny—perfect for Sheila—he needed to forget his crush and enjoy himself a little.

Of course, she realized, he probably thought the same thing about her.

"Don't sound so surprised," he said.

"What's her name? Do I know her?"

"No, you don't know her," he said quickly, like a little brother who was getting picked on by his older sister.

"How do you know? Annapolis is a small town. What's her name?"

He blushed. "Candy Canoe."

"Candy Canoe? You're making that up!"

He shook his head, grinning.

"She lives in Annapolis, the sailing capital of the world . . ." Jan began in a teasing tone.

"So they say. . . ."

"And her last name is Canoe, and her first name is Candy?"

Dave laughed.

"Sounds promising."

"I'll tell you one thing. . . ."

"What?"

"She sure was sweet."

Jan rolled her eyes. "I'll bet she's never heard that one before."

Sheila poked her head in. "Heard what?"

Dave's eyes lit up as he turned toward her.

"Dave was just about to launch into the lurid details of his dating life."

"Oh?" Sheila said, stepping inside the room and encouraging him. As usual, she looked great, dressed in an Armani cotton suit and cool as a cucumber despite the heat. Jan had always respected a person with a sense of style. She simply didn't possess the ability Nick and Sheila seemed to take for granted. Clothes just weren't her thing. Over the course of her career she had invested in several suits which she planned on wearing until they fell apart at the seams. It's not that she didn't want to look pulled together, but planning outfits and shopping took time, and she would rather use her energy for other things. Keeping up with the current styles wasn't high on her priority list.

Sheila tucked a strand of long, silky brown hair behind her ear and said, "Go on."

"He went out with a woman named Candy on Saturday night."

"Candy, huh? And?"

"I don't think we want to know."

"I want to know," Sheila said, sitting across from him and crossing her long bare legs.

Dave laughed uncomfortably, as he blushed and glanced away. "Her name is Candy and she's sweet."

"Very clever," Sheila said. "Speaking of dates, I just met Hank's new partner." She pretended to fan herself as she smiled and winked at Jan.

"A knockout?" Dave said, playing along as if he wasn't jealous in the least.

"He's all right," Jan said.

"So you've met him," Sheila said, leaning forward.

"Briefly. I, uh, ran into him as I was leaving work on Friday."

"And?"

"And what?" Jan asked, still not looking at her.

31

Sheila grinned.

Jan glanced up at her.

"Am I missing something?" Dave asked.

"What?!" Jan asked Sheila.

"I heard he has great legs," Dave joked.

Sheila said, "I don't know about his legs. But he sure has a nice—"

"Hank!" Jan called out with relief as she noticed her friend hurry by her door.

Hank paused just long enough to give them a quick wave. "Morning all," he said, hurrying off.

"Hey," Jan said, calling him back. "What's your rush?"

"He's got a meeting with Max and Nick," Sheila said.

"What's up?" Dave asked.

Sheila said, "They pulled a floater out of the bay yesterday."

Jan glanced at Hank, who had been silent until now. "Where?"

"Bay Ridge," Sheila replied.

"Suicide?" Jan asked.

Sheila shrugged and glanced at Hank.

"No comment," Hank said uncomfortably, backing up. "Nick in his office?" he asked Jan.

"Don't look at me," Jan said. "So, was it suicide?"

"I need to talk to Nick first," Hank said.

"Has the victim been identified?" She thought about Harbert running around loose, preying on prostitutes.

"No comment," he said, already out the door.

"Hank," she called out, trying to stop him with her voice. "It's not a prostitute, is it?"

"No comment," he yelled from down the hall.

"What's all this 'no comment' baloney?" Jan asked Sheila and Dave. "We'll find out sooner or later."

"From what I heard this isn't a suicide," Sheila said. "They think it's the woman that's missing from Glen Burnie. She's a waitress at . . ."

"Lucky's," Jan said. She had been following this case. Her sister Frannie had been a waitress when she was attacked and that similarity alone was enough to bring back haunting memories. At least Frannie's life had been spared—temporarily. "How was she killed?"

"They're not sure yet. But they know it was murder."

"Why?"

"I heard that she was missing clothes. And she was beat up pretty bad. Of course the crabs had been at her. . . ."

"Oh God," said Dave, grimacing. "I hope they weren't the same ones I ate on Saturday."

Lucy Haverdale had disappeared on Thursday night, the same day Harbert was released. "Any leads?"

"Max has the crew going door to door today," Sheila said, referring to the support staff which consisted primarily of uniformed cops. They canvassed the victim's neighborhood and workplace for clues.

"This is Max's case?" Jan asked as she sat behind her desk.

Sheila nodded. "But don't expect him to give you any information."

"Why?"

"Why? 'Cause Hank always talks and if he's not talking, then you know that something weird is going on. And Max doesn't strike me as the type to gossip."

"I'm not looking for gossip," Jan said.

"You know what I mean."

"C'mon Sheila," Dave said. "Let's let GI get back to work."

Jan knew she'd have a tough time concentrating on anything else until she learned more about this floater. She needed to talk to Max. After all, if this was Harbert's work, she was the expert.

Max glanced down at the medical examiner's report as he drove along Route 50, heading back toward CID. The examiner had confirmed his suspicions. Lucy Haverdale had died from a severe contusion to the back of her head. Her slender wrists had been tied together with duct tape and excepting a small pair of black panties, her body had been stripped of its clothes. She had been dead for almost an hour before someone had slipped her battered body into the warm bay water. Lucy had put up a valiant struggle for her life, bruising her knees and tearing off a fingernail in the process.

Her remaining nails had been scraped and sent to hair and fiber, her vagina had been swabbed and the samples sent to the lab for analysis. Even though the coroner had found evidence of sexual assault, Max doubted they'd be able to get anything. Her body had been in the bay almost forty-eight hours, long enough to wash away any DNA the killer might have left behind.

The only obvious clue the killer had left had been intentional: he had cut her hair. Max had noticed the missing hair when he first examined the body, but he had just assumed that she lost it in her struggle—the killer had grabbed on to her by the hair and pulled it. According to the coroner, he was mistaken. Lucy's hair had been cut with skill and the perp had used either scissors or a knife.

Max slammed on his horn, narrowly avoiding a small yellow car that cut in front of him. As he pulled into the other lane, the driver, a young woman in her twenties, turned and flipped him off. Max shook his head. Some cops he knew would take this opportunity to slam the siren on top of the car and pull the driver over to teach them a lesson. But Max wasn't like that. He was more interested in solving crimes than acting tough.

He exited the expressway on General's Highway and focused once more on the killer's clue. It was possible he had cut Lucy's hair because he knew her and was trying to add insult to injury. Perhaps he felt that killing her simply wasn't good enough. Max thought back to one case in which a man had attacked his girlfriend in a park, stabbing her in a jealous rage. He had then taken her bloodied body and thrown it in a Dumpster—but first, he cut off her long blond hair and hung the hair around a neighboring tree. They may never have found the body if a man walking his dog hadn't noticed the hair amidst the leaves. Her boyfriend had later said that he was sick of his girlfriend always primping and carrying on about all the compliments that she always got about her hair. To him, her hair symbolized her appeal to other men.

There was another possibility, however. In many of the murders Max had worked on, especially those committed by a perp that preyed on strangers, the murderer had kept something that belonged to the victim. In one case the killer had kept the bras of his victims, in another case, the earrings. The killers would actually pull out the memento and admire it every now and then, just as someone would treasure a souvenir. Perhaps, Max thought, Lucy Haverdale's missing hair was serving the same purpose.

Max checked his watch as he pulled into the station. His analysis would have to wait. Tonight was Senator Thurman's retirement party and the sergeant had made it clear that he wanted his homicide detectives there. Max was half an hour late as it was.

He caught himself hoping he would see Jan Garret tonight. He tried to brush the thought from his mind. After all, why should he care if he saw her or not? He had only met her once. But still, he had to admit he had been impressed. It had been a long time since he felt that powerful, immediate attraction to a woman. Jan Garret was just his type, petite with delicate features,

no makeup to hide behind. Smart, feisty, and dedicated.
Stop it.

He was not in a position to get involved with anyone right now in any case—even if she was interested. Heck, he had spent the past few years dodging relationships and the last thing he needed was to start off his new job by having a fling with an important attorney with whom he would be closely working. No, he reminded himself. *No way.*

He parked the car and grabbed his file.

He knew his interest in Jan was dangerous, especially since it was being denied. It could only fester and grow. The best thing to do in a situation like this would be to avoid her, but that was impossible. She had already called him twice that day. He knew that she was just trying to get information, but it was information which he was not at liberty to give. And from what he could tell, that would make little difference to a woman like her. She would stay on him until she got what she wanted.

Unfortunately, it wouldn't make his mission any easier.

Jan grabbed a glass of wine and leaned against the wall, her arms crossed stiffly in front of her. She hated big events. They made her feel almost claustrophobic: all the people closing in around her, all the awkward conversation. She had come only out of respect for the senator. Frannie had just finished an internship in his office when she died, and the senator himself had attended her funeral. She had long been impressed with his politics and found him to be a warm and charismatic man in person, with the same easy charm his protégé, Nick, possessed.

But Nick was more than just a protégé to the senator—he was a second son. John Thurman had become close friends with Nick's father when they were both privates in the marines. When a plane crash claimed both of Nick's parents, the senator had stepped in to ensure the orphaned nine-year-old was taken care of. Nick hadn't needed money—his parents had been millionaires and Nick inherited everything—but he did need a family. The Thurmans had included him on family vacations and long weekends at their beach house. Everyone knew Nick was devoted to the senator.

Her eyes settled on Nick. He was directly across the room, smiling and laughing, all the while shaking hands like the natural politician he was. He really enjoyed these events and it showed. She knew that if she was just meeting Nick for the first time tonight she would consider him superficial—too good-looking and polished. But she was able to see beneath his smooth veneer to the scared little boy who craved acceptance and love. She understood Nick like only a fellow survivor could. They both shared the tragedy of losing everything. Nick had made Senator Thurman into his father, just as she had made Nick into the big brother she never had.

Nick caught her eye. The smile faded from his lips as he raised his glass to her. She nodded and smiled, as if encouraging him to continue with his politicking. She had no desire to join him. Not with all those women ogling him.

She glanced away, looking back toward the door. She was not looking for a familiar face—there were plenty of those. She had lived in this town for seven years and she felt like she was at least acquainted with half of the people crowded into the ballroom. Annapolis was like a small town. Everyone seemed to know everyone else.

She had been happy here the last seven years. She had always loved history and she enjoyed the old brick streets and historical homes and shops in the downtown area. She also appreciated the fact that Annapolis was situated on the mouth of the Chesapeake Bay and the entire county was rich with the creeks and rivers that flowed from it. And if she craved the big city, she had her choice of going to either Baltimore or Washington, each only forty-five minutes away.

She stood up straight, her eyes trained on the door. Max stepped into the ballroom, searching for a familiar face as he shoved his invitation back into his suit coat.

A smile crept up Jan's lips as she remembered running into him the other evening. As much as she hated to admit it, she could still feel the firm pressure of his hands against her back as he held her in his arms.

She took a sip of her wine as she forced herself to look away. She had thought that perhaps he had been flirting with her, but she had been mistaken. After all, he had not even bothered to return her phone calls. He was probably the type of guy who was used to having women fawn over him, and used to calling the shots himself.

Well! she thought, her adrenaline stirring. She wasn't used to being brushed off like that. How dare he not return her calls? She wasn't interested in a date, this was business. She pushed herself off the wall and made her way toward Max, who was now standing at the bar.

She walked up behind him and as he waited for his drink, she ordered another glass of white wine.

He recognized her voice and turned around to face her, stepping away from the bar as he handed her the glass of wine. "Jan," he said, nonchalantly. "How are you?"

"Fine," she said crisply, waiting for him to tell her why he hadn't bothered to call her back. He didn't.

"I called you this morning," she continued. He nodded, as if waiting for her to continue. "I was curious about the girl they found yesterday. Lucy Haverdale. Hank tells me you're handling the case." She had already found out that Lucy had not been a prostitute, nor had she been a drug user—typical of Harbert's victims. But she still hadn't ruled out that Harbert had been involved. The timing of her death with Harbert's release was too much of a coincidence for her to overlook.

"I'm the primary investigator," he said modestly.

"Well, I have some questions."

He paused as he took a sip of his drink. Jan hesitated. He was purposely making her feel as though she was stepping over the line. "Did you make your appointment the other night?"

"My appointment?" she asked. "Oh, yes—thank you. About that floater . . . was there evidence of assault?"

"I don't know much more than was in the paper this afternoon. We haven't finished our investigation yet," Max said. "In fact, we've barely started."

"I usually don't have to get my information out of the paper," she replied, looking him in the eye. The state's attorney's office had an extremely close relationship with the police. They socialized together, their kids played together, they even, on occasion, dated and married each other. They were on the same team: the good guys. Without the police, there wouldn't be any arrests. Without the state's attorneys, criminals would be right back on the streets. Maybe Max needed someone to explain the rules.

"I don't have much to share."

She bit her lower lip as she glanced over his shoulder. Sergeant Frank Netzer, the head of CID, was wandering toward the center of the room carrying a plate filled with little fried balls harpooned with red fringed toothpicks. "Sergeant," she said, waving her old friend over. He wasn't the kind of friend she'd go grab a beer with after work, but she had worked with him for the past seven years and she felt that he trusted her to get the job done. She had always done her best to keep his department informed and she was not the type of person to assign blame, even if she secretly felt the department might not have pursued an investigation the way she felt it was supposed to be conducted. "I was curious about the floater that was pulled out of the bay. The Haverdale girl. Was she assaulted before she died?"

"Looks like it, doesn't it Max?"

Max merely shrugged. Jan thought she could see a mischievous twinkle in his eye, as though he enjoyed teasing her.

The sergeant picked up a toothpick off his plate and held it in the air. "What the hell is this?"

Jan peered at his plate. "Looks like a crab ball to me."

He popped it in his mouth. "No crab ball I've ever had," he said, his mouth full.

"So there were signs of sexual trauma?" Jan said, focusing her attention back on Max.

Max shook his head. "Lack of clothing . . ." he paused and nodded behind her.

"Excuse me, Jan?" a tall, dark-haired, handsome man interrupted.

She turned around to face a man she didn't recognize. "Yes?"

"I'm Ed Thurman."

The senator's son. She had seen pictures of him before, but she had never met him.

"I knew your sister, Frannie, " he continued. "I just wanted to introduce myself."

"It's nice to meet you," Jan said. "I've heard a lot about you." She always liked to meet people who knew Frannie. It helped her to remember her. "Did you know her through . . ."

"My dad . . . and Nicky," he said, fondly referring to Nick. "I was home the summer she interned in my dad's office."

"Of course," she said. How nice of him to make a special point of introducing himself.

"So, Frannie mentioned me?" he asked.

She paused, embarrassed. Her sister hadn't mentioned him, but that was not unusual. Her sister had rarely spoken of her friends and acquaintances to Jan. When their parents had died, Frannie had become a pseudo-mother to Jan—even though she was only four years older. Although Frannie had encouraged Jan to confide in her about friends and boyfriends, Frannie had rarely shared the same information with Jan. And Jan, being younger and more self-involved than her sister, hadn't pursued it. It was something that continued to haunt her to this day.

He laughed, as he interpreted her embarrassed silence. "Apparently not."

She smiled. He appeared to be a warm affable guy. Very similar to his father. She knew the senator was proud of Eddie, and rightfully so. Eddie had avoided the trappings that can befall the children of wealthy and successful parents. He had gone to Harvard and had moved to London shortly after graduation, receiving his Ph.D. in business from Oxford. "You live in Europe, right?" she asked.

"I did. Because of my mother's illness, my wife and I decided to move back to the States—at least temporarily." Everyone knew about Betty Thurman's condition. She had been diagnosed with cancer almost a year ago, and her illness had all but shattered her formidable husband. Their marriage was an unusual one in political circles. It was well known that the Senator was crazy about his wife and relied on her opinion more than those of his well-paid aides. Jan had met Mrs. Thurman several times. Although Betty had always been polite and friendly, Jan found her to be cold and distant, hardly the image projected across the covers of magazines.

"Eddie! You wandered away."

Jan turned around and found herself staring at the star himself, Senator John Thurman. He was in his late sixties but he still carried himself like the marine he once was. He was a handsome man, tall, with a full head of silver grey hair which he kept stylishly trimmed. He may be retiring, Jan thought, but he still looks like a warrior.

"Not far enough," Ed said quietly to Jan. Jan glanced away, certain the senator had heard him and mortified to be in the middle of a potential father-son quarrel. Apparently there were some problems in this seemingly perfect family.

"Sarana was looking for you," the senator said sternly, not yet acknowledging Jan's presence.

Ed glanced around the room, his eyes settling on his wife, an attractive, well-groomed woman wearing a tailored blue suit. "There she is," he said calmly. If he was being reprimanded he didn't seem that worried. "I couldn't find her earlier." He turned back toward Jan. "Nice meeting you," he said, flashing her a smile.

As Eddie walked away, the senator said, "It's good to see you, Jan. I've been hearing some very fine things about you."

"Oh, really?" Jan asked, honestly surprised. Who had he been hearing these things from? Nick?

"I think you've got a bright future in politics, if you're interested."

"I, ah . . ." she stumbled. What did he mean?

"What are your plans when Nick leaves?"

She shrugged. "I haven't really decided. I like what I do, but . . ."

"But the money stinks."

"Not that so much. I just, well, I don't want to get burned out."

"Burned out," he said, making a face as though he didn't understand.

Burned out? What was she saying? She should be listing her accomplishments, buttering him up. Anything but complaining.

"Jan just lost a case," Nick explained, appearing behind her. "First one ever."

"Oh, is that all," the senator said, smiling. "I know how you feel, Jan," he added with a wink. "I felt the same way after I lost a bid for state's attorney back in sixty-two. You've got to jump right back on that horse."

"She's already riding," Nick said. It was true. Her caseload was full. "Senator," Nick said. "I wanted to introduce you to someone."

"Of course," the senator said. "If you'll excuse us," he said, smiling warmly at Jan.

Jan nodded. "Thank you, Senator. And congratulations."

She turned around to continue her conversation with Max and the sergeant, but they had disappeared.

"Damn," she said to herself, taking another sip of wine.

"Hey—where are you headed? Sneaking out?" Hank stood on the steps of the hotel, puffing on a cigar.

Max put up his hands, as if surrendering. "I've made my appearance. Now I've got to get back to work."

"You're making me look bad."

"Like that's hard to do," Max teased.

Hank laughed. "It's going to rain," he said as thunder threatened in the distance.

Max nodded as he pulled off his coat jacket and loosened his tie. It was hot and sticky, the kind of night that inspired people to crank up their air conditioners and stay inside. "Maybe it will break this heat."

"I saw you talking to GI back there," Hank said, glancing up as a bolt of heat lightning lit up the sky.

"She wanted to know about the Haverdale woman."

"She tried to nail me this morning."

"She tried to nail you?"

Hank smiled. "I'm not that lucky." He paused. "So what did you tell her?"

"I didn't tell her anything—but it wasn't easy. She's determined to get the details."

"Like I said, she's a pistol, but she's got a good heart."

Max nodded, uncomfortable talking about Jan but at the same time anxious for more information about her.

"She hasn't had it easy," Hank continued.

"You mean in court?"

"I mean because of her sister. She was raped about ten years ago. The night the perp was sentenced she took off all her clothes and went for a swim in the middle of the bay. They found her the next morning."

Max muttered, "Jesus. Suicide?"

"Accidental suicide. She was drunk. They think she got in the water and couldn't manage to get back in the boat again."

Max glanced back toward the hotel. No wonder Jan was so interested in the Haverdale case.

Hank continued, "Her sister was just the icing on the cake. When she was a kid her dad was killed in a car accident. Her mom knocked herself off right after."

"Shit," Max breathed.

Hank nodded. "She's a natural prosecutor. Criminals whine about their sorry pasts, but she doesn't buy it. She's got most of them beat."

"Where is the guy who raped her sister?" Max said finally.

"In the Pen," he said, referring to the Maryland Penitentiary by its nickname, "last I heard."

Jan was in the lobby, searching her purse for her car keys when Max walked back in. After hearing what Hank had to say, Max knew he couldn't just keep his mouth shut. He had to reassure Jan that she had nothing to worry about.

He stopped in the doorway as he glanced at her and nodded. "Hi," she said, surprised.

"Hi." He paused, running his fingers awkwardly through his hair as he sauntered over. "I'm sorry if I seemed a little abrupt back there."

"It's okay," she said. "I was distracted anyway." She fished her keys out of her bag and jiggled them in the air. "I've got to get out of here."

"Me, too," Max said, holding the door open for her. "I'm not much for these events."

"I can't stand them."

Max laughed and looked around for Hank. He was gone. "Where are you parked?"

"Over there," Jan said, nodding toward the edge of the parking lot.

"I'll walk you to your car."

"Okay," she said, glancing at him suspiciously. She had seen Max leave the party. Why had he come back in? Was he looking for her? And why the sudden change of attitude? Had the sergeant told him to cooperate with her?

"About the Haverdale case . . . I didn't answer your question. There was evidence of sexual assault."

They were walking through the dark lot, heading toward Jan's red convertible Cabriolet.

"Such as?"

"She was found half naked. . . ."

"I heard. Breasts exposed. Panties on." She had stopped at her car and was leaning up against it looking at Max.

"You obviously have your sources."

She smiled. "I just wasn't sure how reliable they were."

"You leave your top down?" Max asked, nodding toward the car.

"Sometimes."

"Any perp could hide in back. Not a good idea."

"Any perve?"

"I said perp, but perve will do."

Jan nodded, holding back a smile. "Thanks for the tip, Detective."

"Besides, it looks like it might rain."

Jan shook her head. "I don't think we'll get that lucky. It's going to pass us by."

"I hope for your sake you're right."

She smiled. "Getting back to the Haverdale case . . . were there any signs of trauma?"

"Bruises around her ankles. We found bruises and remnants of duct tape around her wrists."

"Any seminal fluid?"

Max shook his head. "No. There may have been, but the water was too warm and she was down too long."

"So I suppose the DNA guys aren't going to have much luck."

"They took scrapings but they didn't think they'd be able to get anything. The crabs had been at her."

Jan swallowed. She had prosecuted many rapes and had dealt with a lot of rape victims, but for some reason, this one was having a particularly potent effect on her.

"Are you okay? You look kind of, uh, green."

Jan nodded as she hurriedly unlocked her car. "I take it that's not a compliment."

"I didn't mean it as a crack—"

"Don't worry about it."

"Can you drive?"

"Oh God, yes." She sat in her car as she said, "In any case, thanks for sharing. Any suspects?"

"Haverdale was engaged. Two nights before she was killed she had a pretty public fight with her fiancé. Seems she thought he was sleeping around on her. She threatened to call it all off."

"So he killed her," she said, relieved to know that Harbert was not involved.

He shrugged. "I'm not so sure. He's got an alibi for at least part of the night. But the guy's got a history of some pretty violent behavior. We're checking it out. In any case, I wanted you to know that this definitely wasn't Harbert's work, if that's what you're worried about."

"You seem pretty sure about that."

"I already looked at him. He's a lazy, spontaneous killer—nothing like this guy. Whoever murdered this woman was pretty systematic. I think he planned this out. Down to the taking of a souvenir."

A souvenir . . . just like Frannie. Jan would never forget the first time she saw her sister after her rape, the ugly and obvious botch of missing hair that had marked her scratched forehead. *He cut it for a souvenir,* Frannie told her. *He said he wanted to remember me.*

Max rested his hands on the edge of her door and leaned in the car. For a moment Jan thought he might just kiss her. Instead he said quietly, "Be careful driving."

"I always am," she heard herself say.

He gave her a little nod and straightened, turning away and running his fingers back through his tousled hair. "Detective," she said, stopping him. She paused. "This might sound weird, but . . . well, that souvenir you mentioned. Haverdale wasn't missing any hair, was she?"

She wasn't sure what made her ask that question. In the hundreds of rapes she had prosecuted it had never occurred to her they might have been committed by the same man that raped her sister. And she wasn't sure why she would think that now. After all—her sister's rapist, Curtis Custin, was in prison—at least for another six months.

Max was too surprised to answer. He had told no one about the missing hair. Not even Hank. He hadn't had a chance—the medical examiner's report hadn't even been finished until that afternoon. So how did Jan already know about it? Max tilted his head slightly as he stepped back into the light, back toward her car.

Jan was watching him carefully. "You know, like a lock of hair."

"What do you mean?"

She blurted out, "You said he took a souvenir. Was that souvenir a lock of hair?"

Max hesitated just long enough to confirm her worst suspicions.

"Max?" she asked hopefully. *Say no*, she willed him. *A lock of hair? How ridiculous! Why do you ask?* But he didn't say anything. He just stood there, looking surprised. "Oh God," Jan whispered.

"Wait a minute, Jan—"

"Goodnight," she said as her foot hit the accelerator.

5

He cut her hair. . . .

She had seen a picture of Lucy Haverdale in the paper. She was a petite woman, with short brown hair just like Frannie. And like Frannie she had been working in a bar . . . like Frannie she had been attacked when she had returned home after her shift . . . like Frannie she had ended up floating in the bay . . . like Frannie the rapist had cut off a chunk of hair. . . .

Slow down.

Despite the similarities, the rapes couldn't be connected. Frannie's murderer was gone, safely ensconced in jail. He wasn't even up for parole until February.

Weird coincidences. That was all.

Jan turned onto Bender Lane. She could feel her body relax as she drove down the winding road. Years ago she had stumbled upon it when she made a wrong turn. She had been impressed by the woods and the serenity that seemed to engulf this quiet stretch of country on the edge of the South River. This part of town was still relatively untouched by Annapolis' rash of development. Here small, drafty cottages built as summer homes in the nineteen twenties still maintained their original form, with a few improvements. Like hers, most had a single bathroom. Jan made a left off Bender, turning onto a small gravel drive marked by two plain black mailboxes. Her driveway was almost like a street. It wound back into the woods for nearly a mile. Only one other house was back there, an almost identical cottage owned by a feisty old lady named Lily Fletcher. Jan's cottage was just past the last curve in the driveway, perched on top of a hill overlooking Red Creek.

Jan slowed her car, enjoying the sweet smell of honeysuckle that hung in the air. Her headlights picked up scattered, brightly colored wildflowers that framed both sides of the drive, compliments of Mrs. Fletcher. Jan guessed that Mrs. Fletcher was close to eighty, yet she was out in her gardens almost every day and still mowed her own grass. Their houses may have once been identical but Mrs. Fletcher had turned her simple cottage into a fairy-tale-like cabin in the woods.

Mrs. Fletcher's house was a constant reminder to Jan of what could be if only she had a little more money or time to put into it. She had thought of hiring a lawn service but every year she told herself that this summer would be different. This summer she would mow her yard once a week, no matter what. But her schedule would always interfere and despite Jan's good intentions, she was lucky to mow her yard twice a month. As to the flowers . . . well, at least this year she had planted some annuals. Because she hadn't had the time to water them, some had died, but some were still valiantly struggling for their lives. Tomorrow, she thought, tomorrow morning first thing I'll water them.

She pulled up in front of her house and raised the top of her car. She didn't think it was going to rain but she still didn't want to take any chances. She finished fastening the top and stood still for a minute. Usually the woods were filled with the sound of crickets, but the threat of stormy weather had brought on an eerie quiet. She glanced up at the starless sky once more.

The drone of a mosquito broke the silence and Jan swatted at it, almost relieved. She made her way toward the door, glancing down in the dark at her key chain. Once again she reminded herself to get a motion detector installed on her porch. She had a note taped on her fridge but she kept forgetting.

She stepped into the large wrap-around screened porch that enveloped the tiny cabin. It was the porch and the property that had sold her on the house. The cabin was perched on a cliff and the creek ran beneath it, cutting a path through the woods that surrounded the cottage. When Jan had bought the house she had imagined long hours sitting on the porch sipping iced tea as she admired her peaceful surroundings. Although she did enjoy the beauty of the place, she had moved here a year ago and still hadn't found time to unpack all of her boxes, much less sit around and admire nature.

Jan unlocked her door and stepped inside, turning on a small lamp beside the couch. She glanced around. The previous owner had knocked out walls in an attempt to make the cottage more open, and he had succeeded in creating a small, yet airy retreat. The house consisted of one large room with hardwood floors which functioned as the living room, kitchen, and dining room. In addition there was a separate bedroom and a small bathroom. In the summer the house seemed much bigger because the sliding glass doors that surrounded the main room opened to the porch. Even the bedroom opened up to a wooden deck.

Despite the previous owner's renovations, the house still had the musty smell of an unused cottage, and keeping it closed up all day with the air conditioner on didn't help. She turned off the air and walked around the room, opening up windows in a weak attempt to catch an evening breeze.

The house was perfect for her, but there was not room for a family—or even a husband. When Jan had bought the house she realized that she was conceding that, yes, she was single, and yes, she would probably stay that way for a while.

She slipped off her shoes and headed back out to the

porch, curling up in a large wicker couch that she had filled with soft pillows.

There were more comfortable places to relax, but this was her favorite. Just as she was beginning to get comfortable, the sound of a branch cracking outside of the porch made her jump. She heard a meow and realized it was just Mrs. Fletcher's cat prowling around her bushes.

Although she laughed silently at how jumpy she was, she stood up and walked back in the house, locking the door behind her.

He cut her hair. . . . She couldn't help but dwell on the similarities between the Haverdale woman and her sister. Frannie had worked at the Blue Crab, a bar that used to be a hangout for the watermen, men who made their living catching crabs on the Chesapeake Bay. It was an unusual job for a woman who was working her way through law school, but Frannie had enjoyed it. In fact, she had been returning home from work when she had been attacked. He had committed the type of rape that was extremely rare, the jump-out-of-the-bushes-at-a-stranger rape. Someone, Jan thought bitterly, should have explained to him that the majority of crimes against women were committed by someone the women knew. Frannie had never met Custin, yet he had seen her once at the bar, and that was enough to make him follow her and plan an attack on her. He had stripped her naked, tying her wrists with duct tape. He had left her bleeding and nearly unconscious in the woods, but before he left, he had cut off a piece of her hair. It was a large noticeable clump of hair, cut right down to the scalp. He had marked her, physically and emotionally. It was as if he wanted her to remember him every time she looked in the mirror. It took months for Frannie's hair to grow back. When she died, the missing clump was still noticeable.

Jan had never quite recovered from losing Frannie. The mysterious circumstances surrounding her death haunted Jan daily.

When Frannie was raped Jan rushed to her aid, spending the summer at her sister's side. Unfortunately, Frannie's rapist wasn't due to be sentenced until September, when Jan was scheduled to begin her first year of law school. Jan wanted to stay for the sentencing but Frannie insisted she not miss any school.

Still, they stayed in close touch by phone. In fact, Jan spoke with Frannie the night before the sentencing. Frannie had sounded stronger than she had in a long time. More upbeat. She was looking forward to finally facing her rapist and being able to put the whole ordeal behind her. Jan never would have suspected that she was about to take her own life.

But, according to the coroner, that's exactly what she did. She was found with fluid in her lungs, a victim of drowning. The police told Jan that after the sentencing Frannie returned to her house. Later that night, she took several sleeping pills, grabbed a bottle of wine, and paddled her neighbor's rowboat out into the chilly bay.

Her naked body was found floating in the bay the next day, an empty wine bottle still in the boat.

On the insistence of her friends and, Jan imagined, pressure from Nick and perhaps even the senator, her death had been ruled accidental; although Jan discovered later that the coroner and the police had determined it was a definite act of suicide.

After her sister's death, a therapist told Jan that she believed her sister's strange actions were a symbolic attempt to cleanse herself, an attempt to wash her body of the atrocity it had suffered. At the time, Jan found that theory hard to believe—she just didn't buy the suggestion that her sister would kill herself without leaving so much as a suicide note. It was true that Frannie had been depressed, but she had been in high spirits before the sentencing, looking forward to putting the whole ugly mess behind her and starting fresh. So why, after the sentencing, would she kill herself? Even if she had been depressed, Frannie knew the agony their mother's suicide had caused. Jan couldn't imagine Frannie would ever inflict that kind of pain on her.

It was not until she finished law school and started working at the state's attorney's office that she fully realized the scars that rape and violent assaults leave on women. Whether Frannie had intended to kill herself or not, Jan knew that she had been murdered. The man who raped her, Curtis Custin, may not have been convicted by a court but as far as Jan was concerned, he was guilty of murder in the first degree.

6

THE MAN SAT AT A DIRTY TABLE IN THE BACK OF THE DARK, smoke-filled bar. It was almost two in the morning and the place was nearly empty. He picked up his beer and took a swig.

He focused once again on the cute brown-haired waitress behind the bar. She looked similar to Lucy, but prettier. A couple of weeks ago when he was scouting prey he had come here first, but this woman hadn't been working. So he had gone to Lucky's where he found Lucy. Too bad, he thought, still staring at the waitress. He settled on Lucy simply because she was the best of a bad lot. He had to make due with what he had.

Lucy. . . .

His eyes shifted toward his beer as he remembered his failure. It had been a disaster from the start. He was out of practice and it showed. The capture had been simple, but somewhere along the way he lost control. It was unfortunate. After all, she had such promise. Yet she died before he had a chance to fulfill his fantasy. And so he had written her off as a trial run. This time he would be successful.

"Can I get you anything else?"

He glanced into the eyes of the waitress he had been admiring. She smiled at him politely.

"No, thanks," he replied, pleased that she was flirting with him. She turned away and his eyes drifted admiringly toward her firm behind and slender legs. She was just his type: small and sexy, with short brown hair and big brown eyes. He had been "courting" her from a distance for a while now, but tonight was the first night he had actually spoken with her.

As usual he had done his research. Her name was Sarah Tomkins, and she was a part-time graduate student at the University of Maryland, studying archeology. She lived in Edgewater, in a small cabin not far from the beach. She lived by herself—not even so much as a dog or cat to keep her company.

She walked past him once more, flashing him the same tentative smile. He knew women found him attractive, even this phony mustache didn't seem to deter them. He stood up from his stool and raised a hand, giving her a slight wave goodbye. *It won't be long, my sweet Sarah. It won't be long.*

7

HE'S OUT.

The words reverberated through her, echoing in her mind.

"I'm sorry?" Jan whispered into the receiver. Surely this woman was mistaken.

"Curtis Custin was released on June twentieth."

"That's not possible," Jan breathed. "He's not up for parole until February. . . ."

"Hold on, please," the woman said, placing Jan on hold. This was a mistake. It had to be. Jan had called the prison this morning, just for reassurance that Curtis Custin was safely ensconced in the Maryland Penitentiary.

The woman came back on the line. "Yes, ma'am. He's out."

"I don't understand," Jan said. "I wasn't notified about an early release. . . ."

"I'm looking at his file and there's nothing about victim notification."

"The victim is dead," Jan said quickly. "But I'm an assistant state's attorney and I'm telling you that the state's attorney, Nick Fitzgerald, specifically asked to be notified."

"I see that," she said. "And we sent him a letter . . ." She paused, pulling up the information on her computer. "Just this past March telling him he was about to go."

"And he never replied?" Jan asked, surprised.

"Correct."

Jan regained her composure enough to say, "I don't understand why he's out in the first place."

"We're overcrowded, ma'am. And he was let go."

Overcrowded!? Jan thought as she set the phone back on the receiver without saying goodbye. Nick had known how important this was to her. Why didn't he respond to that letter? He could've argued against an early release.

Jan walked down to Nick's office and went inside, not bothering to knock.

He looked up and smiled at her. He was wearing what Jan referred to as his Good Humor man outfit. White shirt, white linen pants and jacket with a red polka dot bow tie.

His smile faded as he noticed the expression on her face. "Jan," he said. "What's wrong?"

She shut the door behind her. "Custin's out."

He paused. "How do you know?"

"I just got off the phone with the Maryland Penitentiary," she said, upset. "They released him."

He was silent.

"They said that they notified you and you didn't respond."

"Look, I know you were focused on his release. I thought it might ease your mind if before his official scheduled release, I told you he'd already been out for months. You'd see the world hadn't crumbled at your feet. That nothing had changed."

Jan was quiet. She glanced at the floor, willing the tears away.

"Jan," he said, standing. "We kept him in there as long as we could. He's served most of his sentence."

"He served half of his sentence. His mandatory release date wasn't for another five and a half years." Custin had been sentenced to twenty years. As it was, he had been released just short of his ten-year anniversary.

"Like you said—he was up for parole in February. He would've been released then and you know it. And they didn't set him completely free—he's got supervised parole for another five years."

"That doesn't make me feel any better."

Nick sighed. "I wish we could've kept him in there forever."

"I would've liked that."

He pursed his lips together, watching her. Finally he said, "Look, I'll tell you what. On my way home, I'll knock off a liquor store for you. I'll bring you the booze and we can frame Custin. We'll get him back in the Pen so fast he won't know what hit him."

Jan smiled despite herself. Nick hadn't offered to frame someone for her for a couple of years now. Used to be, whenever anyone would look at her sideways Nick would jokingly offer to knock off a bank or a jewelry store and frame the guy for her. *Otherwise, what's the point of being SA?* he'd say.

Jan laughed again, then started to cry. Just a little, but it was enough.

Nick brushed back a strand of hair that had fallen in her face. "It'll be all right, Jan."

She shook her head. "Maybe not."

"What do you mean?"

"I mean maybe he had something to do with the Haverdale murder."

Nick didn't say anything for a minute. Then he smiled reassuringly and said, "I didn't see anything in the police report that would make me think that. The Haverdale case is a domestic—"

"What about the hair?"

"What are you talking about?"

"The Haverdale woman was missing hair, just like my sister. Someone had cut if off for a souvenir."

"Where'd you hear that?"

Jan hesitated. Nick was still smiling, his voice was

still calm, but something told her he was not pleased. He had lowered his voice just a tad, a bad sign. When Nick was agitated he would speak so quietly people had to lean forward to hear him.

"Max Hale," Nick said when she didn't answer. He sat back down behind his desk.

"He didn't tell me anything. I asked him if she was missing hair. He didn't answer me. But I could tell by his reaction that I had guessed right."

"Sometimes you're too sharp for your own good. You're right, hair was missing, but it wasn't at all like what happened with Frannie. As far as I know, Haverdale lost her hair during a struggle."

"Oh," Jan said, uneasy from the way he was speaking. He wasn't looking at her. Instead he was focused on the papers on his desk even though he knew how important this was to her.

She said, "I guess, I just, maybe jumped to conclusions. . . ."

"You made an educated guess, nothing wrong with that." Nick smiled at her and said, "Look at you. You didn't get much sleep last night, did you?"

Jan shook her head.

"You hear that the Haverdale woman is missing some hair, then find out that Custin has been released . . ." He smiled sympathetically. "Your head must be spinning."

Jan said, "Both petite with brown eyes and short brown hair. Both were working in a bar when they were attacked. . . ."

"Look, kiddo. You need to calm down. There's a lot that you don't know about this case. You're trying to read between the lines and the book hasn't even been written yet."

She squinted at him. Nick often said things like that. He thought they were profound. She called them politese, a term she had pegged for political BS.

"There's something you don't know about the Haverdale case," he announced.

"What?"

"We have a suspect."

The fiancé. She asked, "Since when?"

"Since the very beginning."

"Then we're getting ready for an arrest?"

"Lucy Haverdale had broken off her engagement with her boyfriend two days earlier. Apparently, he was having a tough time with it."

"Really?"

"Yeah. This guy's got a history. He's been known to tip the bottle and he's been arrested before. Assault."

"Any history of domestic abuse?"

"We're looking into it."

"Who'd he assault?"

"It was some kind of bar brawl."

"Any hard evidence?"

He hesitated. "I don't want to get into that with you. I'm only telling you this to ease your mind. This has nothing to do with Frannie or Custin. It's totally separate and unrelated."

"I want to prosecute this case, Nick." She knew it was a stretch. After all, there was a clear division between the attorneys who handled sex crimes and those who worked on homicides.

He shook his head as he sat on the edge of his desk. "No way."

"Why not? I can handle it."

"It has nothing do with your capabilities and you know it. I need you on sex crimes and—"

"I want this case," she repeated stubbornly.

"It'll swallow you up. As your friend, I would advise you against it for personal reasons. As your boss, I'm telling you for professional reasons: not a chance."

Jan started to speak but stopped. Nick met her eyes with a look that said the conversation was over.

Max sat in the back of the church, his eyes focused on his number one suspect. Tom Neff was sitting with his arms wrapped around the shoulders of Lucy Haverdale's mother. His twenty-year-old face contorted with grief as he stared at his fiancée's closed coffin.

Tom Neff was their number one suspect by default—there was no one else who might want Lucy dead. And, although there wasn't any hard evidence against him yet, there was plenty of circumstantial. The first was motive. According to friends, Neff had been furious when Lucy broke off their engagement, and had told several people she would regret it. The second damning evidence was lack of alibi and a history of alcohol abuse. Neff had been out drinking the same evening Lucy was abducted. He had left his friends at eleven, claiming he was going home to sleep it off—which gave him an hour to kill before Lucy arrived home from work. Neff was also employed in a boat yard and they suspected the murderer had access to a boat. The final piece of information that might prove a connection to the case was that Neff's father was a barber—which might explain Haverdale's missing hair. Perhaps it signified anger at his father, mixed up with anger at Lucy.

As Max watched Neff, he found himself growing increasingly agitated. Despite the evidence, he had a hunch that Neff was innocent. Was he just fooled by Neff's cherubic face? Or was he being suckered by the way Lucy's family treated him . . . as though it never occurred to them that the man who sat there comforting them might be the reason for their pain. Perhaps it was the fact that, try as Max might, he couldn't see how someone who was, by all accounts, as inebriated as Neff was the night of Lucy's murder would be capable of carrying out such a planned and intricate attack and abduction.

The sister of the victim stood at the podium, swallowing back tears as she began to speak. There was not a dry eye left in the church, including Max. Damn it, he thought. This was exactly why he didn't like attending funerals. He liked to pursue his cases methodically, unemotionally. At funerals he always seemed to get caught up in the family's grief and sadness. Emotion clouded his thinking.

Besides that, he hated being in church. Every time he was forced to set foot in one his Catholic guilt caught up with him, and although he considered himself an atheist, he found himself praying to God, asking for his forgiveness.

He wouldn't even be here today if the damn video camera had worked. Killers often appeared at the funerals of the victims, even if they weren't personally connected with the victim before the crime. Homicide detectives either attended the funeral or videotaped it. Max preferred videotape, but today the damn machine had jammed.

Lucy's sister was sobbing now, leaning over the podium and staring at her sister's casket. Oh, Christ, Max thought as he tried to hold himself together. He had a propensity for crying—most of the men in his family did—and while a good cry brought welcome relief, it could be disastrous in a professional situation. Max irritatedly swatted away a tear as he focused on the facts. Lucy Haverdale had moved to Annapolis with her parents when she was seventeen years old. She graduated from Annapolis High School three years ago, and since then, she had been working as a bartender at Lucky's. According to her friends, Lucy had been saving her money to enter cosmetology school in the fall.

The last person to see her alive had been Trudy Newich, the manager of the bar where Lucy worked. Newich stated that Lucy had left work shortly after midnight. She made it back to her house—they knew that because her car had been found in her driveway, and her purse and keys were found on the ground in front of her door. Lucy had been the victim of a blitz attack: she had been surprised from behind before she had a chance to open her door.

Robbery had not been a motive in the attack. There was no sign of attempted forced entry and besides that, her wallet was in her purse, with a wad of bills, sixty-five dollars—her tip money from the night—tucked into the worn leather folds.

That information alone gave him a rough portrait of the perpetrator. Max knew that he had been working alone—otherwise a blitz attack would have been unnecessary. Max guessed he arrived there by boat. Street parking was not allowed and if he had parked in her driveway, Lucy would've noticed the car. After he immobilized Lucy (the sexual nature of the crime convinced Max this perp was a man) he either led her or carried her down to his boat—a feat which, considering the steepness of the ravine, would require a certain amount of strength and skill.

The crime also required familiarity, not only with the terrain but with the victim. The murderer might not have been someone she knew, but Max had little doubt that *he* knew *her.* He knew she would be alone that night, knew what time she would return home from work. He had been waiting for her.

There were other unanswered questions, however. There were several houses not three hundred feet away from Lucy's driveway. If he arrived by boat, why hadn't anyone heard a motor?

Unless he hadn't used the motor. Perhaps he had tied Lucy up and sailed or paddled his way out of the creek.

One thing was certain: whoever killed her had planned the attack very carefully.

But had he intended to kill her? Or was this just a rape that had gotten out of hand? Had the killer just been trying to teach her a lesson—like perhaps an old boyfriend who was at the end of his rope?

If that was the case, the rookie murderer had been extremely lucky. Lucky to have not left any DNA behind, lucky to have dumped her body in the bay where the water would wash away crucial forensic evidence.

They had scoured the woods around Lucy's home, but as of yet they hadn't found anything, not so much as a drop of blood.

Max scanned the pews, looking at the guests. Frederico Warner, the owner of Lucky's, was sitting toward the back of the church. He was holding what appeared to be a heavy gold cross in his left hand. Every now and then he'd take his right index finger and cross himself, muttering silently. Frederico was a

slim, small man in his seventies. He was bald on the
top of his head but attempted to compensate that by
growing the hair on his left side long and brushing it
over his bald spot, then using what looked like grease
to keep it in place. He had lived in Annapolis his entire
life and his bar had been a well known watering hole
and local hangout for fishermen for years. Frederico
was also without an alibi but he didn't fit the bill.
Lucy's killer needed to be strong enough to hold her
down and then transport her dead body from spot A to
spot B. Also, if it was Frederico, why would he wait
until she came home to attack her? Why not just do it
in the restaurant?

Max felt his pager go off and flicked it on, checking
the number. It was a call from the state's attorney's
office. Jan? he thought hopefully. He had called her this
morning but she was in a meeting and he hadn't left a
message. He felt a little foolish for calling her in the first
place. After all, the only reason he wanted to talk to her
was to make sure she was all right. She had seemed so
upset when she found out that Haverdale's murderer
had taken a souvenir.

He turned off his beeper. He had a feeling it wasn't
Jan. More than likely it was another attorney hungry
for details. Annapolis didn't have many murders and
the prosecutors were eager to get their hands on this
one.

Max shifted uncomfortably in his seat, glancing
around as if searching for a friend. Lucy had been dead

for almost a week, and Max knew that with each passing day the chance of catching the killer became slimmer and slimmer.

As the priest resumed his place at the podium, Max prayed, not for forgiveness, but for help. He needed a break and he need one fast.

8

ANOTHER WOMAN WAS MISSING.

Max glanced over the report, not even realizing that he was shaking his head. The similarities between the Haverdale case and this one were frightening.

Sarah Tomkins had been reported missing by her mother, who had gone to her house when Sarah neglected to show up for work on Sunday night. Sarah's car had been parked in her driveway and her mother found her purse outside her daughter's locked front door, one hundred and eight dollars of tip money rolled up and tucked inside.

Max agitatedly ran his fingers through his hair. He had seen Mrs. Tomkins when she came in. She was still trying to tell herself that her daughter was all right, that she had knocked her head—maybe suffered amnesia. That soon she would come walking though the door, apologizing for worrying everyone.

Of course, Mrs. Tomkins knew about Lucy Haverdale. She read the papers. Maybe she even saw the similarities. But Max knew from experience that people never believe fate can turn against them, and when it does, they're so blindsided that it takes a while for the horror to set in.

Max walked outside, cursing his rotten luck. It was raining. After almost a month of drought, Mother Nature had chosen today to let loose a torrent of water which was sure to wash away evidence outside Sarah's house. He slipped into his car and turned on his headlights. Edgewater was about twenty minutes away, and he wanted to get there as soon as possible, while the trail was still warm.

Other detectives were already there, already searching for evidence. This was not his case because the precinct was still officially treating Sarah Tomkins as a kidnapping. Max could only hope they were right.

9

"Hello?" Sheila said, peering into Jan's daydreaming eyes. "Are you listening to me?" They had both worked late and decided to grab something to eat at Arnold's Tavern, a restored inn from the eighteenth century and one of the many places George Washington had slept. Usually Sheila and Jan preferred to sit on the wooden porch overlooking the downtown dock, but tonight the rain forced everyone inside. Boaters and tourists were crowded around the mahogany bar talking boisterously as they drank their beer and swapped sailing stories. Sheila and Jan were lucky to snag a table. "You haven't heard a word of what I've said, have you?"

"I'm sorry," Jan said. "I was just thinking about that woman that disappeared. It's weird, her disappearing so close to the Haverdale murder."

"It might just be a coincidence. Hank said they think this Tomkins woman might show up."

Jan shifted her eyes, thinking for a moment.

Sheila stuck a finger in her drink and swirled her ice cube back and forth. "Actually, I thought you might be distracted for personal reasons."

Jan glanced at her friend, surprised. Had Nick told her about Curtis Custin? "You know?"

Sheila nodded. "The minute I met him I knew—"

"Met him? What are you talking about?"

Sheila leaned forward and grinned. "Max. It's written all over your face."

"Max? Give me a break!"

"You just admitted—"

"I thought you were talking about Custin."

"Custin?" Sheila repeated, leaning forward. "The guy who attacked your sister? What about him?"

"He's out."

"Oh my God," Sheila moaned. "When did you find out?"

"Last week," she said quietly.

"Why didn't you tell me?"

"I guess I was trying to forget about it. Pretend it didn't matter."

Sheila sighed. She was probably Jan's closest friend, yet Jan rarely confided in her. It was almost as if Jan maintained an invisible wall around herself, a normal attribute of people who had experienced horrific loss. Still, it frustrated her. "What happened?"

"They gave him early parole. Apparently the prison was overcrowded."

"He's got supervised parole though, right?"

Jan nodded. "At least, according to Nick."

"Speaking of Nick," Sheila said. "Did he mention anything about Rachel Wyons when you talked to him?"

"Rachel? No, why?"

"Oh," Sheila said, as she nervously tried to change the subject. "Nothing. Hey, did you see those scratches on his face today? Ouch!"

Nick had arrived at work that morning with three long scratches down the side of his face, wounds that he proudly announced had been achieved in a rugby game.

"I can't imagine him playing rugby, can you?" Sheila rattled on. "Wonder what he wore . . . his white outfit or his blue. Probably Bermuda shorts and loafers—"

"Spit it out, Sheila," Jan interrupted. She knew that her friend was keeping something from her.

"What?"

"We already talked about Nick's scratches—with Nick. Remember?"

"Oh, yeah." Sheila picked up her straw and twirled it in between her fingers. "Well," she said, hesitating. "I could be wrong, but I heard that Rachel, well, Nick gave her the Moriarty case and now he's supposedly promising her the Haverdale case as well."

"What?" Jan asked. The Moriarty case was a high profile case for them involving a popular car dealership owner who was shot by a disgruntled employee. When Nick had given that case to a leggy twenty-six-year-old two years out of law school, eyebrows were raised. But to promise her the Haverdale case? He wouldn't even give it to Jan and she had five years of experience on Rachel Wyons.

Jan glanced down at the table. Why would he do this? It didn't make any sense.

"Maybe Rachel misunderstood," Sheila said brightly. "I mean, that's what she's saying, but she probably got it wrong."

"Maybe she's the one who scratched him up," Jan said quietly. She knew the minute she saw Rachel that Nick would fall for her. Is that why he had promised her the case? It was hard to believe he would be so unprofessional, but still . . .

Sheila interrupted her train of thought with, "How did you find out about Custin?"

"I called the prison."

"Why?"

"What do you mean?"

"Did you have a sense he was out? ESP?"

Jan told her friend about the similarities between her sister's case and the Haverdale woman and why she thought Custin might be involved. Then she said, "Too many coincidences, but Nick doesn't think there's a connection. He thinks this Neff did it but I'm not sure. I'll feel better when I find out where Custin is." Jan picked up her straw and bit the end. "So what did you mean when you said *it* was written all over my face?"

Sheila shot her a devilish smile. "Oh nothing."

Jan paused a minute and then said. "I'm not interested in him, you know."

"Whatever," Sheila said, feigning indifference.

There was a lull in conversation. Finally Jan said, "I'm just a little curious about him, that's all. He doesn't seem to want to cooperate with, with . . . our office."

"Hmm," Sheila said, glancing around the bar.

"Have you heard anything about him? I know he was a homicide detective in Baltimore. Do you know why he left?"

"Burned out. Tired of all the crime."

"A detective tired of crime," Jan mumbled. "Great."

"Yeah. He came to the right place, huh? Anyway, Hank says he's a nice guy. Doesn't talk much."

Jan took the straw out of her mouth. "What else?"

Sheila smiled as she raised an eyebrow. "Well, he's not involved with anyone, if that's what you're getting at. And he's twenty-nine, just in case you're interested."

"Too young."

"Give me a break. You're only thirty-two."

"I don't like younger men."

"What about bagel boy?"

Jan grinned at the memory. She had been desperate

for a date last year for the office Christmas party and had asked a man who just happened to have a part-time job working in the bagel shop down the street from the office. "Just because he sold bagels . . ."

"He was a kid."

"He was a doctoral student. Besides, it was just a date. And he was cute—and sweet."

"Don't tell me you don't find Max attractive. I mean, come on! Those eyes—oy! He's got that rough and sexy look, that just rolled out of bed—"

"So he's good-looking. Big deal," Jan said succinctly.

"Okay, here's what you do," Sheila said. "Tomorrow wear that light blue blouse with your snug white pants. Call him and tell him—"

Jan rolled her eyes. "Come on, Sheila."

"Well, you need a little push."

"Forget it. He seems a little cocky to me."

"What are you talking about?"

"Just a vibe I'm picking up."

"I disagree. I mean, I've had few dealings with him and he was perfectly nice, just a little abrupt. No," she said quickly, reconsidering. "*Abrupt* isn't the right word. Rushed. But who can blame him? Things are probably pretty hairy over there. You just need to have some one-on-one time with him. Think of a way to get him alone. After a few minutes of your charm—he'll fall for you."

"Forget it. "

"Just—"

"I've had some one-on-one time with him and I didn't make such a great impression."

"What!?"

"I was hammering him with questions at the senator's party last week."

"Oh no." Sheila had tried to fix her up so many times, but Jan always seemed to either sabotage it or find a reason why it wasn't worth pursuing.

"Yeah. I think he thinks I'm a pain in the ass."

"Oh my God," Sheila said, whispering furiously. "He's here—NO! Don't turn around!"

"Bagel Boy?"

"Max!" She leaned forward and said sternly, "Be pleasant. And if he makes a joke, laugh. No eye-rolling."

Jan turned around.

"I said don't turn around," Sheila commanded again.

"Sorry," Jan muttered.

"I'll see if they want to join us."

"Sheila," Jan began, but Sheila raised a hand to silence her. She strutted over toward them and a few minutes later she was back with the two men in tow.

Max took a seat next to Jan, sliding in the booth so that their legs were touching. Jan knew that it was an accident, but the feel of his leg casually resting against her made her nervous.

"How are you doing?" he asked Jan.

"Great," Jan said, flashing him a polite smile.

He paused a second and then said, "You seemed a, well, little distracted when I last saw you."

Sheila cut in nervously and said, "Funny running into you guys here." She looked directly at Max and said, "Jan and I were just talking about you."

Jan shot Sheila a nasty look.

Sheila ignored it and said, "Jan's got a lead for you in the Haverdale case. She's so smart. She's always—"

"It's not really a lead. . . ." Jan interrupted.

"What?" Max asked, leaning in toward her.

Jan glanced away. "The guy who raped my sister got out of prison last month. I just think that it might be worth taking a look at him. I don't even know where he is."

"In Florida," Max said.

"What?" Jan replied, shocked.

"I told him about your sister, uh, the case," Hank said awkwardly. "He's already working on him."

"You read Frannie's file?"

"Not yet. Archives hasn't been able to locate it. But like I said, Custin's in Florida, so I think that rules him out as a suspect."

"That's good information, isn't it, Jan? Your reputation precedes you, Max," Sheila gushed, looking not at Max but at Jan. "We heard that you were a very thorough detective, didn't we, Jan?"

Jan ignored her mooning friend. "Florida?" she said, thinking. When a convicted criminal was released on supervised parole he could return to his original place of residence, even if it meant crossing state lines. Once there, however, he was not allowed to leave the state without permission. "He's from Sebring, right?" she asked, referring to a city south of Orlando.

"That's where he is now."

"How do you know this?"

"I called the jail, then spoke to his parole officer down there. He reported within seventy-two hours of his release, just like he was supposed to."

Jan began to absentmindedly nibble her cuticles.

"So, he's in Florida," Sheila said, nudging Jan with her foot and discreetly motioning for Jan to stop. "You must be so relieved."

"Does he have an alibi for the night Lucy Haverdale was murdered?" Convicts broke parole every day. Just because Custin was supposed to stay in Florida didn't mean he actually was.

Max said, "As a matter of fact, yeah. He met with his parole officer in Sebring at eight o'clock in the morning on July twenty-fifth. Lucy was abducted the night of the twenty-fourth."

"Oh," Jan said simply. She started to bite her cuticles again but stopped, venting her nervous energy instead by tapping her foot. She had thought such news would make her feel relieved, but instead all she felt was tired. Very tired. "Thanks. I'm glad to know where Custin is and I'm glad he's far away."

"Yes, it's good to know," Sheila piped in.

Jan stood up. "If you'll excuse me," she said, motioning for Max to let her out, "I'm going to head home. I've got to be in court first thing tomorrow morning. I'll see you guys later."

After Jan left, Hank glanced down at his beer and said, "Maybe we'll make an arrest soon and she can put this whole thing behind her."

"Unless," Max said quietly as his thoughts drifted back to Sarah Tomkins, "whoever killed Haverdale isn't finished."

10

Thursday, August 6

MAX RECEIVED THE PHONE CALL HE HAD BEEN ANTICIPATING A little after six A.M. A woman's body had been found in Harwood, floating face up in the Chesapeake Bay.

Half an hour later, he parked his car and walked toward a private dock in the middle of nowhere.

"Where is she?" Max asked the uniformed officer who was standing at the foot of the dock.

"ID?" the cop asked.

Max flipped open his wallet to reveal his badge. He hadn't worked there long enough for all of the beat officers to know him, and even if they had seen him before they might not have recognized him. Max was not a morning person. He had rolled out of bed with four hours of sleep, pulled on jeans and a sweatshirt. At that

87

early hour, a shower and a shave was not in the cards, neither was a suit.

"She's down here, Detective," the uniformed police officer said, motioning toward a boat that was tethered to the dock. The boat was a forty foot luxury yacht, the kind that had more than one bedroom and bathroom.

"What happened?" Max asked the uniformed patrolman as he walked with him to the end of the dock. A crackle of thunder and a flash of lightning made them look up. It had stopped raining several minutes earlier but it still looked as if it might start up again any minute.

"A husband and wife found her. A . . ." the officer said, still walking as he pulled out a small notebook from his back pocket, "Mr. and Mrs. Richard Smith. They were docked off shore. The husband got up early to check the anchor and saw something floating in the water. When they realized it was a person, the husband jumped in to try to save her, thought she was a drowning victim or something. Anyway, they pulled her out of the water, onto the boat.

"Where are they now?"

"Down here," Hank said, appearing out of the hull. His face was a pale white, his expression grim. "Ahoy there."

Max caught sight of a blanket pulled over a lumpy looking object. "Is that her?" he asked.

"What's left of her."

"Who put the blanket on?" he asked with some concern. The less the body was touched the better. Who knew what evidence they had contaminated just by bringing the body onto the boat? And the blanket . . .

"The husband. Didn't want his wife to have to have to look at it anymore."

Max climbed onto the boat. He yanked on a pair of rubber gloves. "Shall we?" he asked Hank.

He pulled back the blanket.

It was the body of a woman so badly bloated that it was impossible to recognize her as the pretty girl with big brown eyes whose picture was up in the police station.

Like Lucy Haverdale, all of her clothes had been removed with the exception of a small pair of white panties. And like Lucy Haverdale, her eyes were open in a horrified stare. But there was one major difference between this body and Lucy Haverdale. This woman had a bullet wound in the middle of her forehead.

Max picked up a cool, spongy wrist. No obvious evidence of duct tape—but then again, she had been in the water a lot longer than the Haverdale woman.

He glanced at her head, looking at her hair. She had short hair and although she had been out of the water for close to an hour, it was damp and tangled with dirt and grime. He leaned in closer, looking at the front left side of her scalp. He could see the rough jagged edges left from the scissors that had chopped off a large chunk of hair. He glanced up at Hank, who gave a nod.

Hank also understood the significance of the ragged hair.

"What do you think?" the officer asked.

Our problems are just beginning, Max thought, his eyes drifting toward the neat, clean bullet wound. Max said, "I think we better hope that evidence collection gets here soon. In the meantime, try to keep her out of the rain."

11

By THREE O'CLOCK THAT AFTERNOON THE CONFERENCE ROOM had turned into a makeshift war room. One side of the room was reserved for Lucy Haverdale, the other side for Sarah Tomkins. Pictures of them in life were pinned alongside pictures of them in death. Their houses, their yards—everything was posted on the walls. Almost everyone in CID was now working on the cases in some way. The narcotics officers were interviewing neighbors, sex crimes were searching down past boyfriends and employers. Homicide was following up the tips and leads that continued to be called in.

The sergeant was standing on the Sarah Tomkins side, staring at a close-up of her dead face. "Same guy?"

"Looks like. Lots of similarities. The type of women, where they lived, the initial blitz attack . . ."

"The missing hair."

"Exactly."

"But the manner of death . . ."

"Can be explained. Lucy Haverdale's death could have been an accident—maybe he didn't plan on killing her. Maybe she hit her head and died before he had a chance. Or there's another possibility. Jack," he said, referring to Jack Haggerty, the department's hair and fiber expert, "said he found some fibers under Sarah Tomkins' fingernails. He hasn't finished analyzing them yet but he said they look like black wool. . . ."

"Meaning this guy was wearing a mask, she pulled it off. . ."

"And he killed her." He glanced at Lucy Haverdale's high school graduation picture. "So there's a chance he didn't originally intend for either victim to die. Murder may not be part of his MO."

"Have you gotten anything off the wire?"

"Nothing. Which is strange, since I'd be willing to bet he's done this before. Certain elements were just too swift, too professional."

"But if your theory is right and he didn't mean to kill them, then maybe he's not so professional."

Max shook his head. "When things got out of hand he didn't panic. He knew exactly how to dispose of the bodies to get rid of evidence."

"Maybe you'll find some answers in Neff's house."

Max shrugged. "Maybe." A search warrant had finally been approved and a team would be searching Neff's house within hours.

"What?" the sergeant asked, reading the expression of doubt on Max's face. "You don't think he did it?"

"It's possible. But if he was as drunk as everyone says on the night Haverdale was murdered, I think it's doubtful. I think he would have had a tough time controlling Haverdale. We would've found evidence."

"Sarah Tomkins' murderer had a gun. Maybe Neff controlled Haverdale with a gun."

"I don't think Lucy walked down that ravine by herself. We didn't find any sign of broken branches on that ravine . . . nothing. I think she was subdued somehow and carried down." He walked over to the picture of Lucy's ravine and pointed to the cabin near the water. "This cabin was rented out that night and no one heard a boat motor."

The sergeant was now looking at a picture of Lucy. Max continued, "Which means that the perp either sailed or rowed his way in and out."

"And Neff can't sail." The sergeant shook his head. "It's not enough. After all, he could've used a rowboat or a canoe. He might have killed Tomkins to throw us offtrack. Make it look like a serial killer was out there."

"Let's assume that Neff did kill Haverdale. He would have had to have been waiting for her when she returned home from work. She never made it in her house. Her purse was found outside her front door along with her keys. Neff already had a key to her house. Why didn't he go inside? Why attack her outside where there's a chance the neighbors might see?"

"Maybe it was spontaneous," the sergeant said, playing devil's advocate. "Maybe they were in a fight and things got out of hand."

"So they start fighting, she falls down, hits her head and dies. He panics and somehow gets her body out of there, pulls off her clothes and dumps her in the bay, hoping to make it look like a sexual assault." Max shook his head. "The neighbors didn't hear anything that night. Plus—we checked his car. No blood. And there's no way he could've rowed far enough for her to end up in Bay Ridge. The only other possibility is he somehow managed not to get blood on his car—or used someone else's car to transport the body. But remember—the coroner said there wasn't any damage to the body from hitting the water, which meant she wasn't thrown off any bridges. He would've had to drive to Bay Ridge, park along a busy road and dump her body off a well-lit dock." He hesitated and shrugged. "Maybe the son-of-a-bitch just got lucky. And maybe he got such a thrill from it and was so cocky that he went out a week later and did it again. If that's the case, this Neff is a lot smarter—or luckier than he seems."

The sergeant glanced around the room, scanning the pictures. "I want to dig up everything we can on Tomkins and Haverdale—let's see if there's any overlap at all in who they knew, what they did. If there's a connection, I want us to find it."

Max nodded. "I agree."

"The press is already climbing all over this place

about the Haverdale case. They're going to go crazy if they find out about the hair connection." The sergeant paused. "This kind of thing just doesn't happen around here." He turned away from the pictures and said, "I want us to keep this as low key as possible. I don't want people panicking."

"Meaning?"

"Meaning I don't want anything said to anyone outside of this department."

"Perhaps someone should explain that to Nick."

The sergeant smiled. "Do you have a problem with our state's attorney?"

"I have a problem with his mouth."

"You saw the news," the sergeant said matter-of-factly.

Max shook his head. "I heard an excerpt on the radio this morning."

"I'll have a talk with him. In the meantime, I don't want you talking to the media—or anyone else."

"People will naturally put the two murders together. There's too many similarities." He stopped. "Does Nick know about the hair?"

As of yet, the fact that Lucy Haverdale was missing hair had been kept away from the media. But of course, if Nick knew . . .

The sergeant nodded. "I just hung up the phone with him. He thinks if we had moved a little faster Neff would have been behind bars by now and Sarah Tomkins would still be alive."

"That kind of half-assed comment makes me think I pegged him right. A mouth with a haircut. He belongs in politics."

"He's not that bad."

Max shook his head, took a step toward the door and stopped. "Just one more thing. . . ."

The sergeant looked up. "Yeah?"

"Frannie Garret's file. Archives didn't have it," he said.

"Frannie Garret? What do you want with her file?"

"Jan mentioned that her sister's rape was similar to the Haverdale case."

"Shit, everybody's got a suspect." He reached for the phone as he said offhandedly, "It isn't the first time archives lost a file."

Max walked back toward his desk. The homicide division was located in the back of the building. Four desks, one for each of the detectives were placed in each corner of the room. Unlike the sex crimes division, the homicide detectives worked in pairs.

He stopped when he entered the room. Jan was sitting at his desk, her arms crossed in front of her as she scanned a newspaper. She practically jumped up when she saw him. "Max," she said anxiously, "I need to talk to you."

"This isn't a good time. . . ."

"Please," she said, almost whispering.

He looked at her, his resolve melting. "Let's find a conference room," he said.

Jan grabbed her purse and followed him out of the homicide office. Directly outside the room where the homicide detectives worked was the burglary unit which consisted of seven men and two women. Jan said hello to some of the detectives she knew as she walked through the center of the room. It didn't escape her attention that most of the force seemed consumed by the latest murder.

Jan started to walk toward the conference room where the sergeant was and Max grabbed her arm, steering her into an adjacent office. "That room's taken right now." As soon as Max shut the door behind them, he asked, "What's up?"

"Tomkins and Haverdale. It's got to be the same guy—Custin."

Max leaned up against the wall folding his arms across his chest. "Custin's got an alibi, he was in Sebring. Tomkins died around midnight and Custin met with his parole officer the next morning."

"I heard they had to approximate Tomkins' time of death—they could have been off by hours."

"It makes no difference. . . ."

"Custin could've caught a flight back that night."

"I checked. The last flight to Orlando left BWI at ten o'clock."

Jan hesitated.

Max said, "The sun set at eight fifty-eight on the day that Tomkins died. That means he would've had to commit the crime in broad daylight, as well as dispose of the body. And there's one other problem with that theory. Tomkins worked until nine o'clock."

"He still would have time . . ."

Max was shaking his head.

"Maybe the parole officer is mistaken. Maybe he's lying. Or maybe he got his days screwed up."

"Come on."

Jan looked at Max carefully. "Was Tomkins missing some hair, too?"

"I never said Haverdale was."

"You told me. Just not with words."

He shook his head as he reached for the door. "Look—" he began.

"Tomkins was missing hair too, wasn't she?"

Max raised his hands, as if refusing to answer any more questions.

They held each other's stare for a moment and then Jan said, "Thanks for nothing." With that, she walked out of the room.

"I was ready to kill him."

It was Friday afternoon and contrary to the activity at CID, the state's attorney's office was quiet. Despite the dismal start, it had turned into a beautiful day and the staff had responded accordingly, the majority leaving right after lunch, anxious to start the weekend. Jan, Dave, and Sheila were the only attorneys left.

"I don't blame you," Sheila said.

"What do you mean you don't blame her? What did he do wrong?" Dave said.

"He should at least check Custin out."

"He did," he said, defending Max. "Custin's in Florida, for crissakes. And he has an alibi. His parole officer."

"So what? Maybe he's lying."

"The parole officer?" Dave asked.

"You guys ever have a case where the rapist cut off a piece of the victim's hair?" Jan asked.

"I knew of a murderer that did that," Dave said. "Wanted a memento of a victim."

"Where did the hair come from?"

"What do you mean? Where was it found?"

"No. Where did he cut the hair from?"

"It was from her scalp, if that's what you're getting at."

"I meant front of the head, back of the head . . ."

"You should be more specific. Hair doesn't just grow on heads, you know."

Sheila threw a paper airplane at him.

"My sister's rapist cut a huge chunk of hair right in the front," she said, pointing to her left temple. "He was marking her. Like making her wear a scarlet letter."

"What was her hair like?"

"It was short, but not too short. Kind of like a wedge cut."

"Like these women," Sheila said.

"Right."

Dave leaned forward on his chair. "Are you serious? These women were marked in the same way?"

Jan nodded.

"And you know this from Max?"

She shook her head.

"Then how?"

She shrugged.

"You called the medical examiner!" Sheila exclaimed.

Jan shrugged again. She had called him but she hadn't spoken with him. She spoke with his assistant. And she used slightly devious methods to get her to spill the beans. Jan had pretended that Nick wanted to confirm the exact location of the victims' bare scalp.

"Very naughty," Sheila said, pleased with her friend.

"This Neff guy worked as a barber, right?" Dave asked.

"Do you know how old Neff was when my sister was killed?" Jan asked.

"Well," Dave said, thinking. "He's twenty now . . ."

"Ten," Jan said. "He was ten years old." She shook her head.

"I agree with you," Sheila said. "This whole hair thing is weird."

Dave stood up. "Well, ladies, I'm sorry to say this but I have to go."

"Where?" Sheila asked.

"I'm meeting up with some friends. The Red Lion. You guys are welcome to come."

"It's a pickup place," Jan said.

"That's what I'm hoping."

"Yuk. No, thanks."

"How about you Sheila?" He paused, his gaze softening a little as he caught Sheila's eye.

She shook her head. "I'm married, remember?"

"Yes," Dave said, no longer kidding as he looked her in the eye. "I remember." He paused as he shifted his gaze. "How is old Mark?" he asked, referring to her husband.

"Fine. He's been out of town. He's due back tonight."

He nodded as he stood up. He gave them a quick salute. "Adios. Have a good weekend." He stopped at the door and turned around. "Jan, you call me if you need anything, okay? I mean it. Anything at all."

Jan smiled at him. After Dave left she glanced toward Sheila. The expression on her friend's face was one of regret and sadness. "Where's Mark been?" she asked. Sheila's husband was a sales rep for a computer company and he was rarely home. Even when he was in town he worked long hours.

"Arizona . . . supposedly."

"Supposedly?"

Sheila's eyes filled with tears. She shrugged.

"What's the matter?" Jan asked gently.

"Nothing," Sheila said. "Nothing I can't deal with."

"Is everything all right?"

Sheila paused. "I think he's having an affair."

"Oh, Sheila," Jan said, touching the top of her friend's hand. "I'm sorry."

"Yeah, well. I've suspected it for quite a while. It's just that . . . I don't know. The bastard left a hotel receipt right in his suit coat, along with a condom."

"He does travel a lot," Jan said weakly.

Sheila glanced up. "I'm on the pill. And the hotel receipt was for the Marriott. Right here in Annapolis. Last Thursday."

"Have you spoken with him about this?"

"I haven't decided what to say yet. I'm trying to figure out if I want to stay with him or if I want a divorce."

"You know, Sheila," Jan said, trying to be careful. "I know that this is a delicate situation, but, I just . . . I think a lot of you. You've got so much to offer. You deserve better."

"It's not that simple."

"Maybe not, but I know that there are a lot of guys that would kill for a chance to make you happy."

"Oh, yeah," she said sarcastically.

"Dave for instance. You must know how he feels about you."

"Oh, we just flirt with each other. It's just in fun."

Jan shook her head. "I think he really cares about you."

Sheila sighed. "I don't know. I'm confused right now."

"I know this isn't easy, but well, I think you should give your husband a kick in the ass—right out the door."

"No offense, Jan," Sheila said before she could stop herself. "But you're hardly one to give advice."

"What?"

"You know what I mean. You can be tough at work, but when it comes to relationships, you're certainly no expert."

Jan glanced away, surprised and hurt. She nodded sadly and said, "You've got a point."

Sheila hesitated, feeling remorse for her loose tongue. "I'm sorry," she said. "I can understand your hesitation to get in a real relationship. You've suffered so much loss. But I just wish you would deal with it and move on. You need to get out, start dating a little. The way you live your life—consumed in work . . . it's not healthy."

Jan thought for a moment. "I don't really want to talk about this."

"You don't have to say anything. I only brought this up because I'm worried about you."

"Well, don't worry," Jan said defensively. She appreciated Sheila caring enough to say something, but she wasn't a basket case. At least—not yet.

"Don't be mad," Sheila said.

"I'm not mad," Jan said, avoiding her eyes. "And to prove it," she said, forcing a smile, "I'll buy you dinner."

"No, thanks. I might run into my husband having a romantic dinner with his date."

"Come on," Jan urged once more. "Let's go out tonight. Let's go do something wild."

Sheila shook her head. "Thanks. But I think I should

go home. I've got to make some decisions." Sheila stood up. "Do you have any plans for this weekend?"

Jan raised an eyebrow. "Is that a joke?"

Sheila shook her head. "You're working."

"Yes, but I really have to," she said defensively. "There's so much to do—"

"That's okay," Sheila said sympathetically. She smiled sadly. "Have a good one."

"Yeah, " Jan said weakly. "I'll be thinking about you."

After Sheila left, Jan worked another two hours then pushed some papers into her briefcase. She switched off the light in her office and headed down the dark corridor. She yanked open the glass door that led to the foyer and froze. Nick and Rachel Wyons, the new assistant state's attorney, were standing by the elevator. Nick had his arm loose around Rachel's waist. She was leaning up against him with her whole body, running her fingertips down the rough scratch marks on his face.

Rachel leaned backward, giggling. As she turned her head she saw Jan. She nudged Nick and motioned toward her.

Nick twisted his head in time to catch Jan's stare.

Mortified to have been caught gawking, Jan quickly recovered and pushed open the door. "I'm sorry . . ." she mumbled, "I thought I was alone."

Nick had pulled away from Rachel, embarrassed. "I

just finished discussing the Moriarty case with Rachel," he said.

Jan nodded as she racked her brain for a reason to go back to her office. She didn't want to ride down in the elevator with Rachel and Nick. "How's the Moriarty case coming?" she heard herself ask.

"We have a lot of research to do," Rachel said, giving Nick a sly smile. "We'll probably be at it all weekend."

Jan could feel herself blush as she stepped onto the elevator. She stood silently in the corner, avoiding looking at either of them. What was her problem? After all, it wasn't as if she was interested in Nick. He had made his advances and she had rejected each and every one. Yet she was feeling jealous, jealous of the fact that they had each other, and once again, she was spending the weekend by herself.

She didn't usually succumb to feelings of self pity—after all, as she liked to remind herself, if she wanted to be with someone she would. But she wasn't content with settling for anyone—not even Nick. She wanted fireworks, passion, a physical and emotional connection. Perhaps, she realized, glancing at Nick, she wanted too much.

The elevator doors finally opened and Jan escaped with a quick and cheerful, "Have a good weekend."

She fled outside, trying to beat them to the parking structure. She ran through the lot and up the stairs to the fourth floor. It was not until she was in her car that she allowed herself to breathe.

So what was she going to do now? Return home full of self pity, go to sleep and have nightmares of Custin running around murdering women? Wake up tomorrow morning and head back into work, all the while trying to forget about Custin?

She turned onto the highway, glancing at the sign to the airport. She thought about Custin living in Florida. Moving on with his life, starting fresh, while Jan was still mired in the past, trying to make sense out of all the destruction. It wasn't fair.

Did he even know that he killed her? She wanted to see Custin, to tell him what happened to Frannie. You remember Frannie, she would say. *You should. You killed her. . . .*

Her anger was growing stronger by the second. She forgot all about her sad dating life. Everything seemed insignificant in comparison to the hatred she felt for the man who had taken her sister away. How could they have let him go? Had he gone back to his old ways? Was he destroying other women just like he had destroyed her sister?

If he was, this rookie cop Max certainly wouldn't be able to stop him.

She tapped the steering wheel impatiently. She was suddenly full of energy—a panicked energy which made her want to take action immediately.

If only she could see Custin for herself—perhaps that would be the closure she needed. She could confront the monster. Deal with the anger and pain that swirled around her heart and move on. But did she have the nerve to do it? She had dealt with more rapists and murderers than she could count off the top of her head, but this guy was different.

And anyway—what would she do, just fly to Sebring, Florida, and show up at his doorstep? Hell, she was the type to book non-refundable tickets months in advance, and arrive at the gate with a solid hour to spare.

Yet it would be so simple, she realized as the exit approached. She could rent a car at the airport, get a map and drive to Sebring. She had no plans this weekend . . . no one would even miss her.

The exit to the airport was in front of her.

If she was going to go, she needed to do it now. Because by tomorrow, someone—maybe even herself, would have talked some sense into her.

12

MAX OPENED A BEER AND PLOPPED DOWN ON HIS COMFORTABLE sofa. It was close to midnight on Friday, and he had left a team of detectives still busy at work. He would have been right there with them if Frank hadn't insisted he go home and get some sleep.

Max glanced out of the open French doors which led to the balcony. It was a perfect night for a sail. There was a full moon and a soft breeze was blowing across the Chesapeake. Staring out at the water, he could almost feel the subtle rocking of the boat. It was this waterfront location that had sold Max on this small one bedroom, one bathroom apartment. The building was situated on a bluff overlooking the Chesapeake Bay, and his balcony was perched right above the water, giving him an expansive view of blue green water.

It was to the soothing, steady hum of a small, portable fan that he now picked up the file labeled

Garret. The file that Jan had messengered to him during the day.

He hadn't had the time to go through this earlier. After Jan left he had hurried over to Neff's house, where they had confiscated hammers, screwdrivers, anything that could be considered a weapon. A pair of barber shears had been found in a bathroom drawer. Duct tape had been found in the basement, a black ski mask in the front hall closet.

Some preliminary tests had already been done on the items and Lucy's hair had turned up on the scissors. Neff's lawyer was insisting that the scissors didn't even belong to Neff. Lucy had brought them over to cut his hair and had trimmed her own bangs when she was finished. The explanation made sense only because Neff's hair had been found on the scissors as well.

He opened the file, his mind drifting back toward Jan. She seemed convinced that Custin had something to do with the recent murders—even though Max had proved to her it was nearly impossible.

Anyone else might have been irritated by the way she was hounding him about Custin, but he understood. After all, he had been there.

Kelly.

He had planned on marrying her. She had been a sophomore at the University of Michigan, a year younger than him. They had planned to meet at his apartment at eleven o'clock, for a Valentine's Day celebration. But on the way home from the library, Kelly stopped at a convenience store not a hundred feet away from his apartment complex. She interrupted a robbery, and ended up dead when the robber panicked and discharged his gun.

Her murderer had been prosecuted and sentenced to life in prison. Three years after Kelly's death Max was working the beat in Baltimore when he was called to the scene of a robbery in progress. A man was robbing a convenience store off Pratt Street, and he had taken a young woman hostage. The woman had looked nothing like Kelly, but it didn't matter. For all intents and purposes Max had flown back in time. To save her would be like saving Kelly. The guy surrendered, but Max went berserk—punching the perp and threatening to kill him. If his partner hadn't been there to stop him, he just might have. He had taken a walk back to hell, and it almost cost him his career.

And now Jan was taking the same risk. He wanted to put her mind at ease, to reassure her that Frannie's rape was not related to the most recent murders. He was hoping to find something else besides the parole officer's word—anything that would prove that Custin was not responsible for the recent murders.

Max thumbed through the papers, searching for the initial police interview with Frannie. He found what he was looking for, a piece of paper stamped confidential, and pulled it out. Lieutenant Jeff Brown had interviewed Frances Garret at three A.M. on May eleventh.

He had interviewed her again later that same day, at ten o'clock in the morning.

Frances Garret, age twenty-six, had returned home from her job waitressing at the Blue Crab shortly after midnight. She lived with a roommate in a small cottage on the Severn River, about five miles south of downtown Annapolis. Her roommate was staying at her boyfriend's house, and when Frannie pulled into the drive, the only thing she noticed out of the ordinary was that her porch light was off. She walked up to the front door, still not noticing anything unusual. It was then, as she pulled out her keys, that she was attacked from behind.

At first I didn't realize what was happening. It was dark, and he was dressed in black. I couldn't really see him. Even though he was twisting my arms behind me, forcing me to walk, I didn't feel any pain. I wasn't even afraid. I just—I thought I was going to throw up. And I kept trying to will it away. . . .

According to Frannie's statement, he had taped her hands together and led her into the woods, threatening to kill her if she struggled. Once in the woods, he . . .

Cut off my shirt. Literally cut it off, with scissors. He used the scissors to cut off my bra.

Scissors? Sarah Tomkins and Lucy Haverdale had been found without shirts or bras. Had the killer cut them off with scissors? Perhaps the same scissors he had used to cut their hair?

Max skimmed forward, looking for a description. It

was not until she was raped that she had a chance to see the part of his face that wasn't covered by his mask.

I remember focusing on his eyes. They were blue. A soft blue. Almost pretty. And his voice. He spoke to me, saying things like, "Good girl, Frannie. Good girl. . . ."

He knew her name.

Max leaned forward and put down his beer.

He had a nice voice . . . polite. Educated. Smart. He spoke softly, almost like a boyfriend. . . . I couldn't see his face but I had a sense that he was handsome. . . . I had a feeling I had met him before. . . .

Max had surmised that Sarah and Lucy had also known their killer. Perhaps they had met him at the bar in which they worked. Perhaps he had spoken with them, even flirted with them.

Was he reading the words of the dead Haverdale and Tomkins women? Had they heard those same words, felt the same terror?

He stopped himself from going further. If he wasn't careful, he would walk right into Jan's private nightmare. Frannie Garret's rape had been solved. Curtis Custin had confessed, and he had an alibi for both the Tomkins and Haverdale murders.

Nonetheless, something was bothering him, maybe the same thing that was bothering Jan. The similarities among the three cases were striking.

13

HICKORY DICKORY DOCK . . . *THE MOUSE RAN UP THE CLOCK* . . .

He stopped at the red light, humming to himself as he tapped his fingers on his stick shift, beating out the tune he couldn't seem to get out of his head. Today was the first day he had been in a reasonably good mood all week. He prided himself on his moods. He was known as cheery and upbeat, the kind of guy that puts on a smile regardless of what's going on inside.

It was the last girl that got him down. *Not my fault*, he reminded himself. After all, he hadn't meant for her to be killed. But she had pulled off his mask and recognized him. The one before that . . . an accident. Just an accident.

He had gotten lazy without practice. Slack.

If he wasn't careful, he would be sent away. He would stop. It was that simple. He had no choice.

A good-looking girl driving a white convertible

pulled alongside him. He nodded hello, flashing her a dazzling smile. She grinned and turned away. The light changed and the girl sped ahead, cutting in front of him as she gave him a little wave.

She was flirting with him. He was tempted to write down her license plate number even though chances were slim he would follow up on it. He just had a gut feeling that she wasn't the right one. When the right one came along, he'd know.

He chuckled to himself. The brief interaction with the girl had caused the adrenaline to churn in his stomach. Despite the warning, he couldn't stop now. He wasn't a quitter. He had to get it right at least once. *One more time,* he whispered to himself. *One more time.*

14

SHORTLY BEFORE NINE, JAN'S RENTED BLUE TERCEL TURNED OFF
Route 21 and onto Willbury Road. She glanced down at
the map spread out beside her. Willbury to Blue Ridge
then left.

Her anger had abated somewhat by the morning
and in its place was a raw, nervous anxiety that made
her question whether she could follow through with
her plan.

Everything so far had gone well. She hadn't had any
difficulty buying an eight hundred dollar round-trip
ticket spur-of-the-moment. She was proud that she
hadn't snapped back into reality the minute she heard
the price of this adventure.

She had arrived in Orlando at ten, rented a car and

checked into the first Holiday Inn she had seen, one not far from the airport. She had thrown her pantyhose in the trash, washed her underwear in the sink and set it on top of the air conditioner to dry. By the time she drifted off to sleep it was close to two in the morning.

She woke at six, and after throwing on the damp underwear and crumpled blue suit, she stepped out into the oppressive heat. With the directions from the car rental place spread out on the seat beside her, she headed off toward Sebring, not even bothering to drink the luke-warm complimentary coffee offered in the hotel lobby.

Now, at nine o'clock in the morning, Jan was almost there. She turned into a wealthy community of palatial suburban homes, each with about an acre of elaborately landscaped lawn. She picked up the map, holding it in her hand as she slowed down. According to the map, she was on Custin's street, at least, she was on the street that *a* Curtis Custin lived on. Jan was overcome with a sense of disappointment. There had been a mistake. This was not the same Curtis Custin that had just been released from prison. This was not the neighborhood that a guy fresh out of prison could afford.

Damn it all! She had just assumed that Max knew what he was talking about when he told her that Custin was living in Sebring. She didn't doubt that there was a Custin living here, but he obviously wasn't the one she was looking for. How could Max have screwed up like this? For all she knew, Custin wasn't even in Florida.

She shook her head. She was a fool. She had gone off on a wild goose chase, tracking the wrong man.

She pulled up in front of 112 Blue Ridge, a large, white colonial which was the residence of at least one Curtis Custin.

The house, like the rest of the street, was quiet. A brand new red Trans Am was parked out front.

Before his incarceration, Custin had been a perpetual drifter from a poor family in Florida. He wouldn't be able to rent a room in this place, much less own it. She had come all this way for nothing.

Was it possible that this man was a distant relative of Custin? Perhaps his namesake? If he was, perhaps she might be able to get a lead on where Custin was now.

So why didn't she just get out of the car and go ring the doorbell? What was stopping her?

Common sense, perhaps?

There was knock on her window. An adolescent boy was standing outside her car. He was wearing a white T-shirt with JESUS emblazoned in big, black letters across the front. A pair of giant, black sunglasses were wrapped around his delicately featured face.

She pressed the button for the automatic windows. As her window slid down, he leaned over and peered inside her car suspiciously. "Can I help you?" he asked authoritatively, his voice surprisingly deep. She guessed he was older than he looked. Probably a thin and fragile fourteen.

"No," she replied, surprised. "But thank you for asking." She shot him a little smile before she began rolling the window back up.

He grasped on to the top of the moving window and said, "How come you're just sitting here?"

"You seem to be a nice kid, but everything's fine. Go play."

He pointed to a sign on the other side of the street. "We have a neighborhood watch. My dad told me that I'm supposed to patrol the streets until noon."

"Look, will you go away if I give you a dollar? I'm really busy." She fished a crumpled single from her wallet and pushed it at him. He snapped it up with his greedy little hand.

"So what are you doing here?"

Jan hesitated. "Listen—"

"Are you going to tell me why you're here or do I have to go get my dad?"

"Look," Jan said, about to jump down his throat. Instead she took a deep breath. What did it matter? "I, um, I'm here to see the man who lives there. . . ." she said, nodding toward Custin's house.

"Custin? What are you, in insurance or something?"

"Me? No, I . . ." she paused.

Before she had a chance to answer the boy leaned in the car and barked "What's your name?"

She couldn't help but laugh. He had worn her down. She joked, "Are you a lawyer?"

"The name's Randall. What's yours?"

This time she didn't hesitate. "Jan Garret."

"Why do you want to see Mr. Custin, Mrs. Garret?"

"I'm an attorney."

"An attorney," he said with a knowing smile. "How can you tell when a lawyer is lying?"

Before Jan had a chance to answer, he said, beaming from ear to ear, "His lips are moving."

"Ha ha," she said. "Where'd you learn that one?"

"In juvenile detention."

"Great," she replied. This kid couldn't be real.

"What do you have to see Mr. Custin about?"

"Some, uh, personal stuff."

"What is it, messy divorce?"

"What?"

"I've seen his"—he leaned forward and raised his sunglasses so that she could see him wink—"friend."

"Friend?"

"Girlfriend."

"Oh, really?"

He nodded as he looked toward the house in admiration. "She's got a nice set. I mean, I prefer them smaller but I wouldn't mind . . ."

"Oh my God," she said, opening the door. He proved surprisingly nimble on his feet, considering that, unbeknownst to her, he had been standing on his skateboard. "I'm afraid I have to cut our interview short, Counselor."

"See you, Mrs. Garret," he said cheerfully. He adjusted his glasses and zoomed off on his skateboard, arms crossed in front of him.

Jan marched up the walk and rang the doorbell. She was so anxious to get rid of the boy, she hadn't even hesitated.

"Keep your pants on," a woman yelled from inside. A minute later the door opened. Jan found herself staring at a pretty, young woman with bleached blond hair and, as the kid had mentioned, two of the largest breasts she had ever seen. The woman was wearing jeans so tight that Jan doubted she could sit down and a T-shirt that said I'M GETTING LUCKY "I'm sorry to bother you," Jan said politely. "But I'm looking for Curtis Custin . . ."

"Curtis!" the woman screamed. "You got yerself a visitor!"

Jan held her breath as she heard a toilet flush in the background.

"What?" a man's voice said.

"Some lady here to see you," the woman said, leaning up against the door as she crossed her arms in front of her, keeping her wary, blue rimmed eyes trained on Jan.

Jan held her breath as Curtis Custin appeared behind the woman. He was the man she was looking for, she recognized him from his black-and-white mug shots. But he was thin and small, not quite the intimidating man she expected. His hair was tousled and he was wearing a sleeveless white T-shirt with a brown stain on the front. He had another stain on his upper lip, what looked like grape juice.

Jan had fantasized about this moment many times over the years. How she would confront her sister's attacker. What she would say. In some fantasies, she would shoot him dead on the spot. In others she would hammer him with questions, beating him down until he asked for forgiveness from her and from God.

But now, standing there looking at her sister's rapist, it was real, finally. And the moment was not nearly as dramatic and emotional as Jan had anticipated.

Curtis gave the woman a little pat on her tight rear end. "Go into the kitchen and wait for me, lambchop," he said with a thick southern twang. He walked up to the screen. "Hello, little lady."

There was something wrong here, something terribly wrong. She had read Frannie's statement and interview with the police so many times, she could recite it word for word. This man was not the man her sister had described. This man was a small, weasely guy with a strong southern accent. With his scrawny arms and pot belly, Jan didn't think anyone would ever mistake him for handsome.

"What can I do you for?" He was calm and cool. He wasn't worried about the police pounding down his door.

"Curtis," the woman's voice could be heard through the hall. "You didn't put the seat down!"

"I's going to," he hollered back.

I could tell he was an educated man . . . a deep, heavy sounding voice. . . .

"What are you—selling something?"

She was staring at his eyes. They were small and dark . . . almost black. *He had soft blue eyes. . . .*

"Lady," he said squinting suspiciously. "What do you want?"

"I, uh . . ."

He must have been at least six feet. I struggled but he was too strong. He kept saying my name, over and over, as if he was trying to seduce me. To calm me. . . .

She tried to speak but couldn't

"Are you another one of those Jehovah's or something? We just had one yesterday and I gotta say, we have our own religion, okay? It comes in six packs and it's all I need, so don't go bothering us no more."

"I'm sorry," she said softly.

He closed the door and she stepped away.

15

Sunday, August 9

"GOOD MORNING, JAN."

Jan waved at the familiar sight of Mrs. Fletcher working in her garden. With her cup of coffee in hand, Jan stepped out of her porch and walked toward her elderly neighbor. At seven-thirty on Sunday morning, the temperature was a cool seventy-nine degrees with eighty-five percent humidity. Mrs. Fletcher looked as if she had been gardening for hours, her fluffy grey hair frizzy and loose under her wide brimmed woven sun hat. She was wearing large, owl-shaped, pink-tinted sunglasses that covered more than half her face.

Jan couldn't imagine she looked much better. Her flight didn't land until close to midnight, and when she arrived home she was so wound up she found it impossible to sleep. She was haunted by the memory of Curtis Custin standing in his doorway. She was almost positive that he was not the man who attacked her sister, but how could that be?

Mrs. Fletcher smiled as Jan approached. "I've been meaning to talk to you about this," she said, using her shears to point toward a vine that was crawling up a tree. "We've got ourselves a little problem around here." She used the shears to chop off a piece and held it up toward Jan. "Polygonum Perfoliatum. Otherwise known as the Mile-a-Minute vine."

Jan nodded. She liked Mrs. Fletcher. She only hoped she could be so active and independent when she was her age. "Mile-a-minute, huh? Seems like it sprung out of nowhere."

"It's all over the woods. There wasn't any a couple of years ago and now it's all that you see."

"I take it it's a bad vine."

Mrs. Fletcher took a step back, as if stunned by Jan's ignorance. She exclaimed, "Bad?! My goodness, Jan, do you know what this will do? This will suffocate your trees, strangle your flowers, consume your house. It will simply take over unless you control it."

"That doesn't sound good."

Mrs. Fletcher went back to her business, yanking at the vine with all her might. "These are terrible. Simply terrible."

"Mrs. Fletcher," Jan interrupted worriedly. She didn't think it was a good idea for Mrs. Fletcher to be exerting herself in this kind of heat. She put a hand on her arm. "I'll take care of this."

"I've got the bastard," Mrs. Fletcher said, giving it a final yank. She fell down on her rump, holding the root up in the air as though it was a prize worth money.

"Oh no!" Jan exclaimed, helping her up. "Really, Mrs. Fletcher. You shouldn't be doing that kind of thing."

"Why? Cuz I might break my hip?"

"Well," Jan said, not wanting to hurt her feelings. "It seems like kind of a tough way to get rid those of things. Isn't there something I can spray?"

"Spray? Good God, you'll kill all your vegetation, it would sink into our water."

"Okay, so I'll do it by hand."

"Just pull it out . . . or hack it off. But you better get started. It's already on your trees. It's vicious. Grows six inches a day."

"Six inches?"

She nodded.

"And I'm sorry about the length of my grass," Jan added. "I plan on mowing it today." She glanced up at the dark clouds overhead. "Provided of course, it doesn't rain."

Mrs. Fletcher smiled at her, giving Jan a glimmer of hope that her elderly neighbor wasn't as angry as she had suspected. "I don't care about your grass. I can take care of that in a flash with my new self-propelled mower. The thing practically drags me behind it, it moves so fast. Sometimes I just jump on the back and go for a ride. But I just worry about this vine. It's nasty," she said, handing it to her.

It looked nasty, Jan thought, staring at the thick, ugly barbed stem. She wondered if the hardware store would carry a machete.

"I'm glad I saw you this morning," Mrs. Fletcher said, nodding for her to follow. "I have something for you."

Jan stepped around the trees and into Mrs. Fletcher's lush yard. She walked over to her garden and pulled some tomatoes off the vine. "A taste of summer."

"Thank you," Jan said. "I love tomatoes."

"Well, I'm going out of town soon with my boyfriend. You come over here whenever you want and pick them."

Jan held the tomatoes close to her chest as she balanced her coffee cup against them. "Your boyfriend?"

"That's how he refers to himself at least. I don't want to get serious though. What do I need an old man around here for? I can barely take care of myself."

"You seem like you're doing pretty well to me," Jan said, impressed.

"He's good for some things. Oh, that reminds me, I've got cukes too. Big ones. You just help yourself."

"That's so nice of you, Mrs. Fletcher. Thank you. Do you want me to take in your mail or anything?"

"Why yes, dear, thank you. That would be nice."

"Where are you going?"

But before she could answer, a black Mitsubishi

came rambling down their driveway, stopping in front of Jan's house.

"That thing sure kicks up a lot of dust," Mrs. Fletcher commented.

"I'll tell her to take it slower," Jan apologized, recognizing Sheila's car.

She said goodbye to Mrs. Fletcher and made her way toward Sheila, who had stepped out of her car and was waving a donut in Jan's direction.

"What are you doing here?" Jan asked.

Sheila handed her a box of Dunkin Donuts. "Just thought I'd stop by."

"At seven-thirty on Sunday morning?"

Sheila shrugged. "All right, I'm trying to kill time. I don't want to go home yet. But I *was* thinking about you. You're not mad at me, are you?"

"Wait a minute. What do you mean you haven't been home *yet?*"

"I stayed out all night."

Jan's eyes opened wide. "Let's sit on the porch."

As Sheila settled into the wicker loveseat, Jan said, "You're going to make me ask, aren't you. Were you with Dave?"

"With Dave? Last night? No," she said, starting to laugh.

"Well, where were you?"

"In New York."

"New York."

Sheila nodded. "After I left you on Friday, I went

127

home and waited for Mark. He came waltzing in at two in the morning reeking of perfume and smoke. I played it cool. I didn't want any theatrics. He walked in the door and I was in bed pretending to be asleep. The next morning I pretended like everything was fine. I didn't even mention it. Didn't ask him where he'd been— nothing. He went to the gym around three o'clock and I wrote a note: *Mark—went out with a friend for dinner. Won't be home late."*

"But you really went to New York."

"I needed to kill some time. So I took the train to New York, went to see a couple of movies and came back. And here I am."

"And you never called Mark."

Sheila shook her head. "Nope."

"Sheila . . ." Jan said as if she was disappointed in her—then she broke out in a smile. "Brilliant."

"Let him see how it feels."

"You can't keep doing this, though."

"You're not kidding. I can't afford it. You know how much a round-trip ticket to New York costs? One hundred and twenty dollars."

"Geesh," Jan said, thinking about her eight-hundred-dollar ticket.

"I'm going to leave him. I've made up my mind. I called my lawyer from Dunkin Donuts."

"Your lawyer works for Dunkin Donuts?"

"Funny," Sheila said, rolling her eyes. "I used the phone there."

"I think this is for the best."

Sheila nodded. "Thank you. You know, on Friday, that little spat we had . . . well, I realized it was a matter of courage for me, too. I think I can do it now. I hate my relationship with Mark, but it's comfortable. I'm used to it. My dad treated my mother that way. . . . It's what I grew up with. But it's time for a change."

"I think that's great."

Sheila nodded as she picked up a donut. "So, what have you been doing this weekend?"

"Well, " Jan said, following suit and choosing a plain donut with white icing. "I went on a little trip, too."

"You did?"

"To Florida."

"Florida? Get out!" she said, swatting Jan's arm.

Jan shrugged and grinned.

"What's in Florida?"

"Not what but who. Curtis Custin."

Sheila put down her donut. "Oh my God," she said slowly.

"I had to—"

"What did you do? Does Nick know?" Sheila asked almost at once.

"I went to Custin's house. And, no, Nick doesn't know."

"What—how did this all come about?"

"It was, well, kind of spontaneous. Friday after work I just decided to do it."

"I can't believe you. How did you even know where to find him?"

"Max had told me Custin was living in Sebring. Information had his address."

"And?" Sheila said, holding her breath.

"I just . . . well, he's nothing like my sister described him. I mean, like she described the guy who raped her. She said the guy was tall, handsome . . ."

"I thought he was wearing a mask?"

"He was. But she could see white teeth, blue eyes. She heard him speak. . . ." Her voice drifted off.

Sheila was silent for a moment as she realized what her friend was trying to say. "You don't think he did it?"

"It's just . . . weird. Custin is living in this huge house with a brand new sports car in the driveway. I'll find out tomorrow if he owns the house, but still, it's strange."

"Do you think Custin took the rap and got paid off?"

After a brief pause, Jan said, "I, well, I'm not sure what to think."

"But . . ."

"But what?"

"Frannie was at the sentencing. If there was a problem, why didn't she mention it then—to Nick? To the judge? To anyone?"

Jan glanced away. Sheila had a point.

"Look," Sheila continued. "This is creepy. Maybe you should talk to Max."

"Forget it."

"He's very sensitive. And he's smart and thorough."

"From now on if I need help I'll talk to Hank."

"I'd talk to Max over Hank."

"You would? Hank's our friend. I don't even know Max."

"Hank's got too many things on his plate right now. I heard he's having some problems with Judy," she said, referring to his wife. "Besides, Max just seems . . . sharp to me. Did you know he's a pianist?"

"Really?"

"Hank said he plays really well. He even has a piano in his apartment."

Jan stood up and said, frustrated, "For God's sake, Sheila. This isn't about my social life."

"I know," she said defensively. "I just thought he might be able to help. What about Nick? Are you at least going to tell him?"

Jan nodded. "Tomorrow."

"Maybe he can shed some light on this whole thing."

"Yeah," Jan said. "I hope so."

131

16

Monday, August 10

"SUSAN . . ." JAN PAUSED, STRUGGLING FOR THE RIGHT WORDS AS she held the phone to her ear. "There's a pattern here. I think we need to focus on your kids . . ."

Susan Brattenburg was a twenty-three-year-old woman who, at age eighteen, had married her mother's ex-husband, a man who had been her stepfather for ten of her eighteen years. Susan was eight months pregnant when they married, and the man who had been an abusive father became an abusive husband. During their brief marriage of five years, Susan had given birth to two more children, and the beatings from her husband, Hal, had intensified. She finally summoned enough strength to file for divorce, and had even found a job working as a cashier at a grocery store when Hal snapped, breaking into her small home and pistol-whipping her with a loaded gun and threatening her life. Susan filed charges and Jan had been assigned to the case. Jan knew that it was difficult to get a conviction for attempted murder when the victim was the wife of the defendant because nine times out of ten the wife changed her mind and declined to prosecute. Without the wife's assistance, despite valiant efforts by the state, the whole case would go quickly down the toilet.

"He said he's changed."

Jan shut her eyes as she continued to tap her pencil on her desk. "If you drop the charges now, and I'm not saying that you can . . . because this thing has been set in motion and we may decide to prosecute anyway," Jan said, although she doubted they would. "If you drop them now, sooner or later, in a week or in a month . . . maybe, if you're lucky, a year, he's going to revert right back to his old actions. I think in your heart you know that I'm right."

"I'm sorry about all of the trouble I caused you," Susan said quickly. "I am. You've been so nice to me. So helpful. I just . . . well, you wouldn't understand. I have to go now."

Jan hung up the phone. She felt like she'd been clobbered over the head. She glanced at the black clock hanging on the wall. It was only nine-thirty. Not a good way to start the day.

Pulling herself together, she picked up her phone to buzz Sheila. She had tried to call her several times last night, but there hadn't been an answer. She was anxious to hear how her confrontation with Mark had gone.

"Hey," Dave said, practically jumping into her office. He was obviously in good spirits. "Good weekend?" he asked playfully, noting her expression.

"Oh, yeah," she said, twirling a finger around in the air. Jan set down the phone. Sheila hadn't answered.

Dave said, "I called you Friday night about ten. No answer. I figured you had a hot date or something."

Jan squinted, remembering. Her conversation with Susan Brattenburg had totally disoriented her. "Friday night I was . . ." on her way to see Curtis Custin. It seemed like a week ago. "Working," she said elusively. She didn't have the strength to get into this whole thing now.

"Working? If I would've known you were going to stay here and work, I would've made you come out with me."

"Why did you try and call?"

"Because I wanted to convince you to come out with us. It was fun."

Jan heard Sheila down the hall and called out to her. Sheila stuck her head in. "What's up?"

Jan smiled, relieved to see that her friend was still walking and talking at the same time. A good sign.

Sheila walked past Dave and playfully patted his shoulder. "New pants?"

He nodded, pleased that she had noticed.

"Are you okay?" Jan asked. She knew she should

probably wait for Dave to leave but she was worried about her friend.

Sheila shrugged. "Fine," she replied noncommittally.

Jan was eyeing her carefully. "Really?"

"Why wouldn't she be fine?" Dave asked, concerned.

Sheila shot Jan a warning glance.

Jan got the message: *Shut up.* "No reason. It's just me. I'm projecting," Jan said, taking the focus off Sheila.

"Still worried about that client whose case you lost? The hooker?" Dave asked.

"Terry," Jan replied defensively. "Yeah, I am," she said, making a mental note to call her. She had meant to stop by this weekend, but her Florida trip had proved too much of a distraction.

"Did you talk to Nick yet?" Sheila asked.

"I haven't had a chance. I just got off the phone with Susan Brattenburg."

Sheila rolled her eyes as she sat in the chair next to Dave. "Don't tell me," she said. "She decided not to testify."

Jan nodded as she leaned back in her chair resignedly.

"I told you," Sheila said, almost excited by her own perception. "I called it. I called it from the very beginning."

Jan picked up her pencil and scribbled something on the open notebook in front of her.

"So what was her excuse?" Dave asked. "Wait, let me guess. He . . . what's her husband's name? Woody?"

"Hal!" Jan said.

"Hal came over and seemed so sweet and so sorry that she just knew that this time, this time he was going to be different."

"More or less. He was dating a friend of hers, probably trying to make her jealous. It worked. He told her that he was breaking off with the friend and coming back to her."

"So she's the lucky winner. The winner of the prize." Sheila shook her head. "What a prize. A big, fat, ugly wife-beater."

She turned to Dave, who had been silent until now. "What are you doing?"

"Thinking of a joke." He paused. "Okay," he said, nodding as it all came together. "What do you get when a man marries his daughter?"

"Children and grandchildren all in one?" Sheila asked.

"No. A tired and cranky assistant SA."

Jan rolled her eyes. "Funny."

"What does a mountain man get when his wife has a girl?"

"A mountain man . . ." Jan began.

"He's trying to be politically correct," Sheila offered.

"A daughter and niece all in one."

Nick's assistant, Iris Patterson, popped her head in. "Jan? Nick wants to see you."

"Thank God," Jan said, picking up the notebook. "Things are getting raunchy around here."

* * *

Nick was sitting behind his desk when Jan entered.

"Hi," she said.

"Shut the door," he replied solemnly.

Jan did as she was told, nervously noting Nick's expression. She hoped he wasn't going to apologize for his behavior on Friday. She didn't want to discuss his relationship with her peer.

"Have a good weekend?"

"It was okay," she said, still standing in front of his desk.

"Do anything interesting?"

Jan glanced away. "Depends on what you call interesting."

"Go anywhere?"

She caught his eye. Maybe this wasn't about Rachel. "Here and there."

He tapped his finger on his desk, high speed, his smile more tense than usual. He was definitely after something, but she could not be sure what. Could he have found out about her trip?

"Custin's parole officer called me at home yesterday. Said someone claiming to be from my office was down there harassing Custin."

She tried not to show her surprise, but she could feel the blood rushing to her face. "Is that so?"

"A woman. A short woman with blond hair and a bad-ass attitude."

"He said that?"

He stopped tapping his finger and with a frustrated shake of his head said, "Jesus, Jan."

"I didn't tell Custin who I was. But I think I might have mentioned it to one of his neighbors. A kid who—"

"What the hell is your problem? How stupid can you be? Did you forget everything I ever taught you? Did you lose all your common sense?!"

"No."

"You were talking to his neighbors? What'd you do, go up the street ringing doorbells?"

"No! This kid came up to the car," she said defensively. "I didn't say why I was there . . ."

"You shouldn't have said anything at all. You shouldn't have even been there."

"Look, I was going to tell you about this today. The whole thing was really unsettling—"

"I bet."

"No. It wasn't like I thought it would be. Custin," she said, hesitating, "He's nothing like Frannie described. He's this scrawny, slovenly guy—she described him as being tall and handsome—"

"Victims often get the description wrong. You know that."

"Not this guy. This guy's a different species from the guy my sister described. Her attacker had a well-educated voice—this guy's got this piercing southern twang—"

"So he disguised his voice—"

"Plus, he lives in a mansion. Custin was a drifter, he

138

was broke. Now one month out of prison he's suddenly rich—"

"Jan," Nick said, shaking his head as if exhausted. "The boy confessed. I was there."

"Something is not right. Definitely not right."

"I'm not going to argue with you about this, but I'll tell you something." He cleared his throat, and then said, "I know you're shaken up by these murders—I don't blame you. There are definitely some serious similarities to Frannie, and the timing makes it even weirder. But I'll tell you what—Neff is a scary guy. I wouldn't be surprised if he knew about Custin. Perhaps he was even trying to make it look like this is Custin's doing."

"I can't believe I'm hearing this."

"Listen, I was right about Goldman, wasn't I?" he asked, referring to a convicted child molester. "You thought he was just a sweet old guy."

Jan was silent.

"I was right about Estes, right?" he asked, referring to a man who had murdered his girlfriend's mother. "There was no evidence until the woman started talking weeks later. You swore up and down he couldn't have known about her mother and the extra key."

"This is different."

"This is not different. It's the same. But you're too impatient, too impetuous to spend time adding up all of the little clues. You're a great prosecutor, but a lousy detective." Nick paused and then continued, "There was a guy in Arkansas, this bank robber named Wes Donhoe, who became an expert at escaping detection. Donhoe would pick a guy fresh out of prison or someone who had just beaten up a cop and commit a crime leaving a few clues behind to frame them. The cops and prosecutors were so anxious to solve the crime, they'd arrest the innocent schmuck and he'd be back in prison before he could blink. Donhoe knew that even if he left out a few details, the prosecutors would be so anxious to nail the perp, they'd be willing to overlook a few things."

"You're saying that you think Neff is trying to frame Custin?"

"I'm saying it's a possibility."

"But highly unlikely. And Neff didn't have anything to do with the fact that Custin is living the high life, that he doesn't resemble my sister's description—"

"Jan," Nick said sternly. "Leave Custin alone. That case was dealt with ten years ago. The man confessed and served his sentence. Custin could press charges and we'd have to put out that fire instead of focusing on nailing Neff."

"Press charges? You've got to be kidding me! For what?"

"Harassment."

"I rang his damn doorbell and then I left."

"He said you harassed him. And the fact that you went down there to see him doesn't help your case."

Jan shook her head as her smile faded. "If you're

telling me I may not be president one day, I'm not worried, Nick."

"Don't get flip with me. I need you to get yourself together and focus on your work. Anyway," Nick said, softening, "you've got a trial this week, don't you?"

"I did. Susan Brattenburg called me this morning. She doesn't want to prosecute."

"More good news," Nick said grimly.

"I know. Without her testimony the case is a wash."

Nick just looked at her and said, as if exhausted, "Is it too early for a martini?"

An hour later, Jan received a fax from Sebring City Hall confirming her suspicion. Custin had purchased the house on Blue Ridge only a week after his release from prison. He had paid $300,000. Cash, she guessed. After all, banks were not in the habit of giving huge loans to ex-cons fresh out of prison.

Jan pulled her copy of the file. According to the police report, Brown initiated the investigation of Custin. He had met Custin once before, during a prostitute sting on West Street the week before Jan's sister was raped.

After the rape, Brown traced Custin, whose car was still impounded, to a hotel in Baltimore. It was there that Custin had initially confessed. Afterwards, Brown brought him back to Crownsville for questioning.

Jan read the testimony again, the same testimony she had studied for hours.

"*What's your address?*"

"*Sebring. Sebring, Florida.*"

"*Your exact address.*"

"*That's as exact as it gets. I've been living with friends. Just till I get back on my feet.*"

"*Place of employment?*"

"*I do odd jobs.*"

"*What were you doing in Annapolis?*"

"*Just here for a couple of days. . . .*"

There were a number of interesting oversights: Why had Custin, a Florida resident, been in Annapolis? Was he visiting someone? Did he know people here? If so, who?

"*Tell us what happened the night of May ninth.*"

"*I went to a bar in Annapolis. I saw this girl. A little thing, damn cute. She gave me one of them smiles, all friendly like. She was into me.*"

"*And?*"

"*So, I followed her home and saw where she lived. Next night I came back and did her.*"

And so he confessed. Nice and easy. Almost too easy. It was as if he was saying what he was told to say. He knew they didn't have anything on him, so why confess? Guilt? It was possible, but doubtful.

And if what he said was true, and he followed her home, that would imply that he did so by car. Frannie had said that she didn't see any strange cars near her drive on the night she was attacked.

Jan picked up a phone book and flipped it open to the

C's. If he was visiting relatives, perhaps they shared the same last name.

Custer, Custis . . . no Custin. But this was the most recent phone book, she reminded herself. She needed one of the old ones they kept at the library.

"Jan?" Iris said, appearing in her doorway.

"Yes?"

"You busy? Nick wants to see you. He's got the senator in there."

"The senator?" Jan asked. "What does he want with me?"

Iris shrugged.

"Can I get out of it? Tell him I'm not here."

"He knows you're here," she said impatiently.

Jan muttered something under her breath, and followed Iris down the hall. She found the senator sitting across from Nick, looking handsome and distinguished, his silver hair combed neatly back.

He looked up and smiled at Jan. "I just stopped by to talk to Nick about his campaign. While I was at it, I thought I'd have a word with you as well. Have a seat," he said, pulling out a chair for her.

She thought about how she might escape, what excuses she might make, then shrugged herself off and sat down.

"As I mentioned the other night I've been hearing some good things about you. We need a strong leader to take over as state's attorney when Nick leaves. As you may know, I'm not thrilled with Steve Farkavey," he said, referring to a local attorney who'd been lobbying for the nomination. "I was hoping that you might be interested."

Jan paused as she looked at Nick. He was nodding. "Me?" she asked.

"I think I mentioned this to you the other night," the senator volunteered.

"You were serious?"

"Of course."

"I, uh," Jan mumbled, "don't know what to say."

"Say yes. Say you'll start campaigning now," the senator said.

Jan squirmed in her chair, hemming and hawing until Nick rescued her. "Why don't you think about it," Nick said.

"Okay," Jan said, standing. "I'll think about it." She probably should have said something a little more eloquent but that was all she could manage.

17

HER AS STATE'S ATTORNEY? AS JAN DROVE TO THE LIBRARY, SHE couldn't help but wonder why the senator had chosen her as Nick's replacement. Okay, he wasn't thrilled with Farkavey for obvious reasons, but what about Nick's two deputies, Chris Kresting and Lisa Chelmitt? They both had seniority over her. Either one would have been a more likely candidate.

This whole business of her replacing Nick had left her with the familiar itchy, uncomfortable feeling she got when things weren't quite right. It was more than she could deal with right now. She didn't have an extra ounce of effort to put into anyone's campaign, much less her own.

The library was an old schoolhouse which had been renovated twenty years earlier. It still had orange shag carpet from the seventies which gave the whole place a sort of retro feel. On a Monday night the place wasn't exactly hopping. Jan guessed that most of the kids were outside, enjoying the brief spell of cooler weather.

Jan tapped on the information desk until an old woman with white hair appeared. Jan peppered her with questions until the smile faded from the librarian's wrinkled face. "Shh," the old woman said, "follow me."

Jan followed her through some glass doors and into a room filled with a collection of books bound in volumes. She walked over to the phone books. "No ten-year-old phone books. We don't even have last year's."

"Do you have anything else that lists the people who lived in the area? I'm looking to see if someone I know had any relatives here."

"Yes, we do. We have city directories. They're similar to phone books, but we only have them through nineteen eighty-five."

Nineteen eighty-five. Three years before her sister's rape. "That would work."

"They're over here," she said, leading her toward a bookshelf in the back. "What year?"

"Nineteen eighty-five."

The woman pulled out a book and set it on a table. "Enjoy," she whispered, and tried to sneak away.

"One more thing," Jan asked. "Do you have back issues of the *Baltimore Sun* and the *Capital* on Microfiche?"

"Micro*film*," the woman said, correcting Jan. "We

sure do. We have that back years and years. Our microfilm room is on the other side."

"Thanks," Jan said. As the woman left, Jan didn't even bother sitting down. She opened the book and flipped to the C's. Custer, Custin. In nineteen eighty-five a Eugenia Custin had lived at 305 Holly Lane.

Holly Lane. Where was that? She walked over to get a better look at the county map on the wall. Holly was a little road off of West Street. Although it was unlikely that Eugenia Custin still lived there, she wondered if some of the neighbors remembered her. Maybe she could get lucky.

With information, that was.

At close to seven, Jan figured she had a few more hours of sunshine left. The home Eugenia Custin had lived in was on a street filled with old dilapidated homes with overgrown yards. The appearance of the house wasn't helped by the old abandoned school next to it.

Jan walked up to the door and rang the bell. While she waited she read the graffiti sprayed across the side of the school.

After a few minutes, she gave up on the doorbell and knocked. A girl who looked to be in her late teens came to the door holding a baby in her hands. "Yes?" she said, peeking out the six-paned window on the top half of the door.

Jan said, "This is probably going to sound strange,

but I was wondering if you knew anything about someone that used to live in this house—a Eugenia Custin?"

The girl shook her head.

"It would have been about ten years ago," Jan said, hoping to stimulate some memory.

The girl squinted her eyes, thinking. She opened the door and said, "Was that when that woman was murdered?"

"There was a murder?"

She nodded. "That's what I heard. But I don't know what her name was. The Ruperts across the street would know, though. They've lived here forever and we just moved in a few years ago. I never would have rented the place if I'd known. It gives me the creeps."

"Yeah, I don't blame you."

"No ghosts though, not yet."

Jan complimented her child's blue eyes, thanked the woman, and crossed the street.

The Ruperts' door was answered by an elderly woman with translucent skin and long, dyed, jet black hair pulled back in a ponytail with a thin, pink ribbon. She wore heavy blue eye shadow and had bright red lipstick smeared unevenly across her lips. Despite her advanced years, she was dressed like a cross between a hooker and a teenager. A pink halter top barely covered her flabby breasts and small black shorts rode up her loose rear end. On her feet were fluffy pink slippers. She reminded Jan of someone—but she couldn't place her.

"Hi," Jan said cheerfully. "I'm hoping you can help me. I'm looking for information about someone that used to live across the street. The last name is Custin—"

"Hold on a second. Who are you?" the woman said, pointing a long, bony finger in her direction.

"Actually, I work for the state's attorney's office," Jan said, pulling her ID out of her purse. "A Curtis Custin was involved in a crime a while back and I was trying to find out if he was related to the Eugenia Custin that lived across the street from you in 1985."

"We don't know any Eugenia Custin."

"What was the name of the person who was murdered? The one that lived there?" she asked, pointing to Eugenia Custin's old house.

"Oh, *Eugenia,*" she said. "We never really knew what her last name was. We always assumed it was O'Malley. At least, that was the name of the fella she was shacked up with."

"Eugenia O'Malley," Jan repeated. "When was she murdered?"

"Oh, Lord," the woman said. "It must be ten years now."

"That has to be her," Jan said, excited.

"Frank," the woman called out. Jan could hear the familiar theme to *Jeopardy* playing in the background. "What is a raisin!" Frank shouted.

"He has to watch *Jeopardy.* Every day," she said, almost apologetically. "Come on in," she said. "He's in the living room."

Baby Jane! That's who the woman reminded her of, Jan thought as she followed her through the entrance way into a small living room. A tall, thin elderly man sat on an old patched recliner. He was pointing a remote control at the two TVs that sat in the corner, one on top of the other. They were both on, each broadcasting a different channel, both with terrible reception. When the man noticed Jan, he slowly pulled himself out of the chair to shake her hand. "Frank Rupert," he said. "Nice to meet you." Like his wife, he looked to be in his eighties. But unlike his wife, he was dressed like a lot of old men in their eighties. Practical, loose fitting pants belted under his breast bone with a light cotton button-down cardigan.

"She's with the state's attorney's office. She wants to ask us some questions about Eugenia from across the street, the one that was murdered," Mrs. Rupert said.

"State's attorney, huh?" Mr. Rupert said.

"I work for him, yes," Jan said as the woman motioned for her to sit down on the couch.

"Coffee?" she asked.

"No, thanks," Jan said. She didn't want to stay there any longer than necessary. Not only was it hot as hell in there, the air reeked of onions and smoke.

"I used to sell you guys paper. All the paper for your typewriters," he said. "I had the account in the sixties, back when Olsen was state's attorney. Who's the state's attorney now?"

"Nick Fitzgerald."

He thought for a minute. "Never heard of him."

"Mr. Rupert," Jan began. "I'm very interested in this Eugenia you knew. What happened to her?"

"She was a tramp," Mrs. Rupert burst in.

"Lillian!" Mr. Rupert exclaimed, as if he was astonished that such a terrible word had come out of her mouth.

Mrs. Rupert shrugged.

"She had an unusual lifestyle," he said diplomatically.

"She was a tramp," Mrs. Rupert repeated.

"A tramp?" Jan asked.

"What my wife is trying to say is that we had reason to suspect she was—"

"A hooker," Mrs. Rupert interrupted. "Married to her pimp. If she *was* married."

"Her pimp?" Jan asked. "What was his name?"

"O'Malley."

A hooker named Eugenia and a pimp named O'Malley. Jan turned back toward Mr. Rupert as if waiting for him to elaborate.

"She had men in and out of that old house. Derelict looking."

"Smoking dope," Mrs. Rupert chimed in.

"So what happened to her?"

"Murdered," Mrs. Rupert said.

"How?" Jan asked.

"Shot. Right through the eyes," Mrs. Rupert said, pointing her index finger to her forehead.

Mr. Rupert rolled his eyes. "We know she was shot in the head. The police thought that she took the wrong fellow home that night."

"But we told the police who did it. Another fellow was staying there when it happened. Just the two of them in that house."

"Where was this O'Malley when she was killed?"

"Dead," Mrs. Rupert chimed in. "He took a heart attack a few weeks before the murder. That's when the kid moved in. She got herself a young replacement." Mrs. Rupert continued. "Didn't take her no time."

Was Curtis Custin this replacement? "What did this other guy look like? The kid?"

"A weasel. That's what."

"Southern accent?" she asked.

Mrs. Rupert thought. "I heard them screaming one day," she said finally. "Him and Eugenia. I seem to recall he did sound a little southern. And of course, Eugenia was from the South."

"Do you happen to remember the name of this kid?" Jan asked. "Was it Curtis Custin by any chance?"

The Ruperts looked at each other, both wrinkling their brow as they tried to remember. "Custard," Mrs. Rupert said suddenly, clapping her hands. "That's it—Curtis Custard! I'd bet my life on it! He was a little pipsqueak. Used to come over and stare in my windows. Hoping I'd get undressed or something."

"Mr. Rupert," Jan said, leaning forward. "Do you

happen to remember exactly when Eugenia was murdered?"

"May. May eighth, 1988," he said.

May eighth. Two days before Frannie was raped.

"I remember the day because it was my brother Charles' sixty-second birthday. We had to go to a big party for him. Couldn't even back out of the drive, all the dang cops were blocking us in, so I had to call my brother and—"

"Talk about crooks!" Mrs. Rupert piped in. "He may be your flesh and blood, but I'll never forgive him for the way he treated me at your mother's funeral—"

"Did the police ever question this Curtis guy?" Jan asked.

"We saw them over there talking to him. They never got him for Eugenia though. Got him thrown away for some rape or something."

"Crime does pay," Mrs. Rupert said knowingly.

"A damn shame," Mr. Rupert said. "That's why I vote Republican. If I had my way, that boy would be toast right now."

As soon as Jan pulled back onto West Street, she picked up her phone and dialed Nick's work number. He wasn't there but his secretary said she had heard him mention something about his boat.

Jan did a U-turn in the street and headed back toward the small private marina where Nick kept the forty-foot sailboat he had christened *Irish Rose*. She had been there once before to deliver Nick some work papers. She flashed the confused marina guard a wave and blew right past him.

She parked her car illegally at the edge of the dock and pulled off her shoes so that she could run without having her heels stick in the wooden slats of the dock. She spotted Nick on his boat, unhooking the mooring. Fortunately, he was alone.

She yelled, "Nick! Wait a minute."

Nick stopped, confusion registering on his handsome face. The day growth of his beard made him appear even more rugged, and his normally perfect hair was tousled from the wind. He was wearing a red Izod shirt and tan Bermuda shorts—his bare feet were tucked into a pair of new looking Docksiders.

Jan began running toward his boat, her dark brown oversized leather purse swinging clumsily over her shoulder, whacking her in the leg.

"What's the matter?" he asked as she stopped in front of his boat.

Without waiting for an offer, she jumped onboard. "Custin," she said simply, pausing to catch her breath.

"What?"

She swallowed, catching her breath. "Ten years ago there was a Eugenia Custin, living over on West Street. She was murdered, murdered on May eighth in nineteen eighty-eight."

He was waiting. "And?"

"Well," she said. His nonchalant reaction had taken

a little wind out of her sails. "The neighbors told me they think Custin's responsible."

Nick shook his head. "That's what you came rushing out here to tell me? Gossip from over ten years ago?"

"Nick?" Rachel came out of the cabin wearing a pair of tight white shorts and a bikini top. Jan glanced at her attire and raised an eyebrow.

"Oh, hi, Jan," she said, giving her almost as warm of a reaction as Nick had.

Jan could feel her face turn red with embarrassment. Play it cool, she advised herself.

"Jan," Nick said reasonably, seemingly unfazed by the fact that Jan had caught him with his lover— once again. "So what? Just because some woman had the same last name as him doesn't mean they're related . . ."

"But . . ."

"And even if they were—what difference could it possibly make today? With the exception of answering your question about Custin's wealth. Maybe he *was* related to this woman and inherited some money when she died. In any case, I'm sure her death was investigated."

"You don't remember it?"

"No," he said, eyeing her carefully. "And considering what the senator mentioned earlier today," he said, obviously not wanting to share any information with Rachel, "I hardly think this type of activity is in your best interest."

Jan was aware Rachel was observing them, trying to figure out what they were talking about. Jan looked Nick in the eye and said, "If he was a murderer, you might have put him away for good."

"Jan, consider your position. The senator wants to help you become the next SA, but if you continue to go off half-cocked—"

"Nick, I'm a lot more interested in getting the guy that hurt my sister than I am in being SA. If you can't understand that . . . screw you!" She clumsily hopped back off the boat, slipping a little as she hit the dock.

Nick hesitated. Glancing at Rachel, he said, "I'll be right back."

He caught up with Jan just as she was jamming her feet back into her Comfort Soles. He grabbed her arm and steadied her. "I don't like to see you so upset." With a sympathetic smile he asked, "What do you want me to do?"

This was Nick again. The Nick that she knew and cared about. At least, the Nick that she thought she knew.

"I want you to help me find out more about Custin. I want to know everything about him. . . ."

"Jan," he began. He shook his head. "This obsession you have with Custin . . ."

He wasn't going to help her. "You just don't get it," she yelled, shrugging off his arm.

He took a step forward, standing so close she could feel his breath on her forehead. She could smell his familiar musky aftershave lotion—or was it cologne? "I just . . . I don't see how this is going to help anything. Custin didn't have anything to do with these murders. You have to let him go."

"I don't think so," she said.

He stood on the dock and watched her walk away. The muscle in his jaw tightened ever so slightly as he turned back toward his boat and Rachel.

18

LUCKY'S TAVERN WAS UNUSUALLY CROWDED. JAN PARKED HER-self on a stool, ordered an oyster shooter and sucked it down.

She had come to watch the crowd and get a feel for the place, in the hope of learning more about Lucy Haverdale. She had to stay focused—she couldn't allow herself to get swept up in the bizarre events of the day. But as she began her second oyster shooter, her resolve began to weaken.

Regardless of what Nick said, she had a feeling Custin was involved with the death of this Eugenia Custin. But what did that mean?

Jan finished off her drink and pushed the glass back toward the edge of the bar. "How long have you worked here?" she asked the bartender as he hurriedly set a drink down in front of a man two stools away from her. He was a big, burly guy working alone behind the counter. Jan wondered if he had worked there for a while, or if he was hired to take the place of Lucy.

"Long enough," he barked, heading off to the next customer.

Jan frowned. So much for her womanly charm.

Her mind drifted to thoughts of Custin, then back to the matter at hand. This was a ratty-looking neighborhood bar with grease-smeared paneled walls and an old tiled floor covered with crushed peanut husks. There were as many women as men, and most were huddled together in small groups where, she guessed, the death of their bartender was still at the forefront of conversation.

Behind the bar were several kegs of home-brewed beer. The sole waitress, a portly woman in her late forties, dressed in a T-shirt and black jeans, squeezed in between the bar stools to place her orders. There were eight bar stools, four of which were presently occupied. Because the bar was located on a pier across from the water, the patrons tonight appeared to be a collection of maritime workers and recreational boaters.

She glanced at the men who appeared to be there by themselves. Two had grey hair, appearing to be in their mid to late sixties. One was heavy, with a bushy mustache and a bald, sunburned head. The other wore a loose-fitting T-shirt and a pair of stained Bermuda shorts. Neither of them appeared to be overwhelmingly prosperous, but in Annapolis, appearances meant little. Boat enthusiast millionaires wore the same T-shirts and stained shorts as their less prosperous peers.

"Excuse me," Jan signaled to the bartender as she set down her beer. "Could I have a seltzer water?"

"Seltzer?" the bartender asked, as though she was speaking a foreign language.

A familiar voice cut in behind her, almost whispering in her ear. "If you're going to work undercover, you might try drinking something that's a little less conspicuous."

She grimaced as Max sat down on the stool next to her. "How ya doin', Ramone?" he asked loudly.

"Good, Max," Ramone said, giving a glimpse of a smile. "What can I do ya for?"

"How about some plain soda water for my friend here and I'll take a," he paused, glancing at the beers they had on tap, "Sam Adams."

"I'm not working undercover," Jan said quietly, hunching on her stool.

He turned to her and flashed her a knowing smile. "No?"

"No. I just, I was in the neighborhood and I'd heard about this place so I thought I'd stop in."

"What a coincidence. Me, too."

The bartender sat the drinks down in front of them and Max turned toward her, giving her his full attention. It made Jan nervous. "I tried to call you today," she said confrontationally, almost in an attempt to set up some distance between them. She was determined to ignore her attraction to him.

"I got your message."

"Thanks, once again, for returning my call," she said sarcastically.

He shrugged nonchalantly, still facing her as he sipped his beer. "I'm not supposed to communicate with you, at least not directly."

"I see," Jan said. "So you've finally decided to start following orders."

"I assumed you were calling me about Custin." He paused. "Was I was wrong?" he said. He was teasing, but there was an intensity to his voice that made Jan blush.

"Is this harassment, Detective?" she said, only half-joking. She had never been good at flirtatious banter, and it showed on Max's face. He seemed off-balance, uncertain. "I, ah——"

"Anyway," she said, letting him off the hook. "I hear Custin's thinking about filing charges," she fired back.

"I spoke to him directly about an hour ago. He said he's not filing charges, but he wants you to leave him alone."

"You spoke to him directly?"

"I called him up. And he answered."

"Why?"

"I imagine he wanted to see who was on the other line."

She smiled despite herself.

"His parole officer told me he thought Custin was going to take some kind of action against you, and I wanted to persuade him not to."

"Thanks," Jan mumbled.

"I didn't do much. He had already decided to drop the whole matter."

Jan shook her head. "What a guy."

"You were right about Custin," he said. "About his house. He owns it free and clear. Along with a brand new Trans Am and a high-speed cigarette boat—all purchased in the past month. I checked up on his girlfriend. She's a topless dancer, unemployed. No money to speak of." He paused as he glanced over at her. Jan was fingering her cocktail napkin absentmindedly. She said, "So you're following my lead."

"It was a good one."

She nodded and said, "I found out some even more interesting news today."

"Oh, boy."

"Two days before my sister was raped, a woman was murdered."

"And?"

"The woman was living in a home that was registered to a Eugenia Custin."

"Uh-huh."

"The murder was never solved, but it sounds like Custin might have been a suspect."

"Why do you say that?"

"The neighbors told me."

He squinted. "That's good police work, Detective."

Normally she would give a polite laugh, but right now she had too much to say. "Custin told the police that he lived in Florida, but they never asked him what he was doing here in Annapolis . . ."

"And you think that was because . . ."

"I think it was an oversight. They already knew why he was here. Because they had already questioned him about the murder."

"There wasn't any mention of that in the files . . ."

"They never prosecuted him. Never even brought charges against him."

"Nick told you that?"

She stiffened at the mention of Nick's name. "No."

"Let me guess—the neighbors."

"Right." She paused and then asked, "What does Custin's parole officer say about his newfound wealth?"

"Custin told him a rich aunt died and left him a small fortune."

"A rich aunt? Hah! Right."

"Do you know differently?"

"Well, no," Jan admitted, "not for a fact. But doesn't it sound kind of suspicious? We'll have to research his family, confirm the names of his parents, find out if he had any siblings, run checks on them. At the very least, you should talk to this Jeff Brown. He was the sex crimes detective who arrested Custin."

Max nodded.

"What if . . ." she said quietly.

"What if what?"

"What if the real rapist was looking for someone to take the fall for him? He chose Custin because he knew he would have nothing to lose . . ." she said, as though the idea had just at that very moment popped into her mind.

"Hmm."

She stared at him to see if he honestly thought she had something or if he was just humoring her.

"So who's the rapist—a cop?" he asked.

"Or someone with connections inside the force. They tell Custin they won't charge him with murder if he confesses to a rape he didn't commit. And to sweeten the pot, they throw in a payoff when he gets out . . ."

Max was looking off into the distance, mouthing the words to the Jimmy Buffet song that was playing on the jukebox.

"Well?" she asked.

"Interesting. There's some holes, but who knows? I'm too tired to be doing any heavy thinking right now, sorry."

"I'll buy you some coffee," she said matter-of-factly.

"Can I take a rain check? I'm really—"

"I heard you searched Neff's house."

He nodded silently.

"And found scissors, duct tape, and a face mask." She rolled her eyes sarcastically. "Even I have scissors and duct tape. Maybe you should interrogate me, too."

He shook his head. "You're a little dynamo, you know that? Where's your off button?"

She grinned and said, "I had it removed."

Max smiled. He had a nice, sexy smile, the kind that could charm the pants off . . .

Jan caught herself. She didn't have time to flirt. She took a drink of her soda then said, "So what's your take on Neff?"

He shrugged.

She said, "I'm surprised there hasn't been an arrest yet."

"There are some complicating factors," he said hesitantly.

"Like?"

He swallowed another gulp of beer.

"Come on," she cajoled him. "You can tell me. I'll find out anyway."

He shook his head and said with a hint of a grin, "I'm sure you will. Basically, I think Neff was too drunk to pull it off."

She shrugged. "Maybe he wasn't drunk at all—just pretending," she said, trying a little reverse psychology. "Nick thinks he might have even planned it well enough to throw suspicion on Custin."

"What?" Max asked, astounded.

Jan nodded. "I'm surprised he didn't tell you. He thinks Neff knew about Custin and my sister and was looking for a scapegoat."

Max laughed. "No way. Neff would have to be a

genius to pull that off and that he's definitely not. Besides, I don't think he was faking drunk that night. I've questioned almost everyone who saw him and they all say the same thing, the guy was sitting at the bar drinking constantly for almost four hours.

"But Nick—"

"Is wrong. I don't know where he's getting his information. And quite frankly," he said before he could stop himself, "I don't trust him."

"Nick?"

"What's with those scratches—he had them the day after Tomkins disappeared."

Jan laughed. "Oh, please. He got those scratches in a rugby game."

"No, he didn't," he said. "There was a game—Nick wasn't in it."

"What?!"

He was silent.

"Oh my God," Jan breathed. "Don't tell me you're investigating Nick."

"Look, I found out about those scratches by accident. A buddy of mine is on the team. Nick told them he got them in a fight."

Jan couldn't see Nick fighting anyone. It just wasn't his style. She thought back to Rachel. Maybe he had been too embarrassed to admit how he really got them. She leaned toward Max conspiratorially and said "I want to help you with this case—I'll do whatever I can. I want to find the creep that's murdering these women."

"The same creep that hurt your sister?"

"I think it's a possibility, yes."

"Look," he said. "I'll make you a deal. If you let me solve the Tomkins and Haverdale cases, when I'm finished I'll help you research Custin."

She grimaced. "Are you trying to get rid of me?"

"Nothing personal," he said diplomatically. "I just work better without interference . . ."

"I'm not interfering. I just gave you all this great information." She paused and said weakly, "I'm helping."

"That's true. I like your thinking, but your boss has a bug up his ass about something. As a matter of fact, he called today. He wanted to know if you had been interfering with this investigation in any way."

Jan was too surprised to be angry. "You're kidding."

"He told me to call him if you tried to find out any details about the Haverdale and Tomkins cases."

Jan reached into her bag and pulled out her cellular phone. She handed it to him. She said, "Four-one-oh, six-two-six, eighty-five-twenty. It's his cellular phone number. He's on his boat. Be my guest."

"Put the phone away," Max said resignedly.

"Forget it. I'll get out of your way," she said, slamming her phone back together. She threw it in her bag and hopped off the stool.

"Look," he said. "I only told you that so you'd know. I have no intention of telling Nick about this."

"You threatened me."

"I know you're hepped up about this, but I wasn't threatening you. As a matter of fact, I was trying to help you out." He waited for the words to sink in, but her steely exterior, her determined, pissed-off expression did not soften a bit. "I'm sorry," he said as she threw a ten dollar bill on the counter. "Whatever I did, I'm sorry. Whatever I'm supposed to be sorry about."

"Fine."

"Hey," Max said, "I'm trying to solve the case. I'm a good investigator and—"

"Don't pat yourself on the back yet. If I'm right, and Curtis Custin didn't rape my sister, then chances are he knows who did. As far as I'm concerned, you're wasting your own time, Detective."

"Can't we just have a normal conversation for two seconds? For crissakes, you're worse than an army drill sergeant."

She shot him a fake smile. "That's sweet."

She turned and rushed toward the door, distractedly glancing back at Max as she pushed against it.

"Watch it," a man said, stopping her before she crashed into him.

She found herself staring up at Ed Thurman. "Oh God," she murmured, embarrassed. "I'm sorry."

"Well, hello," Ed said, smiling as he recognized her.

The man who had been standing behind him, a short, good-looking guy with horn-rimmed glasses, laughed and continued on toward a booth.

Ed looked like the typical yuppie sailor. Sunglasses

were pulled on top of his sunburned face. A short-sleeve rugby shirt hung loose over khaki shorts. He released her and said, "You look like you're in a hurry."

"Ah, no," she said, glancing back to see if Max was watching. He was still sitting at the bar, his eyes on his beer.

Ed followed her gaze to Max and said, "We just stopped in here for a quick beer ourselves. My buddy," he said, nodding toward the fellow with the glasses, "and I sailed in the races tonight. Did you catch any of it?"

"No. But I keep meaning to get down there and watch them." During the summer Annapolitans crowded around the city dock to cheer on the boats entered in the weekly sailing races.

"You should. They're a lot of fun. Get ol' Nick to take you some time."

"Uh, yeah."

He moved out of her way. "I won't keep you. Have a good one."

She caught Max looking at them and she focused her attention back on Ed, flashing him the sweetest smile she could muster. She said, "Nice seeing you, Ed. Or," she added quickly, "do you prefer Eddie?"

"Ed's fine," he replied.

What was she doing, flirting with a married man to make Max jealous? Why did she even care what Max thought? She better get out of there before she made an even bigger fool of herself. "I'll be seeing you," she said. "I look forward to it," he said politely.

Jan drove her convertible across the small bridge, her blond hair blowing freely in the warm wind. She had a destination in mind and although she didn't have an exact address, she knew where she was headed.

Through Frannie's rape she felt she had an innate sense of the perpetrator which made her emotionally incapable of just sitting tight idly twirling her thumbs while the murderer scouted out his next victim.

Despite her frustrations, she understood why Max and Nick had a tough time buying her theory that all three cases were connected. For one, the concept of Custin taking the rap for something he didn't do was a hard sell. Even if they did buy that part, it was tough linking the three crimes together simply because the MO was different in all three cases. For one, Haverdale and Tomkins were homicides—and her sister was simply raped. But Jan felt this could be easily explained. Most serial killers don't start off their careers by murdering people—they work up to it. Perhaps this rapist-murderer was just a beginner at the time of Frannie's rape. Or maybe he had planned on killing her but lost his nerve—or perhaps he was just starting his evil career and at the time a simple rape was enough to satisfy his deviant urges.

There was another possibility, she thought hopefully. Perhaps he hadn't really intended to kill the last two women. Perhaps they had not cooperated or had gotten loose. But, she reminded herself, that theory just didn't fly in light of the fact that Sarah Tomkins had been killed in a cold-blooded execution—the method of death alone suggested a definitive MO. More than likely if he had not lost control of Haverdale she would've died in the same way.

She shook her head as she turned off the expressway. No wonder Max and Nick didn't seem to take her ideas seriously. She was working off intuition and gut feeling, and no jury would convict on that. She needed something identifiable, a sure connection between not only the Haverdale and Tomkins murders but with her sister as well. She needed proof.

She slowed her car down as her headlights picked up the street signs. Harbinger, Bedford . . . she put her turn signal on as she spotted the one she had been looking for: Aris Lane. She made the sharp turn onto the heavily wooded dirt road, driving past the old, small cottages and stopping at the fifth house on the right. The yellow police tape was still stretched out over the driveway, protecting Lucy Haverdale's house from the curious. Just beyond the house was a steep ravine which led to a creek—similar to her own property.

She studied the site for a few minutes and drove off. About ten minutes later she took the Route 2 exit into Edgewater. The sun was setting as she drove past the low billboards and looked for Mayo Road. She signaled, made a left, and drove about five miles, heading toward the water. She made a right on Chicaquin, a left on

Reda and kept going until she found more yellow tape. This time though, she parked her car on the side of the road and got out.

Sarah Tomkins' house sat about fifteen feet off the road. Although she doubted there was much traffic at midnight, the time of her abduction, it still would have been difficult to kidnap Sarah without anyone noticing. Sarah's closest neighbor lived in a small cottage about a hundred feet from her front door.

There was not a driveway, just short brown grass where she guessed Sarah had parked her car. She tried to imagine the events of that night—Sarah returning home from work, tired and hot, stepping out of her car and heading toward her front door. Jan guessed that she had felt fairly safe—after all, even though there weren't many neighbors, the house was close to the road and there were no bushes in which a rapist could hide, no porches to shadow him. The front door was open to the outside. There wasn't even a screen.

Jan headed toward the dark house, stumbling on a branch hidden in the grass. Although it had started off as a clear night, clouds were quickly filling the sky, almost covering the quarter moon. Some detective I am, she thought. Walking around in the pitch dark without so much as a flashlight. Nick was right.

She walked around the side of the house. In the distance she could see the twinkle of boat lights reflecting off the creek. Jan was certain Lucy Haverdale and Sarah Tomkins, like her sister, had died at the hands of a man familiar with the water. He had docked his boat and waited for them to return home from work. When they arrived, he had incapacitated them much the same way as Frannie. When he had them under control he carried them back to his boat where he murdered them.

Jan turned and headed back toward her car, giving the water a final glance before she drove away.

19

Tuesday, August 11

"WAS THE HEAD CUT OFF?"

"Partially. But the eyes were open. He was just staring up at me, like, help me, help me," Kurt said, using a
high-pitched wail.

"What did you do?" Sheila asked.

"I stabbed my fork right into him, picked the whole
thing up and just chomped the head right off."

A groan went up around the room. Kurt Campisano,
a handsome, forty-something sex crimes detective, had
been describing his fish dinner at an expensive DC
restaurant.

Jan glanced around the room. The second Tuesday of
every month they had a meeting of the entire sex
crimes team, including all the prosecutors and police.

They gathered around the large conference table and reviewed the status of their cases.

Usually the meetings went smoothly, but today's had veered off course. The detectives were tired and it showed. Most had been putting in a lot of hours on the recent murders. Everything else had been put on the back burner, much to the frustration of the prosecutors working on other cases.

The conference door opened and Nick stepped in. "Sorry I'm late," he said, taking a seat at the head of the table. Jan glanced at her watch. It was twelve-thirty. The meeting was all but over.

"Have we discussed the Storry case yet?"

Jan caught Nick's eye and he glanced away quickly. She hadn't spoken with him since the previous evening when she had interrupted his date.

"Already did," said Lisa Chelmitt, the deputy SA. "But there's some confusion over whose case it is."

"I want Jan to handle it," Nick said.

At the mention of her name Jan snapped to attention.

Sosha Storry was a sixteen-year-old girl whose mother had died five years earlier. The police had found her lying on the side of the road, bruised and battered, the victim of a brutal rape. The problem was, Sosha had told them her uncle was the culprit, but soon afterwards had begun recanting her story. Even though the DNA proved a match, it promised to be a grueling case.

"Me? But, uh . . ." she mumbled.

"But what?" Nick snapped. "Since the Brattenburg case is not going to trial, you can handle this."

"I'll send you the file," Kurt offered.

"Sounds great," Jan said sarcastically, rolling her eyes as Nick looked down. Some muted laughter followed.

The meeting ended and Jan wandered back to her office. "Congratulations," Dave said, appearing beside her.

"Yeah, right."

"Well, it's a big case."

"Don't toy with me, Dave," she said.

"Ooh," he cried, pretending to be scared.

She sat down behind her desk as Dave continued past. Jan picked up the framed picture of Frannie at the head of her desk. She would find Frannie's killer no matter how many roadblocks were thrown in her path.

As she studied the picture, taken shortly before Frannie's attack, she could feel herself melt, the toughness subside. Frannie was leaning up against her old, beat up car, smiling. Jan had taken the photo herself. She had insisted her impatient sister stand there and pose for it. Jan smiled as she remembered the moment as though it were yesterday. She had been visiting her sister and they had just thrown her suitcase in the car, getting ready to take Jan back to the airport. Frannie had bought Jan breakfast and they had stuffed themselves at the Amish market, cleaning their plates and even ordering dessert.

She wondered where Frannie would be today had she lived. The other question was where would Jan be? Would she be here, sitting in this chair? Or had she become a lawyer to fulfill her sister's dream?

Not that she didn't like her job. But she had gone to law school because she knew that was what Frannie wanted, and she had been too confused at the time to figure out who she was without her sister.

Jan stared at the picture, picking out the similarities between herself and Frannie. They both looked like their mother—petite and small boned with cute smiles and big eyes that were the central feature of their faces. And both had inherited their father's instinct to fight, along with his indomitable will. Their father had been an attorney in private practice. He had done well, but unfortunately spent well, too. They had grown up in a large house with a pool in the backyard and a maid that came once a week. Both had been daddy's girls. Neither one had ever been particularly close to their mother. It was surprising really, considering the amount of time they had spent with her. Though she had been a stay-at-home mom, she had kept to herself, a stoic, unemotional sort. At least, that was what they had thought until their father's death.

She had done it while they were at school. Frannie found her inside the closed garage, the car still running. Frannie notified the neighbors, and her mother's friend met Jan at school to break the news. Frannie had been eighteen at the time, and it was decided that she would become Jan's legal guardian.

The anger Jan had felt toward her mother for leaving them momentarily numbed her pain. It was Frannie's strength, Frannie's resolve which had allowed her to overcome the anger when it surfaced, to recognize that her mother was a decent, simple woman who had loved her husband so dearly she found it impossible to survive without him.

Frannie made an effort to get Jan to remember her mother as the person she really was—a woman Jan was too young to appreciate. It was Frannie who explained their parents' romantic and intense love, and it was Frannie who reminded Jan of their mother's more endearing traits; the cookies she baked, the soft curve of her lips when she smiled, the way she had always insisted on a kiss goodnight.

"Jan?" Nick said, his muscular form filling her doorway.

She was embarrassed to be caught staring at Frannie's picture. It would only cement his obvious notion that her recent actions were simply a sentimental response to Custin's release. She set the picture down and instinctively picked up a folder as he walked into her office, shutting the door behind him.

Nick said, "I just want you to know, I didn't give you that case to be a jerk. I know you've got a lot on your plate, but you're the only one who has a chance to get that S.O.B. I wanted to give it to Lisa, just to give you a breather, but ever since she went on that new reduction, she's been batty. And Chris, I don't know . . . I think he's been drinking again. Anyway, I really appreciate it."

"Okay," she said. He always knew how to soften her up.

"If you get overloaded, let me know."

"Thanks," she said. She looked at him and smiled, wondering if Ed had mentioned that she had run into him.

He looked away from her and said, "There's something else. I just got a call from Frank," he said, referring to the sergeant. "It's bad."

"What?" she asked, leaning forward.

"Your client, Terry Turnbull. She died of a drug overdose this morning."

It was all too much. She broke down and began to sob. She tried to calm herself, but all her pent-up feelings came spilling out, all over her desk, her files, her sleeves.

Nick walked over and squatted beside her, looping his arm around her shoulder. "It wasn't your fault," she heard Nick say.

Rationally Jan might have agreed, but the intensity of the past few days had not helped her objectivity. It took a while, but her emotions finally subsided. He handed her a tissue.

"Thanks," she managed. The last thing she wanted was to look like some kind of basket case in front of Nick just when she seemed to be gaining the upper hand.

He brushed some of her damp hair away from her face, and stood up as he said, "You did your best to help her."

"Was it suicide?"

"There wasn't any note if that's what you're getting at."

"Was there an autopsy?"

He nodded. "Yeah. They found enough heroin and cocaine in her system to take down an entire football team."

Jan ran her fingers through her hair. "She'd still be alive if Harbert was behind bars."

"You don't know that."

"She was worried that these recent murders were Harbert's work. I tried to convince her they weren't but she wouldn't listen to me."

"There was nothing you could do," he said. "You didn't make her a drug addict, Jan. She died by her own hand. And she would've ended up this way even if Harbert was in jail."

"I failed her," Jan said.

"You didn't fail her," Nick said automatically.

"The system did," she said, repeating Dave's words as she stared at the picture of her sister.

20

EUGENIA O'MALLEY, FIFTY-FIVE YEARS OLD. DEATH RULED
homicide. Max read the file, or at least what remained
of it. Unsolved murder files were never officially
closed. But if there wasn't a political or emotional reason for solving the case, they could be shelved indefi-
nitely.

*Found lying on her back, bullet wound in her chest. Bath
towel had been placed over her face. Son discovered body and
called police.* So, Max thought, Curtis Custin—her
son—had been the one to call police.

Max quickly read over Custin's statement. He said
that his mother's TV had been stolen, along with some
cash she had kept in her underwear drawer.

Towel had been placed over her face . . . by whom? When
Max was working in Baltimore and was called to the
scene of a homicide, he always knew when the victim
had been killed by someone they were personally

181

involved with because the murderer would almost always cover the victim's face before they left. It was a strange thing about people. They could snuff out the life of someone they had once cared about and perform cruel acts to the body, but they almost always covered the face to dehumanize them. Couldn't stand to look at them. So either Eugenia O'Malley had been killed by someone who knew her, or else her son had put the towel over her face out of respect. Of course, Max wasn't ruling out that Custin had killed her himself.

"Hey Hank," Max said as his partner entered the room. "You ever hear of a Jim Wingate? He was a detective here about ten years ago."

Hank shrugged. "He was gone by the time I came onboard." Hank had joined the force in nineteen-ninety when his computer analyst wife was transferred to Annapolis from Connecticut. "Why?"

"I ran into Jan last night . . ."

"Ah yes, the little steamroller. What's she into now?"

"She's been researching Custin, the guy who raped her sister. Found out that the day before her sister was raped, Custin's mother was found murdered."

"Back up a minute. She's researching Custin? What for?"

"It's a long story. She thinks that maybe he didn't rape her sister."

A smile formed on Hank's face, as if he just assumed Max was joking.

Max shrugged. "What can I tell you?"

"Is she crazy? I mean, the guy confessed. He went to the Pen."

"In any case," Max said, feeling the urge to defend Jan. "You ever hear about a Eugenia O'Malley?"

"Is that a bar? O'Malley's?"

"I've got her file right here. There's not much in it, considering it was a homicide that was never solved."

"It was this Wingate's case?"

Max nodded.

"Have you asked the sergeant about this?"

"Not yet." And he wasn't looking forward to it. The sergeant had made it pretty clear he regarded the case on Custin closed.

At eight o'clock that night Jan was just finishing dinner when a familiar car pulled into her driveway. It was Nick.

She stood up and brushed her hair away from her face. This was strange. Very strange. Nick had only been to her house once before, and that was to attend a retirement party for one of his deputies. She opened the screen door. "Nick?"

Nick walked toward the porch as the light rain dampened his crisp, starched shirt. He walked past her onto the porch, "Hi," he said. "I just finished having dinner over at Rosie's and I thought I'd swing by and see how you were doing."

Jan stood still. Nick stopped by to see how she was doing?

"Am I interrupting anything?" he asked, glancing around.

"No," she said, snapping back into action. "Not at all. Have a seat. Can I get you anything?"

He shook his head. "No, thanks. I'm fine."

She sat across from him.

Nick began, "I know you were upset about Terry, and I just wanted to check up on you. You okay?"

She shrugged. "I suppose. It's such a waste. She never really had a chance."

He said, "Like I already told you, you tried to help her. And you did a great job."

"Thanks," she said. This was awkward.

"By the way," he said, "I talked to John today," he said, referring to Senator Thurman. "He wanted to know if you'd reached a decision."

"About what?"

"Running for state's attorney!"

"It's only been a day, Nick. I've been kind of busy." She stopped herself before she said anything else. Sometimes she came off more biting and acerbic than she intended.

"Well, I wouldn't wait too long."

"Is he really serious about me? I mean, what about Lisa or Chris? They're your deputies. . . ."

"I know, but they don't have what you have. You've got charisma, you can lead a department. You've got a history of volunteer work, a commitment to a cause. Plus, you're a fresh young face . . . without a family to distract you."

"No family." The words cut through her.

"You know what I mean," he said, moving closer to her. "The senator is serious. He wants you to run."

She shrugged.

Nick sighed. "I'm concerned about you. You're not proving to be a graceful loser."

Graceful loser? Was he referring to losing Terry's case, or was he referring to losing him to Rachel? "What are you talking about?"

"Terry Turnbull. Ever since you lost that case you've been different. You've been flying off on tangents, focusing on cases that aren't even yours . . ." Nick shook his head and then continued. "I didn't tell the senator about your visit to Custin, just so you know."

"I feel awful about Terry but this isn't a matter of me being a poor sport. I mean, come on. Give me a little credit."

"This is all about Custin?"

"I know what you think—oh, forget it," she said quickly. She didn't have the energy to go through this with him again. She'd only be wasting her time.

"Look," he said, as if reading her mind. "I want to help you get through this. Regardless of what you think, I *have* been listening to you. I don't think you're crazy."

She looked at him hopefully.

He continued, "I noticed the discrepancies you're so focused on right away. Of course I talked to your sister about it. She was still convinced that Custin was the man who raped her."

Jan crossed her arms, listening. Nick could be very sincere, very convincing. She nodded, but she still had so many questions.

Nick shrugged as he walked over to the screen, looking toward the water. "I've never really discussed it with you because I didn't want to upset you."

"What did she say when she saw him?"

"Nothing in particular. After the sentencing she was tired. She said she needed to go home. She thanked me, said she felt vindicated but didn't think she'd ever be able to get over it." He paused for a moment and then he said, "She mentioned your mother."

"My mother?" Jan whispered.

He nodded. "She said she missed her." He placed a hand on Jan's shoulder. "Of course, that was before I knew . . ." he hesitated. "Before I knew how she had died. Had I known, I would've insisted someone stay with her."

She got his drift. *Like mother, like daughter.* "My sister didn't kill herself," Jan said, meeting his gaze.

He nodded in a way that said he felt differently.

"She didn't," she said, shrugging off his hand. "She knew how tough our mom's death was on me. She wouldn't have done that to me."

"No one said that she meant for it to happen. It was

an accident, we all agreed. But you and I both know that the coroner's report—"

"My sister wasn't the type to down a few pills, take a rowboat out into the bay with a bottle of cheap wine, strip off her clothes, and go for a swim."

Nick was silent.

"Jesus Christ, Nick, I know my own sister!"

"Whether she was the type or not, that's exactly what she did." He shook his head as she turned away. "What do you think? That I'm making this stuff up?"

"Look, what do you want?" Jan asked quietly. "What are you doing here?" She turned back toward him.

"I just, well—ah, forget it. Christ, I've got enough shit on my plate right now." He glanced up at her and said, "Are we still friends?"

"We've never been anything but."

Nick accepted her response like a slap across the face. "Okay," he said with a quick nod. "See you tomorrow."

"Goodbye, Nick," she said quietly as he stepped inside his car.

21

Jim Wingate lived on the eastern shore of Maryland, about an hour and a half outside of Annapolis. Shortly after Eugenia O'Malley's murder he left the force and went to help his father on the family fish farm.

The rain shower had become a full-fledged summer storm by the time Max pulled into the stone drive that led to Jim Wingate's modest wood-frame house.

He rushed out of the car and ran to the porch. A middle-aged man with peppery brown hair answered the door before Max had a chance to ring the bell.

"Detective Hale?" the man said.

Max nodded. "Jim Wingate?"

"You got it," Wingate said, shaking his hand. "Come on in." He led Max to a small living room. "Have a seat."

"Thanks."

Max sat stiffly on a well-worn brown couch as

Wingate said, "I've got to admit you've piqued my curiosity."

Max nodded and grinned. "That's what I was shooting for. I was wondering if you could shed any light on a murder case from about ten years ago. The woman's name was Eugenia O'Malley. She was found shot—"

"What about it?" Wingate interrupted sharply, his congenial nature suddenly gone.

"Is there a problem?" Max asked.

"Get to the point."

"I'm wondering if it might be related to another case," Max said. "I've been researching a rape that occurred a few days after the O'Malley murder. The man I'm interested in is Curtis Custin—"

"Eugenia O'Malley's son."

"Right."

"He should be out of jail any day now."

"He's out."

The retired detective nodded. He stood up and crossed his arms defensively. "What's he done? Killed someone else?"

Max paused. "So you think he killed this O'Malley woman?"

"Look, what's this all about? It's all in the file. Why don't you read it before you start badgering people. I've gone on with my life. . . ."

"Wait a minute," Max said. "I read the file. There's nothing in it. The murder case is still technically pending but it's been dead for years. I don't think anyone ever really investigated it after you left. It was written off to a botched robbery. . . ."

"Botched robbery, my ass," Wingate said. "I don't know what the hell happened to all my notes, but this was not a robbery. This was a case of a domestic quarrel that escalated into violence."

"Custin killed her?"

"Not a doubt in my mind."

"But the evidence—"

"Fuck the evidence. He had some bullshit story, completely transparent. I would've gotten a confession out of the scumbag if I had to strangle him."

"What happened?"

He sighed. "Higher-ups wanted me to lay off. There were a few . . . problems."

"Like what?"

"Jesus," he said. "I can't believe I'm going through this fucking case again. There was a gun, okay? I'm sure it was the gun that Custin used to kill her. I found it in the trash behind his house. Custin wasn't the brightest bulb, if you know what I mean. He just wrapped the goddamn thing up in toilet paper and tossed it in the Dumpster behind their house."

"I didn't see any mention of a gun. . . ."

"That's because, well . . ." he hesitated. "The evidence was lost."

"Lost?" The sergeant had not said anything about lost evidence. Did he know?

"Goddamn thing disappeared from my trunk."

Wingate began pacing, as though he had walked through the whole ordeal many times before. "I found it. I put it in the trunk. I arrived at the station, told the evidence collection people where it was, led them back out to my car . . . the damn thing was gone."

"Stolen?"

He shot a bitter laugh. "Shit. Anything's possible."

"Damn," Max breathed.

"They canned me, the fuckers. Excuse me, early retirement. Ten goddamn years and that's what I got."

"But you know that Custin confessed to raping—"

"That girl. Oh yeah, I know. The bastard confesses to rape, but his conscience wasn't bothered by killing his own mother."

"It doesn't make sense."

"Nope, it doesn't. That boy should've been shit-canned for good, he was top choice Grade A dirtball. His mother and father were dealers, in and out of the joint. He comes by it honestly."

"So he killed her," Max said quietly, thinking.

Jim Wingate looked out the window. "Not a doubt in my mind."

22

THE RAIN HAD STOPPED. THE WOODS WERE SILENT. THE ONLY noise was the occasional rustling of branches outside Jan's window, blowing in the wind.

It was three o'clock in the morning, and Jan had been lying in bed since midnight, unable to fall asleep. Jan kicked off her covers and got out of bed. Dressed only in a T-shirt and panties, she walked over to the glass door and unlocked it. She slid it open and stepped out onto the porch, listening to the sounds of the night as she crossed her arms in front of her.

She glanced up at the moon and said a silent apology to Terry. Terry had played by the rules and the justice system had failed her, just like it had failed Jan's sister. It was too late to help Terry or Frannie. She couldn't go back in time. But she could learn from mistakes.

She now realized that if there was a serial murderer out there terrorizing Annapolis, she could not trust the police to catch him. He was too clever, too quick. After all, he had slipped in and out of the system before. He had even found a way to control it, arranging for someone else to take the rap. Jan realized in order to catch this killer the police would not be able to play by the rules. They would have to take chances, assume the offensive. Rather than simply waiting for him to strike again and hoping he would leave some clues, they needed to set a trap and wait.

To succeed, they would not only have to be willing to take a chance, they would need a very clear understanding of who they were looking for.

Jan had worked around rapists and murderers for the past seven years. She knew what went on in their crazy, deadly, power-hungry minds. And this perp might be more power-hungry than most. According to Frannie's description, he was over six feet tall with an athletic build, yet he chose petite women. That way he could lord his strength over them, making them feel helpless and insignificant, like a twig he could snap when the mood struck him.

But the victims' personalities also told her something about this man. He liked friendly, almost flirtatious women, women who worked as bartenders or waitresses. They didn't threaten him—but why? Maybe he was intimidated by high-powered career women.

Jan didn't doubt that he had met these women before; even Frannie had mentioned that the rapist had seemed familiar in some way. They had probably talked to him, smiled at him. It was enough for his sick mind to imagine that they were interested in him. Perhaps he even thought that a smile meant they desired him.

His victims had short brown hair—hair that he had shorn, as if to brand them. Why short brown hair? Did they look like a relative? Maybe a mother, a wife, a girl-friend?

What else did she know about him? He owned or had access to a boat. He probably lived on the water, and was able to take his boat out at strange hours without alerting the neighbors . . . unless, unless he had a sail-boat. If he was particularly skilled at sailing, he might be able to maneuver in and out of docks, providing the wind cooperated.

The more she thought about this perpetrator, the more frightened she became. If he had paid Custin to take the rap, then he had to be well-off financially, very well-off. And if he had succeeded in pulling strings so that Custin was never charged with murder, he had to be involved with the police force in some way.

She stepped back into the living room and slid the door shut, locking it behind her. She turned on the light and picked up the photo of Frannie that she displayed on her mantle. It was different than the picture she kept in her office. It was taken the day Frannie had gradu-ated from college. She was dressed in her blue gown, smiling from ear to ear. She had an arm wrapped around Jan as she proudly waved her diploma at the camera. It was obvious that they were sisters. Same color eyes, same body frame. Both petite and small boned, no boobs to brag about. It was the hair that always set them apart. Her sister kept her brown hair in a no-fuss short wash-and-dry style while Jan kept hers long and blond.

Jan fingered the tips of her hair as she suddenly realized how she could seek justice. It would require her to give up everything she'd worked so hard for, to forget *the system* she had fought to honor. It would require her to put her sanity and future in question. Still, she knew that she had to do it. She didn't have any choice.

But what made her think she could succeed when her sister hadn't? Because, Jan thought, she was stronger now than she was when Frannie was alive. She might even be stronger than Frannie had ever been, physically and emotionally. She was older than Frannie now too, older and more experienced. Also, Frannie had been caught unaware. Jan would be ready.

Having made her decision, she turned off the light and crawled back into bed. She would break the news to Nick tomorrow. She would not be gearing up for any political campaign. Instead, she was going to find Frannie's murderer.

23

"I CAN'T BELIEVE YOU'RE DOING THIS." DAVE WAS LEANING OVER her desk, watching as Jan took out a drawer and dumped it into a box.

As it turned out, it had been a perfect morning to resign. The media frenzy was growing and Nick had called a press conference for ten o'clock. She knew what he planned to say. He would deny a definite connection between the Haverdale and Tomkins murders and once again state that an arrest was imminent.

"I mean, I just can't believe Nick is letting you do this."

She shrugged. "It's a leave of absence, Dave. It was either that or I was quitting. He didn't have much choice."

196

"Did you type up a letter or something?"

"Yeah. I had a resignation letter handy in case I needed it. He wasn't happy with this whole leave of absence thing but he gave in." She paused.

"And so he said, 'Go ahead and have a great time'?"

"Not exactly. I think he thinks I'm going away or something."

"What do you mean?"

"Well, he said that maybe a long vacation would do me some good and I didn't bother to correct him."

"I could use a long vacation myself. Maybe I should try that too." He shook his head, admiringly. "So, how long are you going to be gone?"

"I don't know."

"I just don't get it. I mean, things are going great for you here. You negotiated a great settlement in the Hoffsford case. What is it? Just burned out? It's not losing that case, is it? You're not going to like, go join the Peace Corps just cuz of Terry."

She shook her head.

"There was nothing you could do. Sooner or later—"

"Dave," she interrupted. She fished around the box and pulled out a pencil that had a Bozo the Clown face on the eraser. Dave had often kidded her about the pencil and expressed his admiration. "If I give you this will you leave me alone?" she teased.

Dave paused, staring at the eraser. "So, you're going to play hardball." He snapped up the pencil and stood silent, but only for a minute. "Who's going to take me out to lunch and console me about my love life?" he blurted out.

"I'm not quitting, for Pete's sake. I'll be back. And in the meantime, I don't live that far away. I'll still take you out to lunch. "

"It won't be the same. Whose office will I escape to when I've had a crappy morning in court?"

"Sheila's."

"Whose office will I use for all my long distance calls?"

"Nick's."

"But who will massage my feet for me when you're gone?"

"Hey Dave," she said, clapping her hands. "Wake up!"

Sheila stepped into Jan's office, excited. "Oh my God," she said. "Did you see the reporters out there?" She stopped when she saw the box. "What are you doing?"

"She's taking a leave of absence," Dave answered. "Will you massage my feet for me while she's gone?"

"Smooth, Dave. Real smooth," Jan said.

"What?" Sheila laughed, confused.

"I'm afraid he's serious," Jan said. "I am leaving and he does want you to massage his feet."

Sheila shut the door. "What do you mean you're leaving?"

"I just," Jan paused, not sure whether she wanted to get into the whole reason right now. Or maybe she was just afraid that her friend would tell her how crazy she was. Maybe she needed a little more time to live with her decision before she confided in anyone. "I have some personal business to take care of."

"Personal?" Sheila repeated. Dave stepped back, allowing Sheila to move closer to Jan. She turned back toward Dave. "I think we need to have some private girl talk."

"Great," Dave teased, settling into a chair. "Go right ahead."

"Dave. . . ." Sheila threatened.

"I like the sound of 'private girl talk.' Sounds sexy."

"Premenstrual bloating. Tampons . . ."

"Oh, geez, I think I hear my phone ringing," he said as he jumped up. "Me and Bozo have to go." He opened the door and stopped. "Don't be a stranger," he said to Jan.

"Okay, good-looking," Jan replied. Dave shut the door and Jan smiled as she turned to Sheila. "Dave talks like he's in some sort of bad movie or something."

"Jan . . ." Sheila began, all business.

"He really cares about you, you know," Jan said.

"What's this all about?" Sheila asked quietly, nodding toward Jan's box.

Jan sighed. "It's not that complicated. I just, I feel like I've lost control over, well, my life. I need to take a step back and figure out what I'm doing," she said, avoiding Sheila's eyes. It wasn't a lie exactly, it just wasn't the whole truth.

Sheila paused. "Does this have anything to do with your sister?"

Jan took out another drawer and dumped it in the box. She didn't answer.

"Jan? You can tell me."

"There's nothing to tell. I'm not sure yet."

"So let me get this straight. You just decided, 'hey—I need some time off,' went into Nick's office first thing this morning and he said: 'No problem, Jan. Take as much time as you need.'"

"I didn't give him much choice."

"Does Max know about this?"

"Max? What does he have to do with this?" Jan picked the box up off her chair and set it on her desk.

"Don't do this, Jan."

"Do what?"

"What anyone with a pea brain can see you're planning. Don't try to become Nancy Drew."

"We both do have convertibles, you know."

"I hope you know what you're doing, but I don't have a real good feeling you do."

"Look," Jan said. "You're right, okay? If there was any other way for me to do this and stay here I would. But I can't. I can't work for the state and . . . do this."

"Do what?"

"Well . . ."

"Jan," Sheila said. "Think about this. You have bills to pay. How are you going to support yourself?"

"I have some money saved." As Jan stepped out of

her office she stopped as she noticed Nick standing at the end of the hall huddled in conference with Rachel.

Nick looked up. Their eyes met. He paused for a moment, then shook his head. He turned and stepped into the elevator, not bothering to glance back.

Sheila said, "I guess he's not going to try to talk you out of this."

Jan glanced at Rachel as the elevator doors shut. "He's got his hands full."

24

IT TOOK HER LESS THAN TEN MINUTES TO DRIVE FROM HER OFFICE to the boatyard in Eastport where Tom Neff worked. When she arrived the yard was quiet, unusual considering that it was ten in the morning on a workday. Jan stepped out of her air-conditioned car into the insufferable heat, and let out an audible "Ugh." As much as she hated air-conditioning, she was forced to use it today. The clouds had cleared in the night and Annapolis was now enduring a scorching hot day with a full bright sun. She was tough—but even she would have melted without air.

She walked into the open door of a cavernous building that was stocked full of boats.

"Hello?" she asked, pushing her sunglasses up on her head as she peered around the boats haphazardly scattered around the warehouse. She weaved her way toward an open door about halfway down.

Jan could hear something. It sounded like . . . Nick. She peeked around a boat and glanced inside an office. About ten men wearing beat-up looking shorts and T-shirts were gathered around a small color TV watching Nick's press conference.

She stood silently until one of the men walked up and shut off the TV. She saw him put his hand on the shoulder of a young, scruffy-looking kid and say, "Let's get back to work."

Jan took a step forward and the man stopped. "Can I help you?" he asked, walking toward her as the rest of the men began to slowly scatter out of the office.

"I'm Jan Garret. I'm here to see Tom Neff."

"What about?" the man asked, his expression tightening.

"I . . . I think I might be able to help him. I'm a lawyer."

The scruffy looking kid appeared behind him. "It's all right, Fred."

The man gave Jan a warning glance before hesitantly walking away.

"I have a lawyer," Tom said.

He wasn't a bad-looking kid. She knew that he was twenty, but he could easily pass as a high school student. He was thinner than she had expected. His sandy blond hair was tousled and he had a week's worth of beard on his face.

"I know," she said.

"So what do you want?"

"I want to ask you some questions."

"Some questions about Lucy," he said. He shook his head. "You're no attorney, are you? You're a reporter."

She opened her purse and took out her business card, along with her license. "As of this morning I was an assistant state's attorney."

"As of this morning?" he said, wiping his nose with the back of his arm as he glanced at her identification.

"I quit. Basically because I disagreed with the way Lucy's case is being handled."

"They think I killed her."

"Did you?"

"Fuck off, lady."

"I know something that might help you," she said. "But first, I just need you to answer some questions for me."

"Maybe you didn't hear me," he said, leaning forward. "Fuck off."

She raised an eyebrow. "Nick Fitzgerald is out for your ass. If I were you, I'd hear me out."

He stood there for a moment, as if unsure of what to do.

Interpreting his silence as acquiescence, she said, "Let's go outside."

He followed her out by the water. She sat down on the edge of the dock and patted the ground beside her. He remained standing.

She nodded toward a sailboat bobbing up and down

in the water. "Do you sail?" she asked, as though she was making breezy conversation.

He shook his head. "That's fucking helping me?"

Nick was right—this guy was no angel. The prosecutors would have a field day with him. If he wasn't careful he would be cooling off his hot little temper in jail. She stood up and gave him a quick nod. "Goodbye, Tom. Good luck. God knows you'll need it."

She made it ten feet before he yelled out. "I like power boats. Speed, that's my thing."

Jan knew that Lucy's murderer had arrived and left quietly by boat. The motor of a power boat would've been heard. Without the motor it would be too heavy to maneuver. "Where did you go to school?" she said, turning back toward him.

"Little high school on the eastern shore. St. Christopher."

"College?"

He shook his head earnestly. "Didn't even graduate from high school. Lucy was after me to get my GED, but," he shrugged, "never got around to it. I guess I just don't have the patience for that kind of shit."

Lucy's attack had been the work of an intelligent, concise killer. A man so organized and skilled he had planned everything down to the last detail. "Did you ever go to Jay's Beer Garden?"

He shook his head. "Why would I? Lucy gave me free drinks at Lucky's."

"But you guys had broken up."

"Lucy broke up with me," he said, as if correcting her. "At first she said she thought I was fucking around. Then she said she wasn't ready to get married."

"And that made you angry?"

"Shit, yeah. Especially because it wasn't fucking true."

Jan had interviewed a lot of killers, and if someone knew they were suspected of murder, they usually wouldn't admit to a motive.

He paused for a moment and squinted his eyes. "I know what you're fucking getting at. I didn't kill her, okay?"

"Did you take a lie detector test?"

He shook his head and glanced away guiltily. "No. Not yet."

"Why not?"

"'Cause it wouldn't do no good. I passed out cold that night. No witness, dick shit for alibi."

"It would still be worthwhile." She hesitated. "What's the matter, Tom? Are you afraid that because you might have wished her dead you'll flunk the test?"

"I didn't wish her dead," he said quickly. "I was just pissed." He jammed his hands in his pockets and said, "You haven't told me how you can help me."

"I had a sister who was raped ten years ago. Right here in Annapolis. Same kind of attack."

"Really?" He looked at her straight on for the first time since she had arrived.

"Yeah."

"So you know what it's like. You know how it feels."

She nodded.

"They try and pin your sister's attack on you?"

Even the seriousness of the topic didn't stop her from smiling. "Uh, no. They were pretty sure it was a man."

It took a moment, but Neff finally realized the ridiculousness of his question. He smiled too, but his smile faded as he shook his head, his eyes welling with tears. "I mean, Lucy and I, we were on the outs, but," he paused and swallowed, "whoever did this—I'd like to fucking kill him," he said softly.

"Tom," she said, hesitating. She had to ask him one more thing . . . about Haverdale's missing hair. "Are you on good terms with your father?"

He shook his head. "Haven't talked to him in years."

Not a good sign. The prosecution would use that to say that cutting Lucy's hair had been a hostile act, somehow correlating to his poor relationship with his father.

"Did you ever cut Lucy's hair?"

She was watching him intently.

"Fuck no, you think I'm a fairy? The damn police asked me the same thing. Lucy cut *my* hair—and her own. She was real good. She wanted to go to school for it." He paused and then said, almost defensively, "They took her scissors, you know. They took so many things . . . they even took all my silverware, knives . . . my hunting rifle. Everything."

"I know," she said. "Does your lawyer have any experience in criminal cases?"

He shrugged. "He's a friend of my dad's."

"I don't want to frighten you, but I think you're going to need a really good lawyer—one that's familiar with the judges, familiar with the state's attorney." She unzipped her purse and pulled a business card out of her wallet. "I want you to call Simmons and Harwood. They owe me a favor and they'll give you a break on the cost. They're right downtown here. They're the best around."

"You think I'm going to be arrested?"

"Maybe."

He was still sitting on the edge of the dock when she walked away.

25

THE HAIRDRESSER LEANED BACK AND SMILED, ADMIRING HIS creation. Most of his customers were too afraid to make dramatic changes, so he usually found himself bored to tears as he trimmed off the usual two inches.

But not today. This woman had come in looking for a dramatic change, and that's just what she got.

Jan looked in the mirror. She almost didn't recognize herself. Her long blond hair was gone. In its place was short brown hair, cut in a style that required a simple towel dry in the morning.

"Do you like it?"

Jan hesitated, unable to speak.

"Ooooh," said a nearby stylist, admiring Jan's new do. "Love it."

"It's very natural," Jan's hairstylist said.

"It's such a change," Jan said, not even realizing she

was thinking out loud as she ran her fingers over the shorn back of her neck.

"Oh, I can fix that," the hairstylist said, pulling the razor back out. "I thought that was what you wanted."

"It is, " Jan said, practically jumping out of her chair at the sight of the razor. "I'm sorry. I didn't mean it like that. It's just what I wanted."

"Oh," he said with a proud smile, "You scared me for a second there!"

Jan shook her head, running her fingers through her hair. She had to admit she did feel much lighter, much freer without her fake blond tresses. And somehow the whole effect did make her look a little younger. Or maybe that was just wishful thinking.

Well, at least it would be a lot easier to care for. Of course, that wasn't why she cut it. She was trying to look more appealing . . . to one person in particular.

Jan paid her bill and walked out of the salon. She knew that she would have to get a job soon. And as luck would have it, she knew where she might find one.

Max squinted at the screen as Curtis Custin's file came up. He had been in trouble with the law before his visit to Annapolis, but although he had been arrested, he had not been convicted of any crime. He had been linked to several robberies in Florida, but the most serious case involved a prostitute who he had beaten so badly, she spent two weeks in the hospital recovering. A few months before Frannie was raped the woman was killed in a car accident, forcing the state to drop their case.

Max pulled a small Tylenol bottle out of his pocket and swallowed two capsules dry. He closed Custin's file and again opened his own report on Lucy Haverdale. His gut instinct—not to mention what he considered overwhelming evidence—convinced him Haverdale and Tomkins were murdered by the same man. But was it the same man that raped Jan's sister? The statement from Custin's parole officer seemed to make it a no, but there *were* concrete similarities between Frannie's rape and the recent attacks.

Was the signature the same in all three cases?

Maybe. Sarah Tomkins had been murdered by a single bullet which had lodged under her temporal lobe. This might be part of what really excited him—what he had planned to do to Lucy Haverdale had she not died unexpectedly. The examiner had determined that Sarah was badly beaten but alive and conscious when she was murdered. She had been staring straight at her killer, probably pleading for her life as he pressed the gun against her forehead.

Max looked at the analysis of the bullet they picked out of Sarah Tomkins' brain. According to the report, the bullet had been shot from an Undercover .38 with a two-inch barrel, the same gun used by local police. Was it a coincidence?

"Hey," Hank said, striding down the hall.

"How was the press conference?" Max asked, leaning back in his chair.

"That guy sure likes to hear himself talk. Went on and on about how efficient we are. He had plenty of kudos for you."

"I'm flattered," Max said dryly.

"Said there was no concrete connection between the Tomkins and Haverdale murders. Said we were close to making an arrest in the Haverdale case."

"Shit, he's after that poor boy's head."

"The man wants an arrest. And whether you like it or not, you may be taking Neff's fingerprints before the end of the week. And that kid ain't no Cal Ripken. He's a drunk."

Max was quiet.

"By the way, I've got some other news. About your friend, Jan."

Max straightened.

Hank leaned on his desk. "She took a leave of absence, effective immediately. Dumped her cases, everything."

"What?"

"You got it. She's gone. Word has it that when everyone came in this morning, she was clearing out her desk."

Max paused. "I just saw her last night. She didn't mention it."

"Oh?" Hank said with a mischievous smile. "Date?"

Max raised an eyebrow, making it clear that Hank was incorrect. "I ran into her. At Lucky's."

"Lucky's? Where the Haverdale woman worked?"

Max sighed.

Hank understood immediately why Jan had left her job. He whistled through his teeth and then said, with some admiration, "I wouldn't want to be on her shit list."

Max nodded as he glanced down at the pictures of the three women in front of him. "Me neither."

26

"LET'S HAVE A LOOKIE."

Jan bit her lower lip as she watched Rex, the big, burly manager of McRyan's, scan her application. She had chosen McRyan's simply because they were hiring and it fit the bill. All three of the bars where the dead women had worked were small, casual places, located on the water in and around Annapolis. She guessed that the murderer would frequent these bars, scoping out victims. McRyan's seemed to be almost identical to Jay's Beer Garden: same size, same clientele, same easy access to the water.

Of course, she had no idea if this killer would actually show up here. The whole plan was a longshot. Still, she could hope.

She forced herself to breathe as she glanced back at Rex. She wondered if he had pegged her for a lunatic yet. She *was* crazy, no doubt about it.

It made sense that she would lose her mind sooner or later. Every therapist she had ever seen had always told her how impressed they were by the way she had pulled herself together and survived in the face of tremendous adversity. She had lost her father, her mother, her sister, all in sudden and tragic ways, yet she had gone on to college and then law school, graduating near the top of her class. Her life had been a story of survival, of rising above the odds . . . until now. She had obviously been a little more unhinged than her esteemed psychologists had realized. She had suspected it all along, of course. She knew things that they didn't know, like the fact that she had nightmares. Like the fact that she had shut herself down emotionally after Frannie died. She knew she had lost a few marbles. But even she couldn't have predicted that she would set out to trap a serial killer.

"When did you work at the . . ." he paused, squinting as he attempted to decipher her handwriting. He spoke with a slight accent that made him sound kind of Italian, kind of New York. He had a full head of thick black hair which was carefully styled, parted on the side. He was obviously very proud of his hair because he wore his shirt unbuttoned to his waist, allowing everyone a rather unappetizing glimpse of the mass of curls that covered his chest. His father was the owner of this refined establishment, and it was obvious that Rex took his job very seriously. He had a beeper attached to his belt and a portable phone on his lap. "Brown Jug?"

"I was in college."

He set the paper down and squinted at her. "How old are you?"

It was an illegal question, but she had the feeling that this probably wasn't the time to mention it. "What difference does it make?"

"No offense, but you don't look like any college girl. You got that look . . . of, well, been around the block, you know what I mean? Not that it bothers me, no. My mother's got the same look, God bless her, and she's one of the sexiest women on this earth, I kid you not. I swear to God," he said, raising his right hand in testament. "She wears those little minis cut up her ass, showin' off her gams like I don't know what. Nice hooters," he said, cupping his hands and holding them out in front of his chest. "Nothing's sagging if you get the picture."

Oh God, did she ever. "Mr. Bartucci," she began.

"Rex. My employees call me Rex. Nickname. Tough as a bulldog, that's what they say."

She nodded. "Rex," she said gingerly, as though his very name left a bad taste in her mouth. "Why do you want to know how old I am?"

"Just that, seems a little strange. The last job you have on here was in college."

"After school I worked at the state's attorney's office," she said carefully. She avoided telling him she was a prosecutor. "I didn't think it was relevant. I thought you were interested in my experience waitressing or bartending."

"So why did you leave? Good benefits over there, working for the state. But the place is crawling with those sleazeball lawyers. One of them put my cousin Louie away for five years. All on account of him borrowing some guy's car when he was a valet. He just took it out for a spin, got lost, and the next thing he knew, he's in the slammer."

She shook her head, feigning disgust. "I hear you, no justice."

"You said it."

"Anyway, I was laid off."

He nodded. "You got canned," he said, translating.

"You could say that."

"So. What did you do there?" Rex asked.

"I was a, uh, assistant." Good one. Pretty slick.

"Assistant? Pretty big word, eh?" he said, pretending to hold back a laugh. "I.e.: secretary. And now you want to be a drink assistant. A booze assistant." He was laughing now, finding his dim wit hysterical. "A French fry assistant. In the back I have dish assistants . . ." he was continuing, but she was doing her best to tune him out, making sure her phony pleasant smile stayed plastered on her face. The whole time he was speaking she was sizing him up. Was he the serial rapist? Right build. Wrong accent, although he could change his voice.

"Okay, okay. I can tell you got a good sense of humor," he said. "And I got to be honest with ya, even if you didn't, I'd still hire you. I've been having a hard time finding girls who want to work here, on account of that whole murder thing."

Bummer. That thing.

"Lot of girls are afraid. My ma even said, 'Give me an apron and I'll come work for you.' Ain't nobody going to mess with my ma, that's what I say." He paused, as if waiting for her to reply. "You're not afraid?"

"Afraid of what?"

"You know. That there's some stalker or something out there."

Jan shook her head.

He leaned forward and smiled. His mouth was full of perfectly white, straight teeth. "When can you start?"

27

When Jan pulled in front of her house she noticed something very strange. Her grass was short.

Mrs. Fletcher. Jan realized she must've grown so sick of her long grass that she had come over and cut it herself. Old Mrs. Fletcher with white hair and a big hat had pushed a lawn mower over a damp half acre in ninety-degree weather.

Jan stepped out of the car. Mrs. Fletcher was beside Jan's house, chopping at a vine with a machete. Her frizzy white hair was held off her face by a thick white sweatband. She had on a T-shirt over polyester pants that didn't really qualify as slacks or shorts. They stopped at mid-calf, giving an ample view of her rolled down knee-highs and white orthopedic shoes.

Jan jumped out of her car and ran over to her. "Mrs. Fletcher. You don't have to do that," she yelled.

"Hello, Jan," Mrs. Fletcher replied as she continued

to chop. "This vine is going to cover your house if you're not careful."

"Mrs. Fletcher," Jan said, exasperated. "Did you mow my lawn?"

Mrs. Fletcher nodded, yanking and tugging on the thick vine. "I had to do mine so I thought I'd take care of yours while I was at it."

"Thank you," she said appreciatively "But I wish you wouldn't. I mean, it's very nice of you, but I should be helping you, not the other way around."

"Why?"

"Well," Jan hesitated, not wanting to offend. "Because it makes me feel like a slug," she said simply.

"No, dear, you're just busy. I was busy once myself and I know what it's like." She succeeded in pulling off the vine and threw it down on the ground like it was a snake she had killed. She looked at Jan and the smile faded from her lips. "Oh, my. You have a new hairstyle."

She nodded.

"Very nice," she said approvingly. "Much more natural." She glanced at the sun. "You're home from work early."

"Yeah, well," Jan shrugged.

"I hear they arrested that kid for killing his girlfriend."

"They arrested him?"

"Not yet, but they're about to."

Jan shook her head.

"You're not happy?"

"I don't think he did it."

Mrs. Fletcher paused for a minute. "I pulled this vine off, but you really should take care of the ones around your porch over there."

"Yeah," she said. "I'm going to try and get to it today."

Mrs. Fletcher gave Jan a knowing maternal smile as if to say: *yeah, right.*

At six o'clock, Jan was back at the bar. She was wearing her uniform: shorts and a white T-shirt.

She would have preferred some time to prepare mentally, but Rex had insisted he needed her that night. She had agreed simply because she knew that her resolve was weakening and if she waited she might talk herself out of this. As it was, she hadn't even had time to call Sheila. Anyway, she realized it was definitely better this way. Might as well jump right into it.

Rex was standing on a chair, his bulky form stretched up to the ceiling as he changed a light bulb. Of the ten or so tables in the small, dark room, only two were taken, one by a group of elderly men and the other by a young couple.

"Rex?" she said. "Hi."

"Hey, baby," he yelled, screwing the bulb in. "Right on time."

Baby. This was going to take some getting used to. He finished screwing in the light bulb and stepped off the chair. "That's Cindy," he said, nodding toward the woman behind the bar. She was wiping off glasses with a dish towel. "She's a bartender and waitress too, depending on what I need when." Jan followed Rex to the bar. "Cindy, this here's Jan. I told her you'd be showing her the ropes."

Cindy had bleached blond hair which was teased up on top of her head. She looked to be in her mid-forties, but it was tough to tell her exact age. She had a face that reflected years of smoking and lack of sunscreen, but her body was that of a svelte twenty-year-old. She seemed to be aware of her assets, wearing a skin tight T-shirt that bared her midriff and shorts that practically went up her rear.

"You know how to carry a tray?" Cindy asked.

"I think so," Jan said.

Cindy looked at Rex and shrugged. "Seems like she's well-qualified."

"Don't give her no hard time," he said. "You girls get along."

"Can I help you do that?" Jan asked, looking for an extra towel.

Cindy shook her head. "I've got it."

Jan nodded as she glanced around the room uncomfortably.

"I'm taking care of those tables," Cindy said, as though Jan might want to cut in on her action.

"No problem," Jan said. "Do you think it will be busy tonight?"

"Tuesday night. Could go either way. Since . . . since

these girls started getting murdered, it's been pretty crowded. Curiosity seekers. You know, all on account of the bars where the girls worked were a lot like this place. It's like they expect this guy to be in here or something," she said with an uncomfortable laugh, looking around anxiously.

"But you don't," Jan said.

Cindy bit her lower lip and said, "I knew the last one. Sarah."

"You did?"

"I used to work there—at Jay's. Only left about a month ago. I keep thinking, if I didn't—that could've been me."

Jan paused for a moment and then asked, "Did you know her well?"

"Sarah?" she nodded. "She hadn't worked there for very long. Couple months maybe. Nice kid. Fun, you know?"

Jan nodded.

Cindy put down her glass and looked at Jan. "Doesn't any of this faze you?"

Jan shook her head. "The papers said that they're not sure they're related . . ."

She stopped. Cindy was shaking her head. "That's what they say. I don't believe it."

"Why?"

"Too much of a coincidence if you ask me."

"You don't think Sarah was killed by someone she knew?"

She shrugged. "Possible I guess. She dated this guy from the Naval Academy when she first started working there. But that didn't last too long. She dated around a little, had one guy she liked . . . an attorney or something." She shrugged. "Who knows? I don't mean to freak you out or anything."

"No," Jan protested. "Hey, I want to hear. Because I don't want to be working anyplace that's not safe. I'm surprised you didn't get out of this business."

"If I could find another job that paid as well as this one, I would have quit in a minute. Until they get this guy, I'm not going to feel comfortable."

"I can understand that."

"The police were just in here last night asking me questions."

Max. "What kind of questions?"

"You know, asking me about who she talked to and stuff, like I could remember. It gave me the creeps. It could be anyone. Look around, I felt like saying. That's who."

Jan nodded sympathetically.

"Anyway," she said. "I didn't mean to be rude or anything when you first came in, I just, well, I'm a little leery of everyone these days."

"I can understand."

She paused, glancing Jan up and down. "I'm surprised you're not up on all this stuff. Rex said you worked over at the state's attorney's office."

Jan nodded.

"Pay good?"

"Not really. And the work stinks."

"Hmm. I like that guy, what's his name . . . Nick Fitzgerald. I think he's cute."

"Yeah," Jan agreed uncomfortably.

"I just saw him on TV the other night. He says there's evidence that he can't speak of which proves these crimes aren't related." Cindy stopped, suddenly staring at Jan's lower half. "Can I give you a tip?"

"A tip?" Jan repeated. "Sure."

"Your shorts. They look like they're your husband's or something. You'll get bigger tips if your clothes fit, and you might want to show a little skin. You know what I mean?"

Jan nodded.

Cindy gave her a tentative smile. "It's not that bad here. You might even like it if you can just block this Sarah shit from your mind. I mean, it gets really crowded, and Rex cranks up the music. . . . Well, sometimes it can be like a party. It's fun."

Jan nodded again, not quite convinced.

Business was slow that night, and at ten o'clock Rex told Jan to go home. She was exhausted. Not every day do you quit your job, chop off all your hair, and go to work as a bar maid.

When she arrived home, she almost didn't notice the piece of paper wedged in her door. She grabbed it, unlocked her door and slipped inside, not bothering to open it until the door was safely locked behind her.

Jan, I came by to see you—I need to talk to you. Please call me at home when you get in. Nick.

Jan checked her watch. It was almost eleven. Too late? She'd find out. She picked up the phone and dialed Nick's home number. After four rings, the answering machine picked up. She hung up. Whatever it was, it would have to wait until tomorrow.

Jan awoke to the sound of knocking. She glanced over at her clock. It was seven in the morning. "Just a minute," she called out groggily. She stood up and pulled on a pair of shorts to go with the T-shirt she had slept in.

She hurried out to the living room. Nick was standing at the door. She unlocked the door and opened it.

"Jan, my God," he said, staring at her. "What happened to your hair?"

She reached up to touch it. "I got a little trim. Like it?"

He nodded slowly, still staring at her with dismay.

"What's going on?" she said, crossing her arms in front of her, all the while wishing she had put on a bra.

Nick glanced at her attire and gave her a mischievous half smile. "I woke you."

"No," she said, shaking her head. "I was just lying there."

"I, ah, stopped by yesterday."

"I got your note," she said.

"When I didn't hear from you last night, I wasn't sure," he paused. "Can I come in?"

She held the door open for him. "Nick, if this is about my leave of absence—"

He held up his hand. "No. I don't think it's a great idea at this point in your career, but that's not why I'm here."

She was confused. "It's not?"

He shook his head.

"What . . . Has something happened?" she asked, worried.

"Sort of," he said. "Can we sit down?"

"What's the matter?"

"Jan," he began. "I, well, I have something to say to you. I'm not sure how you'll take it, but, ah, I just have to, um, say it."

She sat down across from him as she ran a finger through her messy hair. Something must have rattled him. He was usually quite articulate.

"I . . . I find that lately, I've been thinking about you. A lot. For the past ten years or so, you've been a part of my life, to some degree or another. The other night, when you came on the boat and I was there with Rachel, well, I felt strange. Like I was . . ." he hesitated. "I know this is going to sound ridiculous, but . . . cheating on you or something."

"What?" Jan said, stunned.

227

"After you left, I went back to the boat and asked her to leave. I realized that if I was going to date anyone from the office, it would be you."

"Gee, thanks," she said.

He shook his head again as he stood up. "This isn't coming out the way I meant. Lately I've been aware of some sort of friction between us. I know we've been friends for years . . . more than just friends. I thought of you like a little sister or something, but lately, lately that's changed. I just wasn't ready for it. It took me by surprise."

"What are you saying?"

"That maybe the only reason why I even went out with Rachel was because I was trying to keep you at arm's length. Because I knew in the back of my mind if anything ever happened between us it might be *it*. That scared me. But I can't shut out the truth any longer."

Jan leaned back in the chair. This was terrible. She cared about Nick, loved him like a brother, but she was simply not attracted to him.

They both just sat there, silent for a few seconds.

Finally she said, "Nick, I—"

He interrupted her and said, "I'm afraid I'm in love with you."

I'm in love with you.

Oh boy. This was bad. "Oh, Nick," she said, forcing herself to stand.

"I know this seems sudden, but I've been giving this

a lot of thought. When I was with Rachel I realized it would never be anything. Because," he stopped pacing as he turned to face her, "she's not who I want. You are."

Jan breathed deeply, afraid that she might just pass out. Why was he doing this? True, he had made little overtures throughout the years, but they were always discreet and subtle. He seemed to get the message that she wasn't interested without either one of them having to have an awkward conversation. So where was this coming from? She hadn't said or done anything which might encourage this kind of proclamation. "I . . . I don't know what to say."

"You could tell me how you feel," he was closer now, his lips almost brushing hers. Jan was tempted to push him, to shove him away. "Nick," she began.

"Jan," he whispered, taking her hands in his. "It might have been awkward before, when you were working there, but now with you gone . . ."

"It's just a leave of absence."

"I only have a couple of months left myself."

She pulled her hands away. "I, I care about you Nick, I really do. But I don't think we're right for each other. I mean—"

"You mean that you don't feel the same way about me."

Jan bit her lower lip and nodded.

Nick stared at her carefully and then said, "Okay. I, ah—oh boy," he said, running his fingers through his hair. "Let's just forget we had this conversation. Okay?"

"Yeah, sure. Whatever you want—"

"I should go," Nick said quickly.

She began to nod. She had turned pale white.

"Hey, it's okay," he said. "Really. With any luck I'll learn to love again." He paused and then winked.

28

MAX STARED AT THE FRIENDLY-LOOKING DETECTIVE IN FRONT OF
him. Jeff Brown had retired ten years ago, and from his
tanned face, soft linen shirt and creased khaki slacks, it
looked like retirement agreed with him.

Max was, quite frankly, shocked to see him. After all,
just this morning he had left a message with Jeff
Brown's wife in Florida. She had politely informed him
that her husband was in Maine on a fishing trip and
wouldn't be returning home until some time next
week. Then, just hours later, Jeff Brown had shown up
in person, in Crownsville, at CID. "Boy, you really know
how to return a phone call," Max said.

"I was in DC. When I called home, my wife said that
you had called. I had planned to be in Annapolis anyway, so I thought, what the hell. Stop in and say hi to
the old gang. So where the hell are they? Looks like you

got a brand new gang here. I recognize the sarge, but everyone else looks like a damn kid."

"I just transferred here," Max said politely. "I thought your wife said you were in Maine."

"I was, last week. But my pal's angina flared up so I went to visit another friend of mine back here. I wish I was back in Maine. It's hot as hell here. Christ. Worse than Florida." He tapped his fingers on the table. "So what can I do for you, Detective?"

"I just had a few questions for you on a case you worked on. I really just wanted to get your take on everything."

"Sounds interesting."

"It was one of your last cases. Frances Garret. A young woman that was raped."

"Yeah, we caught the guy."

"Right. Curtis Custin."

Brown nodded, as if waiting for him to continue.

"Well," Max said, suddenly feeling a little silly. He wished the retired detective hadn't bothered to come in for this. "There were some similarities between the Custin rape and a recent murder."

Max thought he could detect a widening in Jeff Brown's eyes that suggested surprise. "Custin's in prison."

"He's out."

"So?"

"So I have some questions about his case."

"I assume you've read the file," he interrupted.

"I couldn't find the file. Archives didn't have it. I got one from the state's attorney's office, but a lot of information seemed to be missing, so I was hoping you could provide some insight. Something that wasn't in the file. Like his personal history, why you suspected him in the first place."

"Let me see . . ." he said, stroking his stubbled chin. "He was a loser. Just in town for a couple of weeks. He was a suspect in the murder of a local woman."

"Eugenia O'Malley. His mother."

The retired detective nodded. "You talked to Wingate?"

"The other day. He's convinced Custin killed his mother. He said something about a gun that was lost—"

"Sloppy detective work. Cost Wingate his job. At least we got Custin for the rape."

"I'm glad you brought that up," Max said. "Why do you think Custin confessed?"

Jeff Brown stared at Max, his blue eyes icy cold. "I don't follow you."

"I mean, if he had an attack of conscience, it seems he would've confessed to killing his mother."

"I think you're right. *If* he had killed his mother. I don't think he did."

"But Wingate—"

"Wingate was a fuck-up. Trust me."

"How did Custin confess?" Max asked. "Did you interrogate him, or did he turn himself in?"

"Do your homework, Detective."

233

"I'm trying. That's why I called you."

Brown was smiling again. He obviously thought Max was just being lazy.

Max continued, unfazed, "Custin doesn't seem to fit the profile the rape victim had given. What made you suspect him in the first place?"

Jeff Brown smiled as he leaned back in his chair, relaxed. "You ever work in sex crimes, Detective?"

Max knew he was being patronized. He gave a simple nod. "Well," Brown continued, "then you know that sometimes the victim is the last person who can give an accurate description of her attacker. She says his eyes are brown, they turn up blue. She says he's short, he turns out tall."

"So, I guess I still don't understand why you thought that Custin might have been guilty."

He shrugged. "I didn't."

"What do you mean?"

"I mean, I didn't. But I didn't have any leads, and I heard that Wingate had a suspect in the O'Malley case. I went to ask Custin if he knew anything about the Garret girl." He shrugged. "He told me he did it."

Max leaned back in his chair. Something about this was not right. "Just like that," Max said, snapping his fingers. "And he never recanted, never tried to get his confession thrown out. Never confessed to killing his mother."

"Like I said, I don't remember much about the case."

"But it was just about your last case, wasn't it?"

The detective wasn't smiling anymore. He leaned forward and said in a low voice, "How old are you, Detective?"

"How old . . ." Max repeated, confused.

"You're not even thirty yet, are you?" Jeff said, interrupting him before he had a chance to finish. "I bet you're a college boy, too. Probably been on the force since you were twenty-two. Started off as a street cop, worked your way up to sex crimes, then to homicide. . . . How long you been in homicide. One year? Two?"

Max didn't answer.

"You're a baby, Detective. You'll learn that there's a lot of fucking weirdos out there, and what they do makes no sense at all. And by the time you figure that out you're going to be so fried from this job you're going to retire. So forget everything you learned in your criminal psych classes because in real life, there are no rules."

"I'm not following you," Max said coldly.

"I'm saying there are some things that just don't make sense. Like life."

"Okay," Max said. He'd had just about enough of this guy. "I know you don't remember much about this case, but would you happen to recall if Custin had been stalking Frannie? I know he said he met her the night before, but the attack was too well planned for that to be true."

"Couldn't tell you offhand," he said, mildly irritated.

He ran his tongue over his sun-burned lips. He glanced at his Rolex watch.

"How'd he get to Frannie's that night? By car or boat?"

"Can't recall offhand."

"Just one more question," Max said. "Do you have any idea how Custin could've come into money?"

"What are you talking about?"

"A month after he was released he bought a big, brand-new house. Brand-new car, brand-new boat."

"Sounds like my boy Custin's back to dealing drugs."

"Maybe," Max said.

"You know, I'm surprised Custin came back here. He was from Florida, I think."

"He's supposedly living there right now," Max said. He regretted admitting that almost as soon as he said it.

Brown was confused. "You lost me."

"At least, that's his official address."

"I don't get it. You think he flew back here to commit the murders?"

Max didn't answer. He didn't have to. He knew how ridiculous it sounded. A serial murderer flying back and forth to commit his crimes. That might be a first.

"Hell of a commute," Brown laughed.

29

JAN SCANNED THE LIQUOR BOTTLES LINED UP ON THE GRIMY DARK wood shelves. She had been at work for an hour but she was having a tough time focusing. She kept thinking about Nick. He had seemed so happy with Rachel. What would inspire him to come over and profess his love like that? It just wasn't his style. Besides, surely he was aware that she didn't feel the same way.

Still, she couldn't stand the thought of hurting him. She loved Nick, she really did, but not like that. She reached up to her throat, feeling for her glands. The whole experience had made her feel physically ill. She even had the chills.

She glanced up at the air conditioner roaring above her head. No wonder she had the chills.

Jan picked up a shot glass and grabbed a bottle of tequila. It was Thursday night and the bar was packed. A group of young men were crowded around, celebrating their friend's birthday. And, unfortunately, Rex had designated Jan the official bartender. Even though she had worked as one before in college, it seemed like a million years ago. She only remembered how to make the basics. And she only knew how to make those very slowly.

Impatient with Jan's slow pace, Cindy ran behind the bar, grabbing a bottle of gin and a glass as she eyed the lineup of thirsty patrons.

That Cindy, Jan thought admirably. She sure knew how to move.

"What do you need?" Cindy barked, noticing Jan's forlorn expression.

"Know what's in a Kamikaze?" Jan asked.

"Lime juice, triple sec, and vodka," Cindy said as she whizzed past Jan, heading toward the blender.

Jan put back the tequila and grabbed the vodka, mixing the drink for the birthday boy. She didn't even flinch when a collective moan emanated behind her as yet another selection from Deep Purple blasted out of the speakers. Rex loved to have Deep Purple blaring as loud as his patrons could stand, but now the boys at the bar were clamoring for a change.

Jan slid the drink in front of the guest of honor. She made a quick decision as she looked into his young, baby face: this would be his last drink. He looked to be about fifteen, but Jan had carded him and his license had stated that he was twenty-two and today was indeed his birthday. He winked and gave her a buck as a tip.

"God help me," Jan muttered under her breath.

Rex must have heard the grumbling about the music because in the middle of the song, Deep Purple was replaced with a fast moving techno-dance rhythm.

"Whooee," Cindy said, setting her tray down on the bar. She put her hands above her head and clapped as she moved her hips to the beat. "I love this song!" Cindy shouted, once again raising her hands over her head.

"Shake it, Cindy!" yelled a guy from the darkness of the bar. Jan could understand why Cindy did so well with tips. She periodically dropped everything to do an impromptu dance, a feat that did not go unappreciated by the large population of males in attendance.

"You have to loosen up," she told Jan when she had arrived for her shift earlier in the evening. "You're never going to make any money with that tight-ass routine you got going. It doesn't hurt to be a little friendly."

Now as Jan watched the men ogling Cindy, she couldn't help but wonder if she had ever prosecuted any of the patrons.

Almost all of the slimy brown veneer tables were full. Jan guessed that Cindy was right, the bar was packed due to the new cachet, the element of danger. Of course, most of the people here didn't have anything to worry about. Nor did Cindy. Her long blond hair, curvaceous body, husband and kids would rule her out as a victim.

As she glanced around the room, her eyes settled on one imposing figure near the door. He was standing still, arms crossed in front of him as he shook his head in disbelief. *Max.*

Jan could see him lean forward and squint, as though he still couldn't believe his eyes. She thought she saw him say: "Jesus Christ," but then again, she wasn't a lip reader.

Cindy jumped behind her, and before Jan could shrug her off, she had grabbed Jan's arms in an attempt to force her to dance. She was moving Jan around as though Jan was a puppet, and the bar patrons seemed to enjoy it, clapping and cheering Jan on.

Jan did her best, self-consciously swinging around as she moved her shoulders. She just hoped she didn't look as ridiculous as she felt.

When the song was over, Jan laughed uncomfortably and broke away, scurrying to tend to some of the orders for drinks from the people at the bar, all of whom had been only too happy to wait until she had finished her dance.

"Nice moves," Max said, not looking too happy.

"Thanks," she said cheerfully, pretending as though nothing was unusual about this interaction. "What can I get you?"

"Can I talk to you for a minute?" he said, a polite smile on his lips.

"I'm a little busy right now," she replied, shrugging.

"If you want to talk to him, go ahead," Cindy said, nodding toward Max. "Believe me, I can handle it."

Afraid that Max would blow her cover, Jan stepped out from behind the bar and nodded for him to follow her.

As they walked outside he said, "What the hell are you doing?"

"Bartending."

"Looks like research to me."

She shrugged, playing dumb.

Max nodded, the muscles in his jaw tightening. "Nice hair cut."

"You like it? I thought it was time for a change."

"You probably didn't know this but Lucy Haverdale and Sarah Tomkins also had short brown hair."

"It's a popular cut these days," she remarked.

Max paused as a big, beefy man with a tattoo of a heart on his neck exited the bar, causing a blast of music to pierce the night. Max said tersely, "Don't be a vigilante."

"What's that, a new band?"

"That's cute. You think you'll be tossing one-liners when the guy puts the knife to your throat?"

She shrugged.

"Look, this is not a good idea, you working here."

"Max, I appreciate—"

"Custin is missing."

"Missing?"

"I spoke with his parole officer again today. He was supposed to meet with Custin this morning. He never showed. Custin's girlfriend claims she doesn't know where he is."

Jan looked at Max, but she'd lost her snappy rhythm.

Max glanced away. "There's more. I'm beginning to agree with you. There's something not quite right about your sister's rape."

She hesitated. "I'm glad to hear you say that."

"Eugenia O'Malley was Curtis Custin's mother."

She nodded slowly and then said, "Since we're being honest with each other, I should tell you I went to see Neff yesterday."

"Why?"

"I wanted to talk to him myself. Confirm what I already knew." She stared him in the eye. "Do you think he killed Lucy Haverdale?"

"I don't want to get into this with you." He paused for a moment.

Jan could see his eyes soften with . . . what? Concern? "You don't, do you?"

He sighed, running out of steam. "Look, Jan. I've got this place loaded with cops. I've got a uniformed man posted outside of Cindy's home—"

"You're wasting your time."

Max didn't say anything.

"This is ridiculous. What are you going to do? Guard every cocktail waitress in Anne Arundel county? Besides, he likes petite, single, short-haired brunette bartenders."

Max ran a hand through his hair. "What makes you so sure he's going to come here, anyway?" he said, nodding toward the bar.

She just smiled and headed back into the bar.

* * *

Jan finished her shift at one. She grabbed her purse and stepped out into the clear, hot night, anxious to get out of the smoky bar. As she headed toward her car, she heard footsteps. She glanced over her shoulder. The birthday boy who had been sitting at the bar for most of the night was behind her. She pulled her keys out of her purse and stopped at her car, slipping the key into the lock.

"Excuse me," he said.

"Yes?" Jan said coolly as she kept one hand on her purse, one hand on the door.

"I saw you in there and I was wondering . . . you think you might want to go somewhere? Get a bite to eat or something?"

Jan smiled politely as she opened the door. "No thanks. I'm beat."

The man grasped on to the top of her door. "I saw the way you looked at me tonight," he said, flashing her a smile that immediately gave her the creeps.

"I think you're mistaken. Goodnight," she said, trying to slip inside the car.

"Hey," he said, grabbing her arm and yanking her back out. "I'm not done talking to you yet."

Jan heard a car door slam in the distance.

"It's my birthday. I should at least get a kiss," the boy said, pulling her in to him. Jan couldn't kick him because the car door was in her way.

Just then, Max appeared. "Police," he said as he flashed his badge.

The boy raised his arms and moved away from the car. "I wasn't doing anything, honest. I was just . . . seeing her off. So, I'll see you later," he said, turning away from Max.

"Wait a minute," Max said, grabbing the birthday boy by the back of his shirt. He leaned toward Jan and said, "Do you want to press charges?"

Jan was sitting inside the car, fuming. She had her arms crossed around her chest. She shook her head.

Max said to the boy, "I don't want to see you around here again, got it?"

The boy swallowed as he nodded.

"Now beat it," Max said, giving him a little shove as he let go of his shirt. As the boy ran away, Max turned to Jan and smiled. "That's my Clint Eastwood imitation. Do you like it?"

"You were waiting for me, weren't you?" Jan asked angrily.

"Hey," he said. "You're welcome. Think nothing of it."

Jan refused to look at him.

He leaned forward and said, "Instead of being so nice, maybe I should be citing you for getting a kid drunk. I'm willing to bet money that kid wasn't twenty-one."

"Look, I know some karate. I can take care of myself."

"Karate's not going to protect you from a bullet."

She started her engine. "Goodnight, Max."

"I know you think you know what you're doing, but

you don't. This kind of trap is going to backfire and get you killed."

"A trap? For who? Don't you read the papers? There's not a serial killer out there. Nothing to be alarmed about."

"Don't do this, Jan." He seemed upset, which surprised her, even spooked her. "Please," he said quietly.

"So let's work together."

"No," he said adamantly. "It's too dangerous."

"Fine. Have it your way. Goodnight." Before he had a chance to speak she hit the accelerator, leaving him in a cloud of exhaust.

A few minutes later she saw Max's car pass her with the siren on. Good riddance, she thought. Go.

Hmph, she mumbled to herself. The nerve of that guy. It was nervy, wasn't it? So if it was so nervy, why had she been almost flattered by his interest in her well-being? Sheila was right—there was something very attractive about him. Not that he was her type, God no. Her type was, well, she didn't really have a type. But there was something about Max which made her wary. He seemed to radiate intensity—he looked at her as if he could read her mind and she didn't like that. She preferred to keep her distance, at least right now.

With that thought, Jan pulled into her dark, unlit driveway. She was warm and sticky from the bar, her clothes reeking of cigarette smoke and booze. She was looking forward to stripping off her clothes and soaking her tired body in a nice cool, perfumed bath. But as

She glanced behind the wildflowers framing the driveway, she had a sudden sense of unease. Had Max's warnings gotten to her?

She stopped her car in front of her house and rolled up her windows. As she stepped into the driveway, a mild breeze blew across the porch, causing the wind chimes to sound.

Jan pulled out her keys. A wave of anxiety washed over her. She could sense something . . . someone.

She glanced around, but she didn't see anything unusual. She walked through the screened-in porch, slid her key in the lock, opened it and stepped inside, quickly locking the door behind her. She leaned forward, resting her forehead against the door as she breathed a sigh of relief. She was safe. It had been nothing. Just nerves.

Suddenly Jan was grabbed from behind, her arms twisted behind her back as she was shoved up against the wall. She kicked back, but the assailant was ready for her, jerking away and knocking her down.

Before she could react he was on top of her, pinning her facedown against the wood floor. He said, "You're no match for him, Jan."

It was Max. He let her go and stood up.

"Are you crazy?" she spat, pushing herself up. "I mean, you must be absolutely crazy. I could sue your ass off."

"You could but you won't."

"Oh yeah? Why?"

"A hunch."

Jan kicked with all of her strength, catching Max in the stomach. As he bent down in pain, she jumped up and hit him in the shoulder, knocking him to the ground. As she paused, he grabbed her, pulling her down with him. Within a second, he was on top of her once again, straddling her as he pinned her arms against the floor.

"What are you doing?" she cried.

He stared at her, not budging. "Trying to save your life."

"Get off me!"

"First promise me you'll give this up."

She was no match for him. Panting and exhausted from her brief struggle, Jan stopped fighting. As she relaxed, both of them became very aware of their physical position. She could feel the strength in his arms as he held her, the pressure of her breasts pushed up against his chest. It had been a long time since Jan had had a man on top of her and she was reminded of urges she had almost forgotten. Embarrassed, she turned her head.

Max let her go and stood up, then extended his hand, offering her help.

She looked away. "I hate you," she said weakly.

"Suit yourself. By the way, that's some great lock you got there. Where'd you get it, the five and dime?"

She sat up, still on the floor, but refused to answer. Each one could hear the other huffing and puffing, still trying to catch their breath. A few minutes later, Max said, "By the way, I do like your hair."

"Gee thanks. I can't tell you how much that means to me," Jan quipped.

Max walked to the window and pulled back the curtains. The moon was full, casting long shadows across her yard. "Nice and secluded." He glanced over to the house next to her. "Who lives there?"

"A retired professor. A wild old lady."

He turned back from the window. "I was kind of hoping for Wyatt Earp."

She smiled, despite herself. "She's as close as you get."

"Look, I want you to be safe," he said. "Do you have a gun?"

She hesitated a moment, then nodded.

"Let's see it."

She disappeared into the bedroom. She reemerged a few minutes later carrying a small silver revolver. She had bought it shortly after Frannie died. Although she had bullets, she had never actually put them in or used the gun.

As if reading her mind, Max asked, "Smith and Wesson, not bad. Do you know how to use it?"

"I guess. You aim it at his crotch and pull the trigger."

"Ooh," Max said, wincing at the image. He could imagine the sensation all too clearly. "What are you doing tomorrow morning?"

"Sleeping. Why? You gonna come over and throw me down the ravine?"

Max laughed. "I'll be here at eight. We're going to the target range."

She hesitated and then said, "Make it ten. I've got some things to take care of first."

Max smiled and gave a little nod of his head as if he was amused by her nerve. He opened the door and stepped onto the porch. Jan got up and followed him out, stopping at the screened door. "Max," she called out. "How do you know I won't tell the sergeant or Nick what you did tonight?"

He shook his head. "I don't," he said, getting in his car.

Jan stood at the door until he drove away. Then she locked and bolted the door.

30

AT TEN-THIRTY IN THE MORNING JAN WAS WEARING HEAD-
phones and goggles, standing in the storefront of the
target range.

"Yep," Max said, looking at her. "Those fit."

Jan glanced at the solitary table in the corner
where several elderly gun enthusiasts were sipping
coffee, their various shiny machines laid out in front
of them.

As Max discussed the different targets with the
manager, Jan pulled the goggles up on her forehead
and glanced at the poster to the side of the cash regis-
ter. It was a picture of a beautiful woman wearing a
cowboy hat and holding a long rifle across giant
breasts breaking out of a tight white shirt. Her auto-
graph was scrawled directly under her breasts.

Assuming she was a famous marksman, she asked, "Who's she?"

He shrugged. "Some woman," he said, picking up a poster-size sheet, illustrated with a life-size diagram of a man's torso.

"Thanks," Jan said. "That wasn't clear."

Max had arrived at her house at exactly ten o'clock. There was something in his demeanor, however, that had changed from the previous night. Jan thought back to the wrestling match on the floor. She had felt something . . . a sexual attraction, and wondered if he had felt it too.

She followed him into the gallery. He was wearing casual clothes, jeans and a clean white T-shirt. He really was handsome, she decided. Some women would say sexy. She wasn't sure why it had taken her so long to notice his thick, wavy brown hair, his big, honest eyes . . . and his well-toned body.

Stop it, she commanded herself.

"Okay," Max said, stopping at the very last stall. There were eight stalls, all of which faced what looked to be an empty warehouse. There was a rope stretched from the top of each booth running the length of the warehouse. Each rope had a piece of cardboard clipped to it.

She watched him press a switch which reeled in the cardboard.

Max clipped the diagram to the cardboard and pressed the switch again, sending the picture back out. "You can basically put this as far away or as close as you want," he said, stopping the figure halfway across the warehouse.

Jan glanced at the booth next to theirs. The man's target was a collection of cards which he was hitting with near perfect accuracy.

"Always, always, hold the gun away from you," Max said, picking it up. "To load it just push in this lever and spin the cartridge out." He took the bullets out and dropped them in the cartridge. He handed Jan the gun. "Go ahead."

"Just shoot it?"

"Well, aim it first."

Jan rolled her eyes. "I figured."

"Give him a what-for, right in the crotch like you promised."

Jan snickered, then took the gun and aimed. She pulled the trigger, doing her best to squelch a scream as the gun exploded. She glanced at Max. He nodded for her to continue. She held the gun in front of her and shot until her five-bullet chamber was empty.

Max peered at the figure. The diagram man was unblemished. Not a single hole in his paper frame.

"Where are your bullets going?" he asked, half to himself as he looked into the range. Still perplexed, he nodded for her to continue. "Load your gun again."

She tried to pull the cartridge open but it wouldn't budge. "It's not opening," she said.

Max took her finger and pressed it against the trigger for the cartridge. "This is it," he said softly.

He paused, keeping his finger pressed firmly against hers. She glanced up at him. Was he flirting with her? Or just teasing her?

The cartridge popped open and Max stepped back, letting Jan load the gun by herself.

She aimed the gun once again and pulled the trigger. "Hold on a minute," he said, "I see what you're doing. You're aiming too high. The bullets are going into the ceiling."

He put his arms around her and lowered her hands. Okay, Jan thought. Maybe this was a date. She felt like she did when she was thirteen and the handsome golf instructor put his arms around her to show her how to hit the ball.

"Now try," he said, removing his hands. Jan shot the gun, quickly firing off the rest of the ammunition. When she was finished, Max reeled in her target for a better look. She had pierced the paper, although she hadn't really come close to the target.

"You do it," she said, holding the gun out to Max.

"I know how. We're here for you."

"I want to see you do it," she repeated stubbornly, handing Max the gun. Before he could protest, she stepped in front of him and reeled the target as far back into the range as it would go. She took a step backward and nodded. "Any time you're ready."

"What is this?" he asked. "A test?"

"I just want to see how you're supposed to do it."

He gave her a smile that said he didn't believe her

and loaded the gun. He took a minute to aim and then fired all the ammunition without hesitation. When he was finished, bullets outlined the man's belly.

"I bet you spent a lot of time practicing that," Jan said.

He nodded. "Girls love it. Sometimes I outline the heart."

She raised her eyebrows, flashing him a sly smile.

"Okay, smart ass," he said, handing her the gun. "Back to you."

Max's skill made her feel competitive. She didn't like being bad at something, especially something that looked so easy. This target was not moving, after all. It was just hanging there. A sitting duck.

Max reeled the target back toward them and Jan took aim. Focus, she told herself. Point the gun and focus as if your life depended on it.

Suddenly, the target was no longer a faceless diagram, it was the man who had raped her sister. The man who had brutally killed two innocent women. Jan pulled the trigger, not stopping until the last shell came tumbling down.

Max stepped up beside her and reeled the diagram back in.

All five of her bullets had pierced his body below the waist.

"Congratulations," Max said dryly. "He's dead. And if he's not, he sure as hell wishes he was."

* * *

"So," Max said, as he pulled back into Jan's driveway. "Are you working tonight?"

Jan shook her head.

"Well, I was thinking," he said, haltingly. "Maybe we could go out and grab a bite after I get off work."

Jan stiffened. Was he asking her out on a date? Maybe he was. After all, despite her protests he had paid for the entire excursion this morning. Bullets and all. "I can't," she said quickly.

"Yeah, of course," he said waving his hand as though he was brushing away his question. "No problem."

A heavy silence suddenly permeated the car as Max pulled up in front of her house.

"Thank you," Jan said, opening her door. "Thanks for taking the time to . . ."

"Sure," he said. "Anytime."

Jan nodded, cursing herself for feeling so awkward. But how else could she feel? Why did he have to go and ask her out, anyway? And why had she been so quick to say no? "Don't forget," Max said, popping open his glove box. "Your bullets." He gave the box a shake.

"Thanks," she said, and put it in her pocket.

"You know where to find me," he said. His message was clear. He had made an overture. Now if she wanted to see him again, she'd have to contact him.

"About tonight—" Jan said, before he could pull away. "I, well, what did you have in mind?"

"Forget it," he said again. "It's no big deal."

"I mean—is it a date? 'Cause if it's a date, then I'll go, but if it's just well, you know—" She stopped and shrugged.

"No," he said, shaking his head as if bewildered. "I have no idea what you're talking about."

Neither did she. What was she mumbling about? Either she wanted to go or she didn't. She said, "Why don't we meet at the Rusty Skipper?"

He grinned as he glanced away. The Rusty Skipper was a small, low-key bar on the water—a place where Jan's serial murderer would be comfortable. Jan had been meaning to check it out but she hadn't found the time. Max said, "Killing two birds with one stone?"

"What?" she asked innocently.

"I'll see you there at eight."

Max pulled away and Jan stepped back in the house, armed to the teeth.

31

"WHAT IS GOING ON?" SHEILA ASKED, LOOKING UP AT THE TWO men walking around on Jan's roof. Sheila had stopped by unexpectedly on her way home from work.

"They're installing floodlights."

"I didn't realize it was such a big production."

"These have a remote. I can turn them on when I get home."

Sheila counted the two already installed and asked, "How many are you getting?"

"Five. Two in the front, one on each side and one in the back."

"Wow. You don't fool around."

Jan smiled. "Come on in. It's too hot out here." As usual, the heat hadn't fazed Sheila. She looked as if she had just stepped out of a magazine. Despite the fact that she had already spent a full day at work, her make-up was perfectly applied and her long brown hair was pulled back in a sleek ponytail. She stepped around the dust, careful not to mess her Charles David sling-back pumps.

Sheila hesitated at Jan's front door. The doorknob and lock were missing.

"This is handy," she said, "in case you forget your key."

"The locksmith is installing a new lock. He had to run out to get one that fits."

"You don't waste any time, do you? I mean, you left your job two days ago. You're supposed to be lolling about the house watching Oprah."

Jan had met Sheila the previous day for lunch, and she had told her almost precisely the same thing. Jan had been tempted to share her plans with her friend, but Sheila had been distracted and upset about her husband, and Jan hadn't felt like it was a good time to bring it up.

"So," Jan said. "What did you get from Mark today?" Ever since Sheila had stayed out all night, Mark had become a different person, arriving home in time for dinner, calling her at work, sending her gifts.

Sheila stepped on a floor board that Jan had purposely loosened. Jan had actually loosened several floorboards the previous morning, hoping that if an intruder were to break in, she would hear him before he had a chance to surprise her. Sheila said, "You should get that fixed while all these workmen are here."

"Yeah," Jan said nonchalantly. "I'll mention it."

"So what did I get? A dozen peach roses, just like the ones that were in my bouquet when we married." Sheila shook her head.

"Wow. That's thoughtful."

Sheila simply shrugged. "So, what are you wearing tonight?"

Jan grinned at her friend, suddenly understanding why Sheila had stopped by. Jan had told her about her plans with Max and Sheila didn't trust her enough to look presentable.

"I have no idea. It doesn't matter. We're going to the Rusty Skipper. I could wear a tube top and cut offs and no one would care."

"I would care. Tube tops have been out for ten years. Anyway, the Rusty Skipper is disgusting. Why is he taking you there?"

"I picked it."

"Why? You should have let him take you someplace nice."

"I didn't want to go anyplace nice. Besides, this is just a casual thing."

"A casual fling?" Sheila said, marching into Jan's bedroom and opening up the closet.

Jan rolled her eyes and followed. "So, this is good news about Mark, right? He really seems to want to work things out."

"Yeah, I guess," Sheila said, thumbing through Jan's clothes. "Now I can divorce him."

"What?!"

Sheila shrugged. "I have the upper hand—but I know this change is temporary. There's no way he can keep this up. And I don't really care. I've had it. I gave my lawyer the green light today."

"Wow," Jan said, standing still as she shook her head in admiration.

Sheila nodded. "Yep, it's for real. It's going to hit him like a bolt from the blue." She pulled out a short black sundress and looked it over. "I've wasted three years on him. At least I've learned something."

Sheila stuck the dress back in the closet and said, "If you don't get along before you get married, the gold band is only going to make things worse."

"Good advice," Jan replied, sitting on the bed.

"Common sense," Sheila said, holding up a pink halter dress.

"I don't think that dress fits anymore," Jan said, shaking her head.

"Why not?"

"Too snug."

"Try it on," Sheila commanded.

Despite the heat, Jan was wearing jeans—and she was wearing jeans for a reason. She realized that if the murderer did somehow sneak past her flood lights, brand new lock and creaky floorboards, she would have to have an escape route, which meant she needed to learn her way around the woods. After Max dropped her off this morning, she spent hours just walking through the brush, trying to figure out the best way to escape from a mad killer.

Jan quickly pulled off her shirt and dropped her jeans. She had the dress over her head when Sheila exclaimed, "Oh my God! What did you do to your legs?"

"Oh," Jan said, pulling the dress down around her hips. "I went for a little nature walk."

"What did you do, crawl through the woods?"

Jan gave a little laugh. "See what I mean," she said turning around to show Sheila. "My butt's too big for this."

"That's the way it's supposed to look."

"Don't you think it's too fancy?"

"Absolutely not."

"But what about my legs?" she said, nodding toward a particularly ugly scratch.

"You should've thought of that before. Now you'll just have to wear hose."

Jan just laughed. "Forget it."

"You're lucky you cut your hair. It really looks cute. You don't even have to do anything to it, do you?"

"Just fluff and go."

Sheila laughed. "You cut all your hair off and dye it dark brown and finally snag your man. I thought blondes were supposed to have more fun."

"If this is any indication I'd say blond hair is over-rated."

"I could've told you that," Sheila said with a mischievous smile as she fingered her brown locks. "By the way, I saw Nick today."

"And?"

"And he seemed to be a little subdued."

"It's probably allergies."

"I think he's brokenhearted because you left."

Jan glanced at her suspiciously. Out of respect for Nick, she had not mentioned his declaration of love for her. She wondered if he had mentioned it to anyone himself.

"Have you talked to him since you left?"

"Huh?" Jan said, as though distracted.

"Nick. Have you spoken with him?"

"Briefly. Why?"

"I heard he dumped Rachel," Sheila continued.

"Oh yeah?" Jan said nonchalantly. "Is she still working on the Neff case?"

Sheila nodded.

"I still think it's strange that Nick would give a big case like that to someone with no experience," Jan said.

"Maybe he'll change his mind . . ."

"I doubt it."

"If you come back."

Jan shook her head. "Sheila, I have something to tell you." With that, Jan explained her plan to catch Frannie's killer. It wasn't necessary to get into her suspicions about Frannie's death, Custin's payoff, the MO of the killer or all the similarities between the three murders because Sheila had already heard Jan rattle on about that. But she hadn't heard about Jan's new job at McRyan's. By the expression on Sheila's face, Jan wondered if she had erred in sharing this new information with her friend. Sheila had enough on her plate right now without worrying about Jan to boot.

When she was finished, Sheila stared at her, dumbfounded.

Sheila said, "This isn't funny."

Jan's initial instinct was correct—she shouldn't have told Sheila. Why did she? Maybe she wanted to be talked out of it, or maybe she just wanted her friend's support. Jan said, "I wasn't telling a joke."

"I knew it," she said. "I knew it when I saw you packing your boxes. I told you not to try to become Nancy Drew—"

"So I cut my hair and became a Hardy boy."

Sheila sat still for a couple more seconds and then said very carefully, "I think you need to get some help. Some professional help. I know a very good therapist—"

"You don't think it's the same guy?"

"I don't know, I just don't think this is the right way to catch him. You could get killed. You think Frannie would want that?"

"Of course not. But I know this guy's the one. And the way they're treating the investigation, I don't think they'll catch him. In the process they're going to end up ruining the lives of innocent people."

"Are you trying to commit suicide?"

"No!"

"You feel guilty for being the last Garret left. You feel bad that it was Frannie instead of you." She shook her head and glanced away, but she kept talking. "You've got a nice guy showing you some attention, and you can't stand to be happy when the people you love are dead."

There was a long pause. Jan wiped away a tear. Finally she said, "Lots of that is true, but that's not why I'm doing this."

Sheila began to reply, but stopped. There was nothing left to say.

32

He stood in the woods watching as Sheila stepped into her black Mitsubishi and drove away.

He scanned the roof where two men were working. He had left the office early today specifically with the hope of finding his prey alone in her nest, but obviously it was not to be. Not that he minded the extra commotion. He didn't. It made him even more sure of his expertise. He had been spying on the house for an hour and despite the men, he had remained undetected.

He trained his binoculars on her bedroom window, catching a glimpse of her as she walked past. He wanted to go up close, to peer inside, but he knew he couldn't. He held his breath as he caught sight of her once more. She was standing in the window, staring into the woods as if she knew he was there. She turned the blinds, and in a second she had disappeared.

She hadn't seen him.

He enjoyed this time almost more than the eventual capture. He was hunting, and every muscle in his body was taut with expectation.

She was unusual prey for him. Normally he was not attracted to high-powered, egocentric, career women— too mannish and tough. He preferred fragile and delicate things. He also liked them young and innocent, which this one definitely was not.

But he had not picked her because of any tremendous attraction. He had picked her because when he had seen her working the bar the other night, seen what she had done and the risks she had taken to attract him, he realized it was all part of the master plan, the game.

But he wouldn't have taken the bait if she hadn't lived near the water. He needed the water.

Still, it was a challenge. The part of the creek below her ravine was too shallow for his boat so he was forced to anchor in a neighboring river and take his dinghy into the creek, not an ideal situation at all. He needed practice. This time, he wasn't going to screw up.

He smiled as he glanced toward the closed window. He wondered what she was doing in there with the blinds drawn. Was she thinking of him? Was she slowly undressing? Or was she in the shower, naked from head to toe? And why had she looked out the window? Had she felt him there? Did she know she was being watched?

Oh, Jan, he thought, taking a deep breath. *I'm almost ready.*

33

JAN SAT AT THE BAR ALTERNATING BETWEEN SIPPING HER WINE spritzer, checking her watch and glancing around for Max. He wasn't really late—at least not yet. It was a little past eight, but she had been there since seven forty-five, and the fifteen minutes she had been waiting seemed more like an hour.

The heat wasn't helping. The bar had a window air-conditioning unit working overtime, but Jan was still warm. She had not taken Sheila's advice on the little sundress and instead was wearing a small white T-shirt and jeans, to cover the scratches on her legs. The only real nod to fashion was her silver dangle earrings and strappy shoes.

"Been waiting long?"

Jan twisted around. Max was behind her, dressed almost identically. "I like your outfit," she said.

"Too bad I couldn't find my earrings," he replied, sliding in next to her.

He ordered a beer and glanced around. "Interesting choice," he said. "It's got kind of a Jay's Beer Garden-Lucky's-McRyan's feel to it."

"You've been here before?" she asked innocently.

He gave her a sly smile. "I'm really not a bad detective."

"I'll take that as a yes."

"Let me ask you something. Is everything you do work-related?"

"Meaning?"

"You know what I mean."

"I don't like to waste time." She winced as the words came out of her mouth. "I didn't mean—"

"I get the picture. You're not sure you want to go out with me, so why not do a little research while you're at it. That way, if the evening's a bust, it won't be a complete waste."

"No—" she protested weakly.

He turned his bar stool around so that he was facing her. "I don't like playing games, Jan, nor do *I* like to waste time. If you don't want to be with me tonight, then I can leave."

Reduced to feeling like an awkward schoolgirl, Jan shook her head, grinning uncomfortably. "What?" she asked, as though that was the most ridiculous thing she ever heard.

"I feel something with you. Last night—at your house . . . I know you felt it too."

"Here's two words I think you should add to your dating vocabulary repertoire: small talk. You know, like ice breaker stuff—'how about this heat wave' . . ."

"Coming from the woman who doesn't like to waste time."

She paused and said, "I'm sorry. I'm just, I'm really no good at this."

"At what?"

"This. You know, dating."

He nodded, looking at her as though deciding what to do with her. After a minute he said, "I have an idea." He smiled reassuringly and gave a nod toward the door. "Let's get out of here."

"And go where?"

He leaned forward and whispered, "Ever eaten here?"

She shook her head.

"Well, I have. Take my word for it, it's an experience you want to miss," he said, throwing a ten on the bar to cover their tab.

Jan followed him out of the bar and down to the edge of the public dock in front of the bar. He jumped aboard a small sailboat and held out his hand. "Your boat?" she asked.

He nodded.

"I don't really know how to sail."

"That's okay," he said.

She accepted his hand and climbed aboard. He held on to her hand for a moment, his attention focused on the long, ugly scratch running across her arm. "How did you get that?" he asked.

She pulled her arm away. "Gardening."

"Looks like it hurt," he said, turning on the motor. He unhooked the mooring and gave the boat a shove away from the dock. "I know this great dinner place."

"Oh?" she said weakly, watching the shoreline and her car creep away. She checked her watch.

"Do you need to be somewhere?"

"What?" she asked, embarrassed. He nodded toward her watch. "Oh. OH. No, no, not at all."

He smiled, his eye on the horizon as he lifted the sail. "Watch your head," he said as the boom swung around.

It was a perfect night. A nice warm breeze sailed the boat into the bay as the water lapped gently at the sides. Jan could feel the tension slipping away as she settled back into the side bench.

After awhile Max sat down next to her and smiled. "It's easy to forget what it's all about, isn't it?"

"What do you mean?"

"I mean, sometimes after a really rough day, I just jump on my boat and head out here, and it's as if I'm transported into another world. No murders, no crime. Just quiet."

"Where did you learn to sail?"

"Summer camp when I was a kid. I've been hooked ever since. What about you? Do you like to sail?"

"Well," she said with a shrug, "sometimes."

"Sometimes?"

"Well, no," she admitted. "I guess I'm not a big fan of sailing. I don't mind times like this when the boat is cruising along, but usually it just frustrates me."

"Why?"

She could see he was disappointed. Obviously he thought an evening sail would sweep her off her feet. She appreciated the effort, but he might as well learn now it wasn't her cup of tea. "It's too slow for me. I guess I just have too much energy. And I hate that rocking when the motor's off and you're waiting for wind. Makes me feel seasick—and trapped."

He thought for a moment as he steered the boat and then glanced at her. "What do you do to relax?"

"I, ah, well, I read."

"What kind of books?"

"Biographies."

"Read anything good lately?"

"Not really," she admitted. "I haven't had time."

He just looked at her.

"I'm pretty boring. Usually I just work till I drop."

"That's too bad."

"Enough about me," Jan said, trying to change the subject. "It's my turn to ask you questions."

"What?"

"Ever been married?"

"No."

"Come close?"

She could see a flicker in his eyes as his features hardened ever so slightly. He said, "What happened to that small talk you keep mentioning?"

Aware that she had hit a sensitive subject, she turned the focus back toward herself. "I've never been married. Never come close."

"Too busy? Or is it because you don't like the idea of being trapped?"

She thought she detected a note of sarcasm in his voice. "Among other things," she said honestly.

He just smiled as he steered the boat into a small creek. "I thought we'd drop anchor over here. It's nice and quiet," he said. He stood up and reached down into the hull, pulling out a large grocery bag and setting it down beside Jan.

"What's this?" she asked.

"Dinner," he said, getting ready to drop the sail and lower the anchor. "I thought it would be nice for us to eat out here, away from all distractions. Is that all right with you? I promise if the boat starts rocking, or you start to feel trapped—we're off."

"Sure," she said nonchalantly, hiding her anxiety by peeking inside the bag. She didn't like the idea of a romantic tête-à-tête with someone she hardly knew. She would've preferred a place with a few more distractions.

"Can you give me a hand with this?" he asked, handing her the rope to the sail. She grabbed the rope and stood up. As he let down the sail, the wind caught it, causing the boom to swing around. Jan ducked in the nick of time.

"Jan!" Max called out, alarmed. "Are you all right?"

"Yes," she said, picking herself up. Max jumped over and checked her forehead. "It didn't hit you?"

"No."

He stopped, still standing in front of her as his worried eyes scanned her face.

Jan felt the same surge of electricity she had felt the night before. Only this time she was on his turf.

"Jan," he said quietly, obviously feeling the same connection between them. He took his finger and lifted her chin, forcing her to look at him. "What are you so afraid of?" He leaned forward, kissing her softly on the lips.

Jan broke away.

Realizing he had gone too far, he said, "Look, Jan. I'm sorry, I just—"

"Don't be ridiculous," she said quickly, pulling a sandwich out of the bag and handing it to him. "This was very thoughtful—thinking of dinner."

All through the meal Jan was uncomfortable, anxiously glancing back toward shore. *What was she so afraid of?* His question rang in her mind. Was she afraid? Maybe so. After all, she had pulled away from him even though she had enjoyed his kiss.

After a couple of attempts at awkward conversation, Max lifted the sail and they set back toward shore.

He pulled up to the dock in front of the Rusty Skipper and began to tie the boat down. "Hold on a minute," he said. "I'll see you to your car."

"No," she replied quickly. "Really, it's all right. Thank you for tonight. I had a wonderful time," she said, jumping back on the dock.

He nodded sadly as he said, "Take care of yourself, okay?"

What was her problem? Jan admonished herself as she zoomed her Cabriolet along Route 2.

Here was this sexy, good-looking guy who seemed to be very interested in her, so what did she do? She panicked and ran away. Tough, invincible Jan. A total coward.

Geez, with her way with men, it was a shocker she wasn't asked out more often.

A large raindrop splashed on her nose. Oh great, and now for the perfect capper to a perfect day, it was raining and she had the top down. As she swiped the water off her nose she realized it wasn't a rain drop—it was sweat.

How attractive. Sweat was rolling off her face.

Jan glanced in her rearview mirror, distracted by the glaring headlights of a car that was practically touching her bumper. She adjusted her mirror as she pulled into the neighboring lane. A date like she had just experienced called for drastic measures. Only one thing would do: a pint of Ben and Jerry's Chubby Hubby. She put on her turn signal and made a left-hand turn, cutting across traffic and pulling into a 7-Eleven. Out of the corner of her eye, she noticed that the car which had been behind her had followed her across lanes and had turned in to the street beside the convenience store. For a split second she wondered if she knew the driver, if perhaps he was actually following her, trying to get her attention.

When Jan stepped out of the convenience store carrying her ice cream, the car was nowhere to be seen. Chuckling at the state of her nerves, she put the ice cream on the passenger seat and started her car. She was back on Route 2 when she noticed it again. The same car. Behind her.

But was it the same car? It looked like it. A silver Nissan. The driver was shaded, but by his husky form she could tell that it was a man.

She focused on the road, shifting lanes in order to let the car pass. It didn't pass. Instead, it followed her into the other lane.

Now Jan was frightened. What should she do? Head to the police station?

Her road was approaching. If this car was following her once she got on the curvy, narrow dirt road, her options would be limited.

Suddenly, Jan swerved her car, doing a U-turn across the double highway. The car that had been following her continued on the road, seemingly oblivious to her move.

Jan laughed. How silly. Obviously he had not been following her. Just a weird coincidence.

Nevertheless, when she arrived home she grabbed not only her ice cream, but her gun out of the glove compartment. Not that she was nervous. No. She was just being cautious. So cautious that she practically ran to her door, unlocking it and slamming it behind her.

The phone was ringing as she made it into her house. She ran over and answered it, hoping to pick it up before her machine.

There was a brief silence, then, "It's Max."

"Max," she said, closing her eyes with relief. He was calling to give her another chance. "Max, I—" she stopped, glancing around her house suspiciously as if an intruder might just be lurking in the darkness.

"Hello?" he said, alarmed by her silence.

She caught an ominous shadow out of the corner of her eye, peeking out from behind the bathroom door. She held her breath as she forced herself to walk over and flick on the bathroom light. Nothing. Just her robe.

"Jan! What's going on?"

"I just, well, I was on my way home when I noticed this car following me. At least, I thought it was following me. And you know those crazy things that go through your head. I thought maybe Custin was after me or something."

"If someone was following you, it wasn't Custin."

"I know, I know," Jan said. "Custin has nothing to do with this."

"Well," Max said after a brief pause. "I thought you should know . . . they just pulled Custin's body out of Lake Okeechobee."

34

"MURDERED?" SHE ASKED QUIETLY, AS IF SHE ALREADY KNEW.

"His boat was found floating loose near the body. It looks like Custin had been drinking, fell off his boat and was too drunk to get back in."

Jan dropped on the couch, weighted down by a sense of guilt that she had somehow set the machinery in motion which led to Custin's death.

"Jan?"

"That's . . . that's how Frannie died."

Max was silent for a minute. "I know," he said. "Look, we still don't have all the details. It might have just been a freak accident."

"What did his girlfriend say?"

"What do you mean?"

"Don't do this to me, Max. She said that she had no idea why he was out on his boat in the first place, didn't she?"

"She said he had a meeting yesterday morning. He told her he wouldn't be long. She went to work. When she came back, he still hadn't returned."

"Did he say who he was supposed to meet?"

"No."

She hesitated a minute and then said, "You think he was murdered too, don't you? That's why you called me."

"I do think it's strange," his voice trailed off. "I'm coming over," he said resolutely.

Jan just nodded as she put the receiver back down. She was still sitting there when Max arrived.

She stood up and opened the door. He said, "I like the lights. Smart move. And I see you got a decent lock," he said, nodding toward her door.

She glanced away, sure that Max would recognize the fear in her eyes.

Max began to walk toward her. He stepped on a squeaky floor board and stopped. He bent down and ran his fingers over the splintered edges. He looked up and smiled. "Why not just throw a bunch of tacks down. Or marbles?"

"I prefer banana peels," she said weakly.

"Come on," he said, nodding toward her bedroom. "I want you to start packing. I'm taking you to the airport."

"Why?"

"You should leave town for a while."

"You think I'm in danger," she said quietly. "You think I'm right about this guy."

"I'm beginning to think so, yeah."

"Good," she said resolutely. "I'm not going anywhere."

He shook his head. He crossed his arms in front of
him and said, "Then I don't have any choice. Got an
extra pillow?"

"What?"

"I'm staying here tonight. I'll sleep on the couch," he
volunteered, fluffing the pillows before settling in. He
lay down, crossed his arms in front of him and looked at
her.

She hesitated.

"Look," he said, raising his hands in the air. "Let's
just forget tonight ever happened, okay? Nothing
gained, nothing lost, or however that goes."

Jan glanced down at the floor. Part of her was
relieved that she could just forget about their kiss—but
part of her didn't want to forget.

"Hey," he said. "I promise. No more dates. We're just
friends."

She nodded, trying to hide her dismay. She walked
into her room and pulled a light cotton blanket off her
bed. When she came back into the living room, Max
was holding the container of ice cream in his hands.
"Looks like I forgot to offer you dessert."

She smiled, handing him the blanket in return for
the ice cream. "You want some?"

"No thanks. I like my ice cream frozen. I'm funny
that way."

She grabbed a spoon and said, "Fortunately, I'm not that particular." Armed with the spoon and ice cream, she walked back past Max and paused at the door to her bedroom. "Thanks, Max," she said sincerely.

He kept his eyes on her door long after it was shut.

Saturday, August 15

Max was gone when Jan woke up. She was filled with a sense of loneliness mingled with panic—as though she had just screwed up. But she didn't have time to dwell on her mistakes. She had a karate lesson at ten.

Halfway into the class, it became obvious that Jan was still unhinged from her experience with Max. She was performing poorly, having trouble with even the most basic of moves. In frustration, she stuck her leg out, purposely trying to trip her partner, the man assigned to work out with her. It worked. He went sprawling across the floor.

"Hold it!" The martial arts instructor looked at Jan and shook his head, disapproving. "Not cool, Jan."

Jan caught her breath. She was breathing heavily— an hour of wrestling with some big burly guy would do that to a girl. Since law school she had taken karate lessons periodically as a way to stay in shape and keep her self defense skills sharp. But over the past few years she had practiced less and less and it showed. She was lousy.

She nodded toward the man she had tripped. She could tell he was angry with her and she didn't blame him. He had been using kid gloves with her, purposely being gentle and she had gone and tripped him like an immature kid. "Sorry," she said.

She turned back toward the instructor. "Look," she said. "I should've been a little more clear when I came in here. I'm not really interested in the feints or moves or katas. I just need to know some good defense techniques. Some real killers."

"Real killers, huh?" He smiled. "Why didn't you say so?"

35

JAN THREW A GARDEN TROWEL INTO HER BACKPACK AND stepped out of the house heading for the woods. This time she was smart—her fair skin was protected by a long-sleeve blouse, jeans, and garden gloves. She walked to the edge of her driveway and stopped.

The path cut a rough, overgrown, serpentine trail from her house down the hill to the water. Yesterday Jan had marched up and down imagining herself followed by a dangerous perp, marking special spots where she might loosen his grip for a moment, or reach out to regain her balance as he dragged her along the dirt. She knew where to hide and how to make a complete circle through the woods so she would end up back at the house. And she found, despite the fallen branches and the vines that grew thick through the trees, she could make her way around the woods in less than twenty minutes, covering an area approximately three quarters of a mile.

As the backpack clanged against her side, she jogged toward the first curve in the trail. Jan had decided to hide some weapons along the path for back up. She would leave nothing to chance. She would not turn up dead in an accidental drowning accident or be found floating at the end of a dock. She would survive their encounter, she would triumph!

With that thought, she tripped over a branch and went sprawling into the brush. A cricket beside her seemed to remark on her failure. In a split second Jan had lost her momentary feeling of confidence. Instead she was left with an ache in her knee and the painful memory of a client she once had, Karen Lokowsky.

Karen was twenty years old when she was raped by a masked stranger in her own house. The case was unsolved, the rapist uncaught. Karen bought a gun and went to target practice religiously. One year later, almost to the exact hour, Karen woke up to hear a familiar voice say: "Did you miss me?" Her rapist had returned. She had a loaded gun underneath her pillow, but she couldn't use it. Despite all her training she had frozen with fear.

Jan pushed the memory from her mind as she picked herself up. She would not allow herself to end up like Karen. For the next week, she would try to do most of her sleeping during the day, her work and her training at night.

She kicked the branch that had tripped her out of the

way and continued walking. At the first curve she stopped and pulled a sharp kitchen knife out of her backpack. She glanced around for an appropriate spot, a place where it would be hidden yet still easy to retrieve. She settled on a green, leafy bush and stuck the knife into its base.

She kept moving along the path, stopping at the second curve. Here she hid the extra remote for the flood lights, hoping that being bathed in bright lights would be enough to frighten the murderer. Just in case that failed, she hid another butcher knife behind a tree around the third curve. She then walked slowly to the fourth and final curve. This would be her final chance, her last ditch effort to save her life.

She set down her backpack and gingerly pulled out the gun she had purchased that morning. It was a .32 Smith and Wesson, a duplicate of the gun she already owned. She popped open the cartridge as Max had shown her and loaded the bullets.

She glanced around her one more time, making sure she was alone. Satisfied, she was bending down to hide the gun under a bush when it suddenly went off.

Cursing, she dropped it as she jumped back. There was another explosion and she realized that it wasn't her gun at all, someone else was shooting behind her. She was crawling on all fours into the brush when she heard a familiar crotchety voice say, "Goddamn you little rodent. I'll get you yet!"

"Mrs. Fletcher!" she screamed. "Stop!"

The old woman came into view, dressed in a light cotton house coat with a large terry visor wrapped around her forehead and new, big, purple sunglasses embossed with a small rhinestone heart in the corner. A large, heavy looking rifle was swung over her shoulder. "Jan?" she called out calmly. "Oh, there you are," she said, spotting Jan sprawled on the ground. She gave Jan a wave and continued strolling down the path as if nothing out of the ordinary had occurred. "Out enjoying the day? You weren't swimming were you? The jellies are here."

"What are you doing?" Jan asked, still catching her breath as she stared at Mrs. Fletcher's big ugly gun.

"What?" Mrs. Fletcher asked, as though she didn't understand the question. "Oh, you mean the rifle. Goddamn squirrels have been eating all my birdseed. I've got a beautiful family of grosbeaks to feed and the damn furry monsters are eating all their food."

"So you're trying to shoot them?"

"Trying's right. Can't seem to get the little bastards. I'm out of practice. I'll get them though, mark my words."

Jan shook her head as she pushed herself up and brushed the dirt off her knees.

"What are you doing here?" Mrs. Fletcher asked.

"I'm, uh, exercising," Jan said.

"You've cleared up this path a little, I see."

"A little," Jan said.

"I wondered what you've been doing around here. I

see you coming up and down from the creek a lot these days."

"It's my work-out."

"Good for you," Mrs. Fletcher said approving. "I noticed you've been doing some work on your house as well."

"I just had some lights installed."

"Well, that's a start." Mrs. Fletcher smiled at her. "How about a nice cool glass of lemonade. I have the good kind. From Paul Newman. I'll buy anything that has his picture on it."

"I'd love some lemonade," Jan said, grinning. The whole scene was so ridiculous she was tempted to laugh. She didn't know which was nuttier, her out there planting weapons in the woods or Mrs. Fletcher ambushing squirrels. Jan was about to follow Mrs. Fletcher when she saw the bag with her gun sitting out in the open where she had dropped it. "I'll meet you up there," she said. "I just have to do a few more push-ups."

"Push-ups?" Mrs. Fletcher repeated curiously. "Right here?"

"There's a slight lean in the path which makes them a little more difficult—ergonomically that is," Jan spit out.

"I'll have to give it a try," Mrs. Fletcher said as she began making her way back up the hill.

Jan grabbed the bag and hurried off the path, hiding the bag under a tree and using rocks to cover it and protect it from the elements. As she turned briefly back toward the water, she saw something which made her pause. A large white boat was parked at the mouth of the creek. It looked just like Nick's boat. But it couldn't be Nick's boat, she reminded herself. Nick was at work.

The thought of Nick playing hooky made her smile as she zipped up her backpack and ran back up the hill, catching up with Mrs. Fletcher at the top.

36

DID YOU MISS ME?

Jan lay on her bed, staring up through the darkness at the ceiling fan whirring above.

For months during the trial she had lived Karen Lokowsky's nightmare. She had woken up screaming, dreaming that she was hearing those words again herself.

Jan remembered when she had first met Karen. It was after the initial rape, and the police were still searching for her masked intruder. Karen had chosen to stay in her house alone, knowing that the man who raped her was still out there somewhere. At the time Jan had thought she was crazy for taking that risk but she respected her, respected the courage Karen had shown in putting her life back together. She was determined that fear would not control her life.

Even after Karen was raped the second time, she had

displayed an inordinate amount of strength and resolve. Karen Lokowsky was no shrinking violet, yet at the moment when action had counted, she had been paralyzed with fear. What made Jan think she was any stronger?

Jan jumped out of bed and began pacing the floor. She snapped the picture of her sister off the mantle and held it to her breast. Could she do this? She might not have a choice anymore. That could well have been him in the car last night. He could already be stalking her.

Was she ready for him?

She put the picture back on the mantle and pulled the gun out from under her pillow. She aimed it at an imaginary foe. Disgusted, she dropped it to her side.

It was a quarter past eleven and she wasn't even remotely tired despite the fact that she had tended bar on top of an already busy day. She didn't plan on sleeping much at night anyway, but she couldn't just wait for him like a prisoner in her own house. She had to conquer her fear.

If he *was* coming after her, she doubted he would arrive by car. He would travel by boat, just like he had for her sister.

She swung open her closet and pulled out a pair of shorts. She was headed for the water.

Jan focused on the ground as she picked up speed, running through the woods. *He's chasing you*, she told herself. *Run.*

This was all part of her training, part of her plan.

Each extra day was a blessing, another opportunity to hone her skills for his arrival.

She raised her gun as she raced across the hard-packed dirt, skipping over branches like a commando in training. She stopped running and paused to catch her breath. She pulled out her flashlight and glanced at her watch. It was almost twelve-thirty. She had been running around for the past forty-five minutes.

A twig snapped behind her and Jan dropped the flashlight as she whipped around, her fingers tightly clenched around the trigger of the gun.

Silence.

She picked up the flashlight and pointed it toward the thick covering of vines and brush.

Nothing.

She stood still for a moment, listening again. The only sound was the crickets humming and an occasional mosquito flying by her ear.

She turned off her flashlight and tucked it back into her shorts. She took a step and stopped at the sound of leaves crunching. The smile faded from her face. She was familiar with the usual sounds of the woods, and this was not one of them.

She heard it again. Distinctly. It sounded liked a shuffle, like someone was out there in the darkness.

She cocked her gun and turned slowly. She moved with cat-like quiet, so as not to advertise her position. *You can fire,* she told herself. When he appears, just shoot.

She heard another branch break, this time in front of her. Whatever it was, animal or man, it was moving. Suddenly she came up with a new plan: run.

Max stepped out of the car and glanced toward Jan's house. The house was dark with the exception of the bedroom light, which burned brightly. Good, he thought. She made it home safely. He could just drive away now but he figured since he was there, he might as well knock on her door and make sure she was all right.

"Jan," he called out from his car so that his sudden arrival wouldn't frighten her.

When she didn't answer, he stepped out of his car, lightly shut the door and walked toward her house. As he took on the second porch step, he tripped on a carefully placed row of marbles and fell ass over tea kettle, landing flat on his back on the driveway. It hurt, but he couldn't help but laugh. She really was too much.

He glanced up, expecting to see her standing over him with a baseball bat in her hands. Just then he heard the unmistakable sound of a gun going off.

37

MAX GRABBED HIS GUN AND BEGAN RUNNING TOWARD THE woods. He didn't have a flashlight and the moon wasn't quite bright enough for him to make out the path. He began to make his own path, using his weapon to knock back the vines that grew thickly through the dense trees.

He stumbled onto a trail and stopped. He could hear the muffled sound of a woman in pain. "Jan?" he yelled at the top of his lungs.

"Down here," he heard her reply.

He followed the trail down to the water. He found Jan at the water's edge. She was curled in a ball, hugging her knees to her chest.

He knelt beside her and said, "What happened?"

She looked up at him, too upset to speak.

"Jan," he murmured, wrapping his arms around her. "Are you all right?"

She nodded.

"Where did the shot come from?"

She nodded toward the dirt behind him where her gun lay on the ground.

Max picked it up as he asked, "Is there anyone else out here?"

"I think so. I'm not sure. I think he was here. Or maybe it was just an animal, I don't know."

"You didn't see anyone?"

She shook her head.

Max breathed a sigh of relief as he tucked her gun in his jeans, doing the same thing with his. He pulled her up and held her close to him. "Come on," he said, keeping his arm wrapped snugly around her waist. "Let's get you home."

Back at the house Jan sipped water as she told Max what happened.

He sat across from her, listening as she explained her plan, with all the built-in safety precautions. He leaned forward as if he wanted to be close to her, near enough to touch her.

A keen sense of admiration for what she was doing tempted him to smile, but he stopped himself, fearing that she would interpret it as condescending. He nodded toward her scraped knee. "Where do you keep your washcloths?"

"In the hall closet," she said. "But I'm fine."

He ignored her and rummaged through her closet,

coming back with a wet cloth. He kneeled down in front of her and gently pressed it to her wound. "You have to get the dirt out."

"Thank you," she said. What would she do without him? Everyone else seemed to think she was crazy except him.

Jan watched Max tenderly clean her wound. She had never met a man like him. He could be tough and aggressive one minute, sweet and sensitive the next. She thought back to his kiss on the boat, longingly remembering the soft touch of his lips.

She reached out and touched the top of his head, lightly resting her fingers on top of his tousled brown hair. "Max," she said softly. "Why did you come here tonight?"

He pulled the cloth away from her wound and slid up on the couch next to her. "I wanted to make sure you got home all right from work."

"Why?" she asked again, looking at him directly.

"Because," he repeated, inching forward. "I was worried about you."

Jan smiled. "Worried about me? Why? Just because I'm buzzing around the woods in the dark with a loaded gun?"

"I know. It was silly of me to worry."

"You've got to have more faith in me," she said, with a grin. "Didn't you know? The force is with me."

"Oh, yeah," he said, amused. "I think Hank mentioned that."

She gently touched the back of her hand to his cheek.

He sat still. "What are you doing?" he whispered.

She reached out with her other hand and gently cupped his face as she kissed him.

He broke away, removing her hands and holding them. He looked at her for a moment as if trying to read her mind. "I should go," he said, standing.

"You should?"

He noticed the frightened look in her eyes as she glanced back toward the window. He said, "Actually, why don't I stay here again. On the couch."

"You don't have to," she said weakly. "Stay here, I mean."

"Go on," he said. "Take a shower, do whatever. I'll keep an eye on things."

She nodded, embarrassed and confused by Max's rejection. "Thanks," she said, escaping inside her room.

Max shook his head as he dropped down on the couch, running a hand through his hair. It had taken every ounce of willpower to pull away. Had he waited one second longer, he doubted he would have had the strength.

He couldn't remember the last time he had felt this way about a woman. It had been, hell, he realized, years. He hadn't felt this strongly about someone since Kelly.

He had been with several women since then, but the relationships had been primarily about sex. He had never been the type of guy to have one-night stands, but his pain had kept him from anything more than a rough, superficial intimacy. He tried to be honest with these women, tried to make them understand that a relationship with him was destined for failure. Strangely enough, that seemed to make them care more. Eventually though, they would accuse him of being too closed off emotionally and leave, or he would start to care and run away. Lately though, he had become tired of running.

And then he met Jan.

Underneath her tough-talking exterior there was sadness, but also resilience. Instead of withdrawing from the world, she had become a fighter, charging through life. He found himself wanting to wrap his arms around her, to rescue her from battle.

He turned around. Jan was standing in the doorway to her room. Her wet hair was combed back and she was wearing a long terry cloth robe.

He gave her a little smile, embarrassed. "How long have you been standing there?"

"Not long." She took a step toward him. "You look deep in thought."

He shrugged.

"I wanted to talk to you about last night—why I reacted the way I did when you kissed me," she said, and sat down beside him.

"It was just a spontaneous—"

"I liked it," she said. "I just, well, I guess I panicked. I didn't know how to handle it." She leaned forward, brushing her hair away from her eyes. Her robe began to fall open and Max averted his eyes, trying to ignore the glimpse of her full white breasts. "I know what you're thinking. I'm thirty-two years old. A little old to be such a coward."

"I hardly think you're a coward."

"Yes, you do. You even said—"

"I never called you a coward."

"Well I am. Not in my job, but—" she paused, remembering that even Sheila had called her a coward. "All I'm saying is that . . . I'm okay with," she swallowed, "whatever happens—with us."

"Meaning?"

"I'm not expecting to fall in love," she blurted out.

He stood up. "I see."

"You said you didn't like games so I'm just telling you how it is. I don't expect flowers and candy, fireworks and the rest of it. I'm too old to believe in fairy tales."

She walked over to the window and absentmindedly ran her finger against the screen. "I think I usually expect too much out of people and because of it I, well, I can count the number of times I've made love on one hand." She paused and then gave a quiet laugh. "Some women my age can't even count the number of men they've slept with. But me, well . . ." her voice trailed off. "I haven't been with a man in six years."

"Because you were waiting to fall in love. I think that's honorable."

"I think it's an excuse. Just because I'm frightened." She shook her head and said, "I don't even know what I'm trying to say. I keep so much inside of me, so many emotions—" Her voice cracked and she stopped, blinking back tears.

He stood up and walked behind her, standing so close she could feel his breath against her ear. "It's okay," he said.

Her voice was barely a whisper as she turned back toward him. "Yesterday you asked me what I was afraid of. Well, I can answer that now. I'm afraid of you. Of my feelings for you."

He paused for a moment, staring into her brown eyes. For a moment, she thought he might leave.

Instead, he reached out and gently pulled the tie to her robe, causing it to fall open. Still holding her gaze he took a step forward and slid his hands around her bare waist, pulling her in to him.

She closed her eyes as he picked her up and carried her into the bedroom, gently laying her on the bed. He knelt beside her as his fingers glazed over her naked body, gently running over the tips of her nipples on their way down to her toes and back up again. "Just relax," he whispered, lightly massaging her neck.

Her body began to tingle and she could hear herself moan as his tongue began to take the place of his fingers.

He paused just long enough to take off his shirt. "If

you want to stop," he breathed in her ear as he leaned over her, "you just let me know, all right? I don't want you to be uncomfortable. I just want you to feel good."

She reached up and touched his arms, fingering the muscles on his back, on his chest and arms. Still exploring, she touched her lips to his chest, and was pleased to hear him inhale with pleasure.

She reached down toward his pants, touching the hard spot between his legs.

"Not yet," he murmured. "We've only just begun." His tongue slid down to her bare belly, circling her belly button and slowly inching its way toward her most private place.

She gently clutched on to his hair as he skillfully licked and kissed her, bringing her to the point where she thought she would explode and then teasing her by slowly inching his way back up her stomach to her breasts. She fought to maintain control but her body began to move as if independent of her mind, ultimately releasing a flood of pleasure more powerful than she could ever imagine.

When her shuddering stopped, he kissed her gently on her forehead and moved up beside her.

She surprised him by reaching for his belt buckle. "Take them off," she said, rolling on her side and looking him directly in the eye.

He grinned, pleased by her sudden brazenness. He slipped off his pants and she wrapped her legs around him, using her karate experience to flip him onto his back and pin him to the bed.

He slid inside her and watched as she began to move on top of him, doing to him as he had done to her. Finally he wrapped his arms around her and held her to him, causing them both to climax at the same time.

Still staying inside her, he wrapped his arms around her and said, "I thought you were out of practice."

"I thought I was." Jan smiled as she blissfully closed her eyes, entwining her fingers through his. They lay there for a while, neither of them saying a word. Finally Jan said, "It's strange, isn't it? I mean here we are, yet I don't know you very well."

He laughed. "You now know me a lot better than anyone else in this town." He rolled over on his side, facing her. Jan followed suit, leaning forward on one elbow and running her finger along his chest. "That's not what I mean."

"What do you want to know, Counselor?" he asked, playfully tweaking her nose.

She shrugged. "What about your parents? Are they still alive?"

He nodded. "Still alive and full of the devil."

"What do they do?"

"My parents?" he repeated. "My father is a doctor and my mother works as a receptionist in his office."

"Your father is a doctor?"

"Does that surprise you?"

She shook her head no.

He smiled, as though he had caught her in a faux pas. "You're surprised that a doctor's kid would become a cop, aren't you?"

"No," she said, not quite believably. "What made you decide to enter the force?"

"I wasn't planning on it. I went to the University of Michigan. My undergrad degree is in Poly Sci."

"Poly Sci? Were you pre-law?"

He nodded.

"But you came to your senses?"

He shook his head, taking her hand and holding it. "Not exactly. I had a friend who died." His voice trailed off, as though the pain was still fresh. "Her death changed me. And I decided to become a cop." He kissed her hand as he closed his eyes, as if to shut out the memory.

"What happened to her," she asked softly.

"Wrong place, wrong time. Interrupted a robbery at a convenience store. The guy panicked and shot her. She died immediately."

"I'm sorry," she said quietly.

"Not many people know that story."

She leaned forward and kissed him, running her lips along the side of his face.

Her mouth drifted down his body and when he was ready, she led him inside once more.

Afterwards, Max held her in his arms. It was not until he heard the deep relaxed sound of Jan's breath that he allowed himself to go to sleep.

38

MORNING SUN SHONE THROUGH THE CRACKS IN THE BLINDS when Jan opened her eyes. She felt disoriented, weighted down, and hot. She glanced beside her. Max was there, his arm stretched over her chest, his hand resting against her breast. She smiled and turned to face him.

As if sensing her, he opened his eyes and smiled at her. "Good morning," he said hoarsely.

"Good morning," she replied. She paused for a moment. "It's kind of funny opening my eyes and seeing you."

"Yeah. I thought you would feel kind of funny about it," he said rolling on his back.

He stretched his arms up toward the ceiling. Jan admired the sinewy muscles, the vein across his biceps.

He looked lean and powerful. He sat up, scanning the floor for his shirt. "What time is it?" he asked, grabbing his shirt off the ground.

"A little after seven," Jan said.

He shook his head as if trying to shake the sleep out.

"Where are you going?" Jan asked.

"To work," he replied.

"Work? It's Sunday!"

"I've got a pressing case."

"Oh yeah?" she teased.

"Besides, not everyone can retire at thirty-two," he teased.

"Come back to bed. You don't have to be there so early."

"I'm going to go home and change first." He paused. "Unless you don't feel safe . . ."

"And if I don't? What are you going to do? Stay here all day? All night?"

He smiled as he walked over to her side of the bed and sat down on the edge of it. "I can think of worse things," he said.

She grinned and said, "Okay, I'm scared. I guess you'll have to stay."

He leaned forward, fully intending to give her a quick kiss goodbye.

Jan arched her head, meeting his lips. She sighed sensuously as the tip of her tongue touched inside his mouth.

He pulled back slightly as he murmured, "I've never met a woman like you."

"Consider yourself lucky."

He laughed. "You don't have a problem with self-confidence, do you?"

"Not this morning at least. Unless you're about to give me one."

He ran his finger around her lips. He wanted to ask when he could see her again but he didn't. *Keep it simple,* she had said. And he would try. He didn't want to frighten her away.

She smiled as she watched him stand up. She pulled the sheet up to her chest.

"You working tonight?" he asked casually.

She nodded.

"I'll probably see you there."

Jan yanked the sheet off the bed and wrapped it around her before following him out of the room. "I don't think that's a good idea."

"This is business, Jan," he said, defensively. "We've been frequenting all the bars this guy has hit—"

"What if he knows you're a cop?"

"Then chances are he knows you're a prosecutor."

Something caught his eye and he moved toward the window for a better look.

The canvas roof of Jan's car had been slit down the middle. Half of it was hanging loose, blowing in the wind like a torn piece of skin.

Jan turned around, following his gaze.

"Oh my God," she breathed, running toward the door.

Max grabbed her arm and pushed her behind him. Jan stood still as Max pulled his gun out and carefully walked toward the car.

The roof was not torn. Someone had used scissors or a knife to make a nice even gash.

Max took out a tissue and opened the car door, careful not to disturb any fingerprints.

Jan rushed behind him. That's when she saw it.

On the driver's seat in a small plastic bag was a lock of light brown hair.

39

"DON'T TOUCH IT," MAX SAID, HOLDING ON TO HER ARM. HE nodded back toward the house. "Go get dressed. I'm calling the sergeant."

Max was at his car, radioing the station, all the while looking around the ground, searching for footprints—anything the naked eye could see.

Jan ignored Max and just stood there, holding on to the sheet as if paralyzed.

"How the hell did he get here without us hearing him?" Max said, after he got off the radio. "He must've parked his car up on the road and hoofed it."

"He came here by boat," Jan said matter-of-factly.

Max glanced toward the creek. "The water's not deep enough . . ."

"He could've docked it in the mouth of the creek and just walked up through the forest. I thought I heard someone out there last night. I guess I was right."

"Jesus," Max mumbled.

Then she turned to walk back toward her small cottage. She should be happy, she thought to herself. At the very least, vindicated. Her killer had acknowledged that she was right. He was out there, stalking women. More importantly, he wanted to play.

"Max," Hank said quietly.

They were standing outside Jan's cottage, supervising the search for clues. They themselves had been looking until only a few minutes earlier. As Max suspected, they had come up empty. He thought there might be a chance for a footprint by the water, but as of yet they hadn't found anything.

"We've got to get GI out of here," Hank said.

While Max agreed, he took his partner's suggestions as an insult. "I can look after her."

"I know, but why? What's the point?"

"She won't leave. She wants him to come after her. She's tempting him."

"But how does he know that?"

Max looked back toward Jan's damaged car and felt a tremor go through him. She had been alone in the woods with this monster. "Maybe he knows her."

"What?"

"Maybe he knows her. Maybe not well, just well enough to realize she's trying to get him. He wants to let her know he's in control. He'll take her when he's ready."

Hank was silent for a minute before he said, "Is there anything else?"

"She thought she was followed the other night."

"When?"

"Two nights ago. She was at a light when she realized, or so she thought, she was being followed."

"And she called you? Why didn't she go to the station?" he asked suspiciously.

"What is this, Hank? An interrogation?"

Hank paused.

Max sighed, noting the hurt expression on his partner's face.

"I'm trying to figure out what's going on. . . ." Hank said.

"Yeah," Max said, brushing the air with his hand. "I know. Look, I've been trying to dissuade her from this. But since I realized that she wouldn't listen to me, I've been keeping an eye on her."

"Why is that a secret?"

"Nobody said it was."

"He doesn't even tell his own partner." Hank shook his head, making a *tch* sound with his tongue. "What were you doing here this morning?"

"That's what I'd like to know," said the sergeant, appearing behind Max.

Max turned around. "Not that I owe anyone any explanation," he said. "But I came here last night because I've been worried about her. I just wanted to make sure she was all right. She told me she thought she had heard someone in the woods."

"But despite what she *thought* she heard, you didn't see anything unusual?" the sergeant said, his cool brown eyes slowly scanning the house as if looking for clues.

"No." He didn't mention the part about her running through the woods, gun loaded. The image of a deluded former assistant state's attorney running around the woods with a loaded pistol would prove tempting gossip.

"So you stayed with her all night?"

Max hesitated, surprised that the sergeant would ask such a personal question. "I don't think that's anyone's business. . . ."

"I don't give a damn about your social life. I want to know if it's possible she did this herself."

"What?" Max asked, incredulous.

"Look," the sergeant said. "I like Jan, too. We all do. But Nick told me that she's been doing some very strange things lately. . . ."

"You think she ripped the top of her car and planted the hair?" Max asked incredulously.

"Nick thinks she might need some professional help."

"No," Max said adamantly. "No way she slit that roof herself. Not a chance. She didn't leave my sight. There's no way she could've done it."

The sergeant was silent for a moment. "We found a goddamn arsenal hidden in the woods, Max. A gun, knives. . . . Jan told us to leave 'em there. Said they're hers. Any idea why she'd be hiding loaded guns in the woods?"

"You'll have to ask her," Max said.

"I did."

"And?"

"She said to protect herself from this serial killer." Max shrugged.

"If I were you," the sergeant said quietly, "I'd encourage her to get some help. It's always the smart ones that go crazy first."

"Then I guess we're safe, huh?" Hank laughed.

The sergeant's half-lidded eyes said he wasn't feeling humorous.

"She didn't do this, sergeant," Max insisted.

He paused and then said with a sigh, "I hope for her sake you're wrong." With that, the sergeant turned around and headed back up the hill.

40

JAN PEEKED OUT THE WINDOW INTO THE DARKNESS. THE YOUNG, uniformed cop was standing outside her door, his arms crossed over his beefy chest like a bouncer at a night-club. Jan retreated into the dark of the house and crawled into bed. This wasn't exactly what she had in mind when she had told Dave earlier that she wouldn't be alone.

She checked the dial on her clock. It was almost midnight.

She had last spoken with Max at about three that afternoon. She had stubbornly refused to leave her house, so he insisted on police protection. She had assumed that he had been referring to himself.

For some reason, the presence of the cop out front made her feel lonelier than ever, as if no one else would ever be allowed in or out. She snapped up the receiver three or four times and started to dial Max's number, then hung up. She had told him she wanted to keep things simple. By staying away, he was respecting her wishes. She became suddenly angry with him for paying attention to her words instead of her needs—yes, he had sent protection but she was frightened, she was living a nightmare and she wanted to be held. She snapped up the phone and pounded his number once again. Before the first ring, she hung up. Her fried emotions had made her irrational. She had to calm down and regain control. She needed to talk to a friend. Someone she cared about and respected. *Nick.*

She was hurt that he hadn't returned her phone calls today. Surely he had heard what had happened to her—she had been on and off the phone with Sheila and Dave all day. Wasn't he worried? She picked the receiver back up and dialed his number.

Before the first ring, she heard a car pull into the driveway. Max. It was about time.

Relieved and happy, she hung up before Nick answered and slipped under the covers.

She heard the muffled sound of men's voices, then the door opened. The couch springs squeaked as he sat down. She slipped out of bed and walked toward the light wearing only her short, white cotton nightgown.

He glanced up at her and gave her a weak smile. "Did I wake you?" he asked.

She shook her head. She was silent for a second and then said, "Tough day?" She was teasing and he knew it.

He grinned. "You could say that." He stood up and kissed her on the cheek, then lay back on the couch and closed his eyes.

"I went to work," she volunteered.

"I heard."

"I wasn't going to, but Cindy called in sick."

When he didn't answer, she sat down beside him. His breathing was slow and even, his eyes were closed. "Hey," she said, and poked him in the ribs. With what appeared to be a great amount of effort, he opened his eyes. He studied her face as if he didn't know who she was.

"What are you doing?" she asked.

"Um, giving you my undivided attention."

"I like it," she said with a smile. "Did Jack analyze the hair?"

He nodded. His exhausted brain seemed to be working slowly. "Right now it doesn't look like it came from either Haverdale or Tomkins."

"You kept hair samples?"

He nodded again. "They were both missing that chunk of hair. If it turned up, I wanted to be sure we could identify it."

"Of course," she said, nodding. "So, what are you thinking?"

"I'm kind of tired—"

"I think the hair is Frannie's. He's just that kind of vicious SOB. He's probably happy that I've connected the three murders. He wants everyone to know I'm right." She nodded toward the ceiling. "I have a box of Frannie's things in the attic. Her brush is in there. Frannie always wore this perfume. I kept the brush because it smelled like her." Feeling a rush of sentiment coming on, she jumped up. "Anyway, I never cleaned it so you can get a hair sample from it. I'll go get it," she said energetically.

"Tomorrow," he said, grabbing her hand. "I don't think we'll analyze it tonight 'cause everybody is already sleeping."

She shrugged. "I guess I'm a little gung ho."

"I'll see if I can find you a used off button." He flashed her a quick smile. "Get some sleep," he said, giving her hand a squeeze and letting it go. "We'll get that brush tomorrow."

Jan glanced at him. He was making it pretty clear he didn't plan on joining her in the bedroom.

Jan swallowed. "Aren't you coming to bed, too?"

"Business before pleasure," he said. "I want to stay out here and keep guard."

"I'll leave the door open," she said. She blushed as soon as the words came out of her mouth.

As she turned away he said, "Look, there's one more thing, and you're not going to like it."

"What?"

"I have to get a hair sample from you, too."

"Me?" she asked, confused. "Why would they need a sample from me?"

She stood in the doorway as a faraway look of confusion passed over her face. After a couple seconds she understood. "You're right," she said, and slammed the door behind her.

41

THE LAST CURSE

"Well, thank you, Suzanna," Jan said. "We wouldn't need a service to do that."

She stood there, conveying a flicker of hurt, a brief jittery pause of her face as if a couple about to share troubled words you to realize, and she turned her doorknob for

Monday, August 17

THE RAIN STARTED BEFORE DAWN. BUT IT WASN'T THE DRIPPING from her overfilled gutters that woke her from a deep sleep. Nor was it the sound of the door closing as Max left for work. It was the phone.

Without opening her eyes Jan reached over and picked up the receiver. "Hello?" she said groggily.

"Jan," said Sheila. Jan could hear the panic in her voice. "What's going on?" Sheila whispered as if terrified.

"What do you mean?" Jan asked, still trying to focus. Jan had spoken with her several times the day before and Sheila had seemed fine.

"Dave!" Sheila said.

Jan was awake now. "What about him?" she asked crisply.

318

"Max came to see him last night. Said he wanted to talk to him about Sarah Tomkins. To *question* him."

"What?" Jan asked, looking at the clock. It was almost nine. "Why?"

"Has Max said anything to you?"

"No. . . ." Jan began. No wonder he had acted so weird last night. He must've felt like a rat for not confiding in her.

"It's a mess," Sheila confessed.

"Why would Max—"

"Dave knew her."

Jan held her breath. "What do you mean he knew her?"

"Just that. I guess he met her in a bar or something."

"Oh my God. And he just told you about it now?"

"No. The police found his business card in her apartment. That woman who works with you identified him or something, said that he was the one who came to mind when the police questioned her."

Cindy. No wonder she hadn't shown up for work last night. She was at CID with Max.

Sheila whispered, "You know how Dave is. He can't handle this."

Despite Dave's tough-seeming exterior, he was an extremely sensitive guy who didn't bounce back from misfortune easily. Just being connected with these murders would be enough to destroy any self-confidence he had.

Jan couldn't think. She rubbed her forehead as she asked, "Where are you?"

"I'm at Dave's apartment. I have to go in to work later, but—"

"I'm on my way."

42

JAN WAS DRIVING A COMPACT CAR, THE ONLY CAR HER INSURance would cover. Her hands were agitatedly tapping the steering wheel as she reviewed the sudden turn of events.

She kept focusing on one big question: Why hadn't Dave confessed his connection with Sarah immediately? Surely he must've realized how disastrous this could be. He should've known that the police would be all over him eventually.

Jan shook her head. It didn't make any sense.

What did she know about Dave, anyway? He had received his undergrad degree from the University of Maryland. He took some time off afterwards and traveled around the world. His parents live in Maryland, which was why he moved back after he finished law school. And she knew that he was in love with Sheila, even if he didn't realize it himself.

This whole thing had to be just a weird coincidence. After all, she reminded herself once more, she *knew* Dave. He certainly wasn't a murderer. How could she even question his innocence?

She paused. Is that what she was doing?

Jan pulled onto Dave's street and parked her car. Dave lived in a modest apartment building about three miles away from the office, seven miles away from Sarah Tomkins' house.

Someone was walking out of his building so she grabbed the door and let herself into the lobby. She walked up to his apartment and knocked.

A few minutes later she heard footsteps behind the closed door.

"Dave?" She hesitated. "Sheila?"

Sheila opened the door. She had been crying. Dave was sitting on the couch behind her.

"What are you doing here?" Dave asked, surprised. He stood up to greet her. From his appearance, one never would have guessed anything was wrong. His hair was perfectly in place as usual. He looked as though he had even dressed for the office. The only telltale signs of stress were the circles under his eyes and the way he kept nervously running his fingers through his hair.

"I called her," Sheila said.

"Why?"

"Because I think you need your friends right now."

"God damn it!" he said. Sheila and Jan both jumped.

They inched their way back when they realized he wasn't yelling at them—he was just frustrated with the entire situation. "This is ridiculous," he added more calmly.

Jan paused. A big question was running across her mind like a ticker tape, replaying over and over again. It might not be the best time, but she had to ask him. "Why didn't you tell Nick about this?"

"It's not like you think."

"Didn't you recognize her picture?" Jan asked. Sarah Tomkins' picture had been plastered all over the TV and newspapers.

"No," he said. He dropped down on the couch. Even though she had not been invited, Jan took that as an indication that she was welcome to stay. She settled into a stiff looking chair by the door.

Dave continued, "I met her—if it was her, and I'm not willing to admit that it was, at Tony's Late Night," he said, referring to the dance club off of Route 50. "I had too much to drink, so did she. We talked for a while. And I left. I never even saw her in the daylight."

"You never saw her after that night?"

"No!"

"So how did Cindy identify you?" Jan said, staring at Dave's eyes. They were bloodshot, making them appear even more blue than usual.

"She didn't identify me, as you put it. Your friend Max was looking for any strange man who had contact with her. Cindy mentioned that Sarah had said something to her about an attorney." Dave shrugged, embarrassed. "Apparently I gave her my card. They found it in her address book." He shook his head. "I fucked up, didn't I? Big time."

"You'll be okay," Jan said automatically. She chewed on her lower lip for a minute while both Sheila and Dave just stared at each other blankly. "Did you talk to Nick?" Jan asked. They must've spoken with somebody over there. After all, it was ten o'clock and neither Dave nor Sheila had shown up at work.

Sheila rolled her eyes. "He wasn't any help."

"What did he say?"

"Oh, he's thrilled," Dave interjected. "Thrilled to pieces. First you go off and disgrace the office, then me. He's beside himself."

"Don't worry," Jan lied casually. "You met her—so what? That's not a crime. They can't turn it into anything else."

"Oh, yeah? They already are. Max has been digging around in my past. He even asked me if I had ever met your sister."

"Why?" Jan asked.

"Apparently we both graduated from the University of Maryland in '86."

Jan waited for a moment before speaking. "So did fifteen thousand other people."

"Exactly."

"And he wanted to know if I can sail."

"Can you?" Jan asked.

"Oh, God," Dave said, standing. "Not you, too."

"He was captain of the sailing team in high school," Sheila volunteered.

Dave shot her a look.

"Dave, don't be ridiculous," Sheila snapped. "You don't have anything to hide."

He held his head as he sank back into a chair. "My head feels like it's going to spin off. You don't have any aspirin on you, do you?"

Jan shook her head. "I'm afraid not." She looked at him. He couldn't hurt anyone. She was sure of it.

"Look, Jan," he said. "Thanks for stopping by, but if you don't mind, I think I'm going to close my eyes for a while. I didn't get much sleep last night."

Sheila grabbed Jan's hand. "Call me later. I'll be here."

"Sure," Jan said. She gave Dave a final look before leaving.

43

JAN CRAWLED THROUGH THE ATTIC, SEARCHING FOR THE BOX with her sister's belongings. She pulled out the brush and held it up to her nose, breathing in her sister's scent. She fingered the wisps of hair still matted inside. She glanced inside the box at the odd things she had saved, a pack of gum that had been on Frannie's dresser, the framed pictures she had kept beside her bed, a stuffed bear.

She forced herself to close the box. She couldn't afford to get emotional right now. She had business to attend to, business of which she was certain her sister would approve. She slipped the brush inside a manila envelope, hurried back down the ladder, and jumped in her car.

A half an hour later she screeched into the station, parking her car at an illegal angle. She waved at the receptionist to buzz her in then stormed through the office, not even noticing the cops that bothered to wave to her or say hello.

Max was behind his desk on the phone. His face registered a brief look of surprise as she entered the room.

"Hi, Jan," Hank said from behind her.

Jan barely nodded, her whole being angrily focused on Max.

Max hung up the phone and said, "Good morning."

"I need to talk to you," she said.

He hesitated. "All right," he said, as though unsure. "Let's find an empty office."

He followed her back through the main office. The detectives working at their desks leaned forward with smiles on their faces, realizing that a scene was about to unfold. They slipped into an empty office and Max said, "I take it Estelle buzzed you in."

"What's going on?"

"With?"

"You know very well. With Dave."

Max was silent. "I'm sorry about this, Jan. I know he's your friend."

"He didn't do it."

"You're jumping the gun here, Jan. All I did was ask him some questions."

"You could've done more research before you questioned him! You could ruin his career—"

"I'm doing what I have to do to solve this case."

Jan glanced away. She knew he was right. In a defeated tone she asked, "Why didn't you tell me?"

"I knew you'd be upset. Besides, I wasn't sure Dave wanted anyone to know—"

"You suspect him of raping my sister? Of murdering her?" Jan said, angrily biting her lip.

"Where did you get that idea?"

"Don't play games. He said you asked him where he went to school. When he graduated."

Max was silent.

She pulled Frannie's brush out of a manila envelope. "This is Frannie's," she said. She reached into her purse and pulled out her brush. "And this is mine. If you don't trust me to provide my own sample, you can pull it yourself."

Max swallowed as he said, "Jan, I'm sorry about this. I really am."

"I know."

"I think you should go home," Max said. "Lie down for awhile."

She shook her head as she wiped away a tear. Keep it together, she ordered herself. She shook her head and said, "The whole world's gone crazy."

As Jan peeled out of CID she couldn't stop thinking about Custin. Perhaps Custin had grown too greedy, approached the killer for more money and the killer had simply disposed of him. After all, Custin was no longer needed. He had already performed his side of the bargain.

As she sped down Defense Highway, she dialed

Nick's office. His assistant gave her the same brush-off she had given her previously. Nick was tied up in a meeting. He would call her as soon as possible.

Jan hung up the phone and ran a yellow light as she once again tapped the steering wheel impatiently. If only she could talk to someone else who had known Custin. Who else besides Nick could help her shed light on his conviction?

Only two people: Jeff Brown, the detective who had arrested him, and Anna Parrets, the judge who had sentenced him. According to Max, Jeff Brown was retired and living in Florida, and she wasn't quite up to another trip to the Sunshine State. But fortunately, she knew where Anna Parrets was. She was still here. Right in Annapolis.

44

SHADY SIDE GROVE.

It sounded like a cemetery, but it wasn't. It was an expensive community of condominiums nestled in the mouth of the Chesapeake Bay, not far from Bay Ridge, where Lucy Haverdale was found. It was in this parcel of pricey waterfront real estate that Anna Parrets lived.

Jan had no problem tracking her down even though the judge had retired in 1991, several years after she had sent Curtis Custin to jail. When Jan explained that she was an assistant state's attorney who had some questions about a rape case the judge had presided over, Anna Parrets had agreed to a brief meeting that day. Jan could tell that she had piqued Judge Parrets' curiosity.

Jan parked the rental car underneath an old willow

tree and walked over to the identical row of modern, cedar shingled townhouses. She pressed the buzzer for 2309.

"Yes?" a pleasant voice answered.

"It's Jan," she replied. "Jan Garret."

The door opened and an elderly, small, attractive woman with brown hair appeared. She ushered Jan inside and offered her some iced tea. Although the judge was polite, she emanated an air of impatience. She cleared her throat and asked, "So what is this case?"

"I brought the file," Jan said. "It actually has to do with a rapist you sentenced in 1998. His victim was my sister, Frannie Garret."

"She was your sister?" She dropped her eyes and said, "I was very sorry to hear about her death," as though it had just happened. "So tragic."

"Yes," Jan said, but neither did she have much interest in chit-chat. "Do you remember Custin?"

"He pled guilty, as I recall. There wasn't much of a case."

"Do you remember anything unusual about his plea?"

The judge's eyes narrowed slightly. "What is this all about?"

Jan hesitated. She didn't want to share with the judge everything she suspected, but on the other hand, the judge was a smart woman. She needed to hear the real reason. "I think there might be a connection between my sister's rape and subsequent death and the recent murders of Lucy Haverdale and Sarah Tomkins."

The judge paused for a moment. "I thought they were domestic cases."

Jan shook her head. "I don't think so." She leaned forward as she said, "I don't know if you remember anything about my sister's rape, but before the rapist left, he hacked off a lock of her hair."

"And the Haverdale and Tomkins women also had their hair cut."

"Right.

The judge nodded. "And you think that Custin is responsible?"

Jan shook her head. "No, I don't think so. He had an alibi."

"I'm afraid I don't understand. . . ."

"Lucy Haverdale was killed a month after Custin was released. That and the fact that the perpetrator had cut some of her hair, was enough to make me suspect Custin. I went to Florida where he was living in a three-hundred-and-fifty-thousand-dollar house, driving a forty-thousand-dollar car. He also owned a one-hundred-thousand-dollar boat which was docked at a club nearby."

"Odd. Did you speak to him?"

"No," Jan said quickly. "I was going to, but, well, when he came to the door, I realized that he was nothing like my sister described." Jan waited but Judge Parrets was silent. "Anyway, a week after my visit, just last Thursday, Custin was murdered."

The judge nodded, taking it in without emotion, as if she were sitting high above her courtroom.

"It was ruled an accidental death—but the circumstances were very similar to my sister's. He drowned in a lake, just feet away from his boat. Like my sister, no one knew he was going out by himself. He simply disappeared."

Judge Parrets continued to stare at her calmly.

"Two nights ago the roof of my car was slashed and a lock of hair was found inside."

"And the hair was traced to . . ."

"They're analyzing it as we speak."

"Very strange. So you think that Custin was innocent of your sister's crime, that someone else paid him to take the rap and then killed him off. And now that faceless rapist is back, but this time he's murdering his victims."

"Exactly. I mean, they didn't have any evidence on Custin, nothing to connect him to my sister. And, like I said, he certainly didn't fit the profile she gave the police. He had the wrong eye color, the wrong height . . ."

"I don't remember that."

"Well, it's in the file. She also didn't mention anything about an accent, and Custin has—or rather, had—a pronounced southern accent."

"Perhaps he purposely dropped it for the assault." She crossed her arms. "What do the police say?"

"They're not even sure all of the murders are connected."

"But you are."

Jan nodded. "Please. Anything you would remember would be helpful."

"Let me think," she said. "The case was handled by Nick Fitzgerald. There wasn't much to handle, of course, because it was a plead. Custin's attorney was Don Shuller, who used to be a very prominent defense attorney here in town. He had a heart attack shortly after this case and died. Anyway, he asked for leniency because Custin had confessed and was repentant. Nick conferred, which," she shrugged, "was a little unusual."

"Nick conferred? What do you mean?"

"I mean, he agreed Custin should get a lenient sentence."

Jan furrowed her brow, confused. "He agreed?"

She nodded.

"What did he say?"

"I don't remember exactly. But I do remember that after I sentenced him your sister became visibly upset. And she tried to call me that afternoon. Several times, in fact."

"She tried to call you?" Jan could feel the blood drain from her face.

"I was in court all afternoon, but she spoke with my secretary. Apparently she was quite adamant that I call her back immediately. I tried, of course, around five o'clock that evening. But there wasn't any answer. So I called Nick to let him know. I assumed he was aware of what was going on." She paused. "Has he ever mentioned that?"

Jan shook her head. "Never."

"He probably didn't want to upset you." She hesitated. "Nick Fitzgerald is a good lawyer. I've known him professionally for many years." She smiled. "I wouldn't vote for him though."

"Why is that?"

"I don't trust him. Something in his eyes."

45

"LOOK, IRIS," JAN SAID, FRUSTRATED. SHE WAS STOPPED AT A light on Forest Drive, talking into her cellular phone. She had called Nick almost immediately, yet once again she was being given the runaround. "This is urgent. I need to talk to him."

"I'm sorry, Jan. He's out of the office."

Jan shook her head, frustrated. "Where did he go?"

"I have no idea."

Jan hung up the phone. She was about a half mile from Nick's house. But he wouldn't be home—would he? Oh hell, she thought. It was worth a try.

The light turned green and she swerved into the right-hand lane, almost causing the car behind her to ride up her rear. She made a sharp right and turned onto Ferry Point road.

As she passed the horse farms and acres of undeveloped property, she was struck with a weird sense of déjà-vu. She had been to Nick's house before, of course. Nick liked to entertain and she had been invited to several parties there. But she had never been there by herself, and she felt strange intruding unexpectedly.

She pulled up in front of Nick's house. The garage door was down, not a good sign.

Still, she parked her car in the driveway and stopped to peek in the garage. Nick's car was there, parked on the left side of the garage.

She walked up to the front door and knocked.

A few seconds later, much to her surprise, Nick answered.

"Nick?" she asked.

He looked terrible. His left cheek was sporting a fresh bruise and his usually perfect hair was tousled. More tellingly, he was wearing an old black T-shirt and a pair of dirty shorts. "Jan," he said, almost as though he was expecting her.

"I know about Dave . . ." she began. Her eyes focused on a spot of red on his shirt. It looked like blood. She glanced up at him and said, "What's the matter?"

Nick walked away from the door, leaving it open.

Jan stepped inside, confused. "Nick?"

He glanced out the door and said anxiously, "You should go."

"Why aren't you at work?" she said calmly. She took a step forward so she was standing directly in front of him. She could smell the alcohol on his breath.

"I'm sick."

"You look like you've been in a fight. Playing rugby again?"

"I fell," Nick said tersely, avoiding her eyes.

"That's too bad," Jan said, fully aware that he was lying. "I met with Judge Parrets today. I spoke to her about Frannie's case. She said that my sister tried to call her several times after the sentencing."

He didn't say anything.

"Do you know why?"

"No."

"Was she upset? She must've been upset."

"I don't remember, okay?" he said, holding the door for her. "Please go."

"What's going on?" Jan asked nervously. "What's the matter?"

He looked as though he was going to say something and then he stopped. "I'll talk to you about this later, all right?"

"But Dave—"

"I'm going to take care of Dave."

Jan took a step and crossed her arms in front of her as if refusing to leave. "How did Custin afford a prominent attorney?"

"Jan," he said quietly, the muscles in his jaw working. "Look, I'll tell you whatever you want to know—later. Please, you have to go."

"I just want—"

"Now!" Nick yelled, his face turning red.

"Nick," Jan breathed, startled.

Nick grabbed her arm, pushed her outside, and slammed the door.

Jan stood there for a moment, stunned. She glanced back toward the door, defiant tears welling in her eyes. One thing was certain, he was crazy if he thought she would just leave gracefully.

As she walked toward her car, she caught a glimpse of Nick watching her from the window. She started her car and drove around the block. When she returned, she parked down the street and craned her head for a view of Nick's house. Within five minutes, a Cadillac pulled in the driveway and Senator Thurman stepped out.

46

"So?"

Jan was back in her car, speeding along as she spoke to Max. She replied, "So, get over there. Something is definitely going on."

"Okay, give me a minute. I'll just gather up the SWAT team and we'll surround the house."

"This isn't funny."

"Come on, Jan. You know I can't just go over there like that—"

"Make up an excuse."

"I can't do that. Besides, I have to go to Baltimore."

"To Baltimore? Why?"

"Because—I need to, that's why."

"Okay, fine," she said testily.

"I thought you weren't talking to me anyway."

"Only for business."

"Oh, I see. Are you working tonight?"

"Yep," she said, narrowly avoiding the car in front of her.

As the driver slammed on the horn Max asked, "What's that?"

"Nothing. This car just doesn't handle like mine."

"I'm hanging up so you can focus. I'll see you after work."

"I don't want—" But it was too late. Max had already hung up.

She knew it had been a long shot that he would be able to help. After all, what she really needed was for Nick to tell the truth. But for some reason, he was determined to lie. Why? Had he screwed up with Frannie? Was he worried that Jan would find out what happened? Is that why he had called the senator over there? Because he needed to confide in his mentor?

Jan went back home and made a pitcher of iced tea. A storm was blowing in from the north and she sat on her porch with her drink, watching the clouds gather. One thing after another popped into her head.

Several hours later she had a caffeine buzz so intense she nearly jumped out of her skin when the phone rang. Certain that it was Nick, she practically threw herself on it, but she was greeted by silence. Whoever had called hung up.

She glanced at the clock and grudgingly headed off to change her clothes for work. The afternoon of thought and caffeine had allowed her to come to an important conclusion: she was through with

McRyan's. The hair episode, Dave's troubles, and Nick's loss of sanity had caused her to reevaluate her strategy. She wasn't in the mood to be a vigilante any longer.

Much to her surprise, however, when she arrived at work, she felt a sense of relief. Rex was washing glasses, chatting amiably with the few patrons that had gathered around the bar this evening. This was life, she thought, real life. There was something about this whole place that grounded her.

"Where's Cindy?" she asked.

He looked at her and smiled. "Hey!" he said enthusiastically. "Jesus H. Christ, am I happy to see you. Cindy called in sick again."

Jan was glad that she wasn't there. She was angry at her for involving Dave in this mess. She knew that Cindy had no way of knowing who Dave was or what he meant to her, but Jan didn't care. Her mother hen instinct had taken over and she was ticked.

"Rex," she said. "I need to talk to you."

"Shoot," he said, handing her a dish towel.

"This is going to be my last night."

"Your last night?"

"I can't work here anymore. . . ."

"Why? The whole thing about this serial rapist shit getting to you?"

He gave her just the out she needed. And he wasn't off track, either.

She nodded, her eyes filling with tears.

"Aw, hell," he said, disgusted. "I'd like to find that guy myself."

Business was slow and by ten o'clock her caffeine buzz had worn off, leaving a brutal headache as a reminder. Hank came in just as she was about to plant herself at one of the tables. "Hey," she said, surprised. "What are you doing here?"

"I'm here to party. It's Saturday night, right?"

"Not quite. Where's Max?"

"Stuck in Baltimore. I'm his stand-in till he gets here."

"Doesn't Judy want you home?" she asked, referring to his wife.

Hank said, "Nah. We're kind of, well, separated. I think that's the official word for it." He shrugged. "I'll get over it. I get to keep the dog, that's the important thing."

"God," she said. "Everything seems to be falling apart. Everywhere."

"Yeah, well, you about ready to go?"

She nodded, walked over to Rex's "office" and banged on the door. "Rex?"

Rex popped his head out. Jan wondered what he did in there all night with the door closed. She didn't care to think about it. "Everything's wiped down."

"I'll send you your check," he said. "Send some friends in, blondes and redheads preferred."

"Send some friends in?" Hank asked as they were walking toward the door.

"I quit."

"I don't blame you. I don't know how you can stand the smoke in here. It's too much for me, and I smoke." He glanced at her. "Poor GI. You look wiped."

She nodded. "I am. Did Max tell you about Nick?"

He nodded. "I've always thought he was strange."

"What do you make of it?"

"He told his office he was taking some time off. If he never returns, it's all right with me." He opened the door and peered out. "Shit, it's really coming down now."

The rain was pelting the street, a steady hard current. "Where'd you park?" Jan asked.

"I didn't. My car's back in the shop. I had one of the boys at the station drop me off."

"How will you get home?"

"Max's car. Either that or we'll have a slumber party."

So it was understood that Max was spending the night. She wondered what he had told his peers about their relationship.

They drove to Jan's house in silence, two old, comfortable friends both too exhausted to speak. As Jan pulled into her driveway she asked, "What time did Max say he'd get here?"

"Any time now."

Jan stopped the car at the end of the driveway and pressed the remote. Suddenly, they were bathed in light.

"Whoa," Hank said. "That's bright."

Jan laughed and opened her door. Hank put his hand on her arm. "Wait," he said.

"What?"

"Give me your keys."

"Why?"

"Because I want to go check the house first."

"Don't be silly. There's no one here. We'd see them."

"I'll flash the lights twice if it's all right," Hank said, unconvinced.

Hank hopped up onto the porch and quickly disappeared into the house.

It made her feel good to know she had friends who would go out of their way for her. Even in the midst of all the tragedy, she had something to be grateful for. As she waited, she opened the glove box, glancing at her gun. It was there. Right on top.

She pulled it out and held it in her hands.

Suddenly, the lights went out. She glanced toward the house, concerned. Hank was supposed to flash them, not turn them off.

She stepped out of the car into the rain. "Hank?" she called out.

The house was still dark.

She heard a door slam shut. "Hank?" she yelled again, reaching inside the car and fumbling around for the remote to the lights.

Suddenly she was yanked backward, her gun knocked on the ground. Before she had a chance to scream, her hands were behind her back and a rough, gloved hand was over her mouth.

Oh my God, she thought. *I screwed up. Big time.*

And then suddenly, she heard a blast. There came a groan, and the hands dropped away.

She looked at the stranger in a heap at her feet, then turned around to see Hank standing in the doorway. He lowered his gun and asked, "Are you okay?"

Before she could answer, he collapsed.

47

A HALF AN HOUR LATER JAN'S QUIET DRIVEWAY WAS FILLED
with screaming sirens and flashing lights. The whole
scene seemed surreal, Hank lying there, blood pouring
from his ear. A stranger dead at her feet.

Hank would be okay, or at least, that was the last she
heard. The bullet had grazed his skull, deep enough to
make him lose consciousness, but not deep enough to
kill him.

The same was not true for the man in the puddle. He
was older than she would have expected, in his early
fifties probably. His tanned, lined face had been
splashed with mud, leaving rivulets of brown water
laced across his mustache. He wasn't a bad looking
man. If she hadn't found the sight of him so distasteful,
she might have even thought him handsome.

The paramedics gathered around the body and
hoisted it up on the stretcher. A few minutes later the

ambulance pulled away. Uniformed cops continued to arrive, moving over her property like ants at a picnic.

Max walked into the porch and took Jan in his arms.

"Was there any identification on him?" Jan whispered, still holding on to him.

Max shook his head. "No. But I know who he is."

Jan pulled back.

"His name is Jeff Brown. He's a retired cop. The guy who arrested Custin in the first place."

"So, he's the one," she said.

"I don't know. It certainly looks that way."

She shook her head. "If he wasn't dead I'd like to kill him."

Max pulled out his keys. "I want you to go to my apartment. Get some sleep."

"What about you?"

"I've got work to do. I'm going to have an officer drive you there. Apartment 103."

"Aren't you coming, too?" she asked worriedly. "It's just that, well, I'm a little shaky right now."

"I know," he said. "I'll be there as soon as I can." He stopped for a moment, his bloodshot eyes staring at her. It was a look of pain, of sadness. And then he turned and signaled the officer.

The uniformed officer came inside Max's apartment with her and did a quick check of the rooms. When he was finished he said, "Max said I should make you a cup of coffee."

She laughed and then said, no, but thanks anyway. She locked the door behind him, glad to be alone. She checked the apartment again, peeking under the bed, in closets, even in drawers. She was still shell-shocked and edgy, so overly alert she thought she might jump out of her skin. On the ride over she had even begun to suspect the young cop of being involved with Brown—that he was figuring out a way to dispose of her. Now that he had left, her suspicions switched to Max. After all, she thought, admiring the spectacular view of the Chesapeake Bay off his balcony, where did he get the money for an apartment like this, for all of these nice things?

Her brain was working overtime and she couldn't stop it. She walked toward the piano and ran her fingers over the keys as she wondered how much the suede couch and blond Haywood-Wakefield table and chairs had cost.

She peeked down the hall. A small kitchen was off to the right. Beyond that was a bedroom and bath. She glanced back inside the bedroom. The double bed was unmade. There weren't any pictures on the wall, although there was one framed photo on his dresser. She walked over and picked it up.

The picture was of a young woman. The style of her clothes and her feathered back hair convinced Jan that either the girl had worse fashion sense than Jan did or the picture was at least ten years old. She looked to be in her early twenties. She was petite, with short brown hair and perfect white teeth—just like Haverdale and

Tomkins. The woman was smiling at the photographer, waving to the camera uncomfortably.

Was this the "friend" who died and left Max in search of justice?

She set down the photo, suddenly feeling very tired. She went into the bathroom and took a quick shower, then wrapped herself in a towel that smelled like after-shave. She then went back into the living room and lay down on the couch, not even bothering to grab a blanket. Her mind raced with the possibility of plots against her, of crooked cops and close friends who really had it in for her. The longer she thought, the more complex the web of intrigue became. As her thoughts approached the impossible, her exhaustion caught up with her and she fell into a deep sleep.

What seemed like only a moment later, she awoke with a start, aware that someone was standing above her. She jumped up, ready to scream.

"Hey," Max said softly.

She looked up at him, her suspicions fading at the sight of him.

He sat on the couch and pulled her down next to him.

"How's Hank?" she asked.

"Stabilized. They've got him out of surgery. Judy's there with him."

"Judy's there?"

Max nodded. "Sometimes crises have a way of bringing people together."

She gave him a little smile and said, "I'm glad

you're back." She leaned toward him, resting her head on his shoulder. "What time is it?"

"I don't know. Four. Five."

"Were you at my house this whole time?"

"Yeah. We were afraid the rain would wash away the foot prints."

"Did you find any?"

"A couple. It was hard to see in the dark."

"Did you ever find his boat?"

"I don't think he came by boat. Too rough. And the Coast Guard looked. Nothing."

She scooted up so she could look at him. "Car?"

"That's what I thought, but we couldn't find it. We searched the entire area."

"What do you make of it?"

"I'm not sure yet."

"Well at least Dave is off the hook."

"Yeah. . . ." he said with some hesitation.

"You don't sound convinced," she said, getting a little angry.

"Listen," he said. "I want you to take it easy tomorrow . . . or rather," he said, glancing at his watch, "today. Just lie in front of the TV. Don't do a thing."

"But," Jan began.

"No buts. They were ready to cart you off to the hospital but I convinced them that you didn't have to go. Don't make me change my mind."

Jan smiled weakly. Her smile faded as she said, "So he killed Frannie."

"We don't know."

She nodded. "I mean, he must've. When she saw him at the sentencing she probably recognized him. So he killed her."

"Maybe." He sighed. "The results came back on the hair we found in your car."

"And?"

"It's Frannie's."

She felt winded, her breath taken away.

"I'm sorry, Jan," he said quietly. He shook his head as he slowly ran a finger across her chin. "When I think about what could have happened to you . . ."

"I'm okay."

"I should have been there with you tonight."

"You sent Hank."

He dropped his hands.

"Hey," Jan said. "This isn't your fault."

She leaned forward and kissed his cheek, then his forehead. He tilted his head and their lips met.

Despite their exhaustion, they needed each other. Clothes were undone and discarded with a desperate urgency. They rubbed their bare bodies up against each other, making love with a slow, comforting rhythm. Afterwards they stayed wrapped in each other's arms as they silently stared out over the water.

48

"JAN! MY GOD. ARE YOU ALL RIGHT?"

Jan finished tying Max's bathrobe around her waist as she held the door open for Sheila. "What time is it?" she croaked. She would still be sleeping if Sheila's pounding hadn't woken her.

"A little after ten," Sheila said, breezing past her.

Jan had no idea what time they had finally fallen asleep last night. All she knew was that Max must have carried her to the bedroom because that's where she found herself moments ago, completely naked. "How did you ..."

"Max. I got your messages this morning. He told me where you were. My God—I can't believe it!"

"How's Hank?" Jan asked quickly.

"He's doing okay. How are you handling everything?"

353

Jan sat down on the couch. "I don't know. I was really freaked out last night. I think I've calmed down a little bit."

"You must feel vindicated at least. Max said it was the guy who arrested Custin. Obviously there was a cover-up."

Jan nodded.

Sheila shook her head. "You could've been killed."

"I feel terrible about what happened to Hank."

"It wasn't your fault," Sheila said, repeating the same words Jan had said to Max.

Jan just shrugged.

"At least it's over," Sheila said, trying to soothe her. "Your sister would be proud."

At the mention of Frannie, a quick smile passed over Jan's lips.

"She would," Sheila reassured her. "You set out to catch her murderer and you did."

"There's still so many unanswered questions."

"But the big one is solved."

Jan nodded, encouraged. "How's Dave doing?"

"Oh, he'll be all right. I think he's relieved that this thing is over." She shrugged. "He was never officially a suspect so his name was kept out of the papers."

"Good."

"Wow," Sheila said, glancing around her. "Look at this place. What a view. This can't be cheap."

Jan blushed, embarrassed for Max.

"And he's neat, isn't he? Unusual for a guy." She

stood up and peeked in the kitchen. "Does he have anything to eat? I'm starving."

"I don't know," Jan said. "Actually, last night was the first time I've been here."

Sheila opened the refrigerator and leaned inside.

"Have you heard from Nick?" Jan asked.

"Screw Nick. When Dave was freaking out Nick wasn't the least bit supportive," Sheila said, still sorting through the refrigerator. "I like this guy. He puts Saran wrap on his leftovers so you can see what it is. I hate it when people put foil on top, you know? You never know what it is until it's too late."

"He told me that he was going to take care of Dave."

"Who—Nick? What do you mean he told you? He wasn't even at work yesterday."

"I went to his house."

Sheila slammed the refrigerator door and stood up straight. "You saw him?" she said.

Jan nodded. "It was really weird. He looked like he'd been in a fight. His face was all bruised. He wouldn't talk to me—he literally pushed me out of his house. And then, a few minutes later, the senator showed up."

"Weird. I guess he's not taking this whole Mrs. Thurman thing very well," Sheila said, offering Jan the rest of the banana.

"What do you mean?" Jan asked, passing on the banana.

"I thought you knew." Sheila paused as she threw the remainder into the trash. "She's in the hospital.

They say it's critical. They don't expect her to live much longer."

Jan stopped. She knew how much Mrs. Thurman meant to Nick. "I don't know," Jan said, shaking her head. "I don't think that's the reason he hasn't been to work."

"It's obviously not the whole reason. I mean, if he was so worried about her he wouldn't have left town."

"What?"

"We got word this morning that Nick was taking extended leave. Someone said he had some personal business out of town or something. He might not even return to work. After all, he doesn't have much time left there anyway. But still, it seems so strange. I mean, to just disappear like that. Not even say goodbye to the staff."

"He didn't mention anything about leaving town to me." Of course, he didn't say much at all.

"Maybe he just cracked. Not being able to have you was more than he could stand."

Jan spoke as if she hadn't even heard her friend. "I think he's in some kind of trouble. You should've seen him."

"Maybe he feels guilty for the way he treated you. Maybe it's caused him to reevaluate his life."

"No, no," Jan said. "Nothing like that. I don't know, I just have this weird feeling that he knew something about Frannie—that he lied to me."

Sheila was silent. "It's possible. I mean, this Brown guy arrested Custin, right? So Nick knew him."

Jan nodded.

"But if Nick suspected him, why didn't he come forward?"

Jan shook her head. "It doesn't make sense."

"Oh God, Jan," Sheila said, crossing her arms as she shook her head guiltily. "I wish I would have been there for you yesterday."

"You had your hands full."

"I guess so," she said. "You know, I give you credit. You really did know what you were doing."

Jan paused.

"So, do you feel any sense of relief?"

"No," Jan said quietly. "None."

49

Friday, August 21, 10 A.M.

IT FELT STRANGE TO RETURN HOME. SHE HAD BEEN AT MAX'S apartment for three days and their lives had assumed a kind of strange domestic tranquillity. Nevertheless, last night over dinner she told Max she needed to go home. It was time. Her brain had cooled down, the conspiracy theories had stopped popping into her head, and after all, the man she feared had been killed. The only way she could deal with the demons that still resided within her was to return to the scene of the crime—alone. Once she became comfortable being by herself, she would welcome Max back.

She drove down the driveway. The yellow tape had been removed, the blood completely washed away. It was quiet. Peaceful. As if nothing had ever happened.

Except for one thing. Her grass was short again. Which could only mean . . . Mrs. Fletcher. Jan smacked her head. She had completely forgotten about Mrs. Fletcher's mail. And from the looks of it, Mrs. Fletcher wasn't happy.

She was in her yard uniform carrying a big bunch of tomatoes in her arms.

Jan stopped in front of her house and jumped out of her car, running toward the older woman. "Mrs. Fletcher!" she said. "I forgot to pick your tomatoes."

"That's okay," she said in a forced sugary voice that barely masked her anger.

"And your mail."

"It was all in my box. One big pile."

"Oh, geez, Mrs. Fletcher. I'm sorry. I am. I just, well, I haven't been here myself."

She leaned forward and nodded. "'Cause of the murder?"

"Yeah."

"I heard about it. God damn, I said to my son. Wouldn't you know it? I'm on some silly tour bus with some old coot in Fredricksburg, missing all the action."

Jan held back a smile. She had never heard anyone refer to their boyfriend as an old coot. She kind of liked it. "Yeah, well, there certainly was action."

Mrs. Fletcher looked at Jan and winked. "Did you shoot him? The burglar?"

"He wasn't a burglar."

"Did you shoot him?" she repeated excitedly.

"No," Jan said. "I'm afraid not. He was shot by the police."

"You know, I've got that M1 under my bed."

"It would have come in handy the other night."

"Damn," she said again, shaking her head. "Wouldn't you know I missed it."

"Thank you so much for mowing the lawn," Jan said. "I'm really going to try and be better about it—"

"I thought you'd been through enough."

"Thank you. I really do appreciate it."

Mrs. Fletcher lifted her big glasses and squinted her eyes as she glanced around. "I haven't seen any blood around here."

"No, it's gone. Washed away."

Mrs. Fletcher glanced back at Jan's house. "Got any pictures?"

The question took Jan off guard. "I'll see what I can do. A stack of pictures, extra blood."

"I'd appreciate it. Now how about a nice tomato?" Mrs. Fletcher asked, happy again.

50

8:40 P.M.

I'M BACK.

He motored his boat slowly down the river, enjoying the breeze as it tousled his hair. The sun was about to set, and the moon had already slid into the horizon. He waved to the boaters cruising past.

He had been afraid after the last altercation that he wouldn't be allowed to return, but *her* sickness and eventual death had paved the way. There was no way he could stay away, no way anyone could keep him from coming back to attend her funeral.

He turned off the engine as he lowered the anchor.

The day had been grueling, and he had found himself looking forward to this moment more than he had suspected. He had not intended to strike tonight. He had been taking his time, enjoying the game. Jan had proved a formidable match, a prey more engaging than any he had encountered as of yet.

But as much as he had enjoyed the game he was ready for the ultimate conclusion.

He pulled off his shirt and glanced down at his finely carved abs.

She was almost his.

51

JAN FOUND HER HOUSE TO BE EXACTLY THE WAY SHE LEFT IT.
Even her nightshirt was on the floor, right where she
had dropped it. After sorting through closets, drawers,
checking behind and underneath the furniture, she
had determined her house was safe once again. She
had tried to read a book but had been thrilled when
Sheila and Dave called and offered to take her out to
dinner.

Now, returning home once again, she felt more at
peace than she had in months. As she pulled back into
her driveway, she hoped her sense of peace would continue.

It was a cool evening and the mist had begun to set-
tle, making it difficult to see despite the bright moon.
She leaned forward, stiffening as her bright headlights

363

illuminated the spot where Jeff Brown had died. *It's over,* she reminded herself. *It's all over.*

She parked in front of her house and turned off her headlights. She pressed the remote for the floodlights, but it didn't work. She took a breath and pressed it again, reminding herself there was nothing to worry about. Even if the lights didn't work, it was just chance, not the act of a murderer. After all, out here in the woods, electrical outages happened all the time. And for all she knew, the police had screwed them up when they were here.

Still cloaked in darkness, she took her time getting out of her car, attempting to ignore the uneasiness churning in her belly. Max had warned her she would feel like this. With her hand still on the door, she hesitated. She reached back in the car, popped open the glove compartment and took out her gun.

She held the gun firmly in front of her as she walked toward the house, loosening her grip only to unlock the door. She stepped inside and froze, her attention focused on the living room window. She was almost sure she had locked the house up like a tomb before leaving, yet the sheer curtains were blowing in the breeze, giving an almost ghostly effect.

She reached on the wall and flicked on the switch to her lamp. It didn't work so she flicked it again. Nothing but darkness.

She took a step toward her bedroom and stopped. Suddenly she knew there was not a power outage. Just as surely as she knew she was not alone.

She could see him in the darkness, his form outlined by the light of the moon shining in through the window. He was dressed completely in black with a mask covering his face. He stood there silently, as if waiting for her to make the next move. To determine how the game was to be played.

She stood still as she slowly aimed her gun. "Stay where you are," she said. "I have a gun."

His blue eyes glistened in the dark.

"Get on the ground, now," she commanded, breaking out in sweat.

He started to bend down, but suddenly lunged at her, knocking her down and sending the gun spiraling across the floor. She twisted around but he grabbed her ankle, pulling her toward him. She screamed as she kicked him in the face with her other leg. She picked herself up and bolted for the door. He grabbed her arm and spun her around. She kicked him in the groin, lurching forward and breaking free. Then she spun on her heels and ran toward the woods.

52

11:12 P.M.

MAX RUBBED HIS EYES. HE WAS WORKING LATE. HE HAD NO REA-son to rush home, after all, Jan would not be waiting for him.

He had enjoyed the past few days despite the crisis they'd endured. The whole terrible incident made him realize what he had tried to deny—he was in love with Jan. It had been years since he had held a woman close all night without feeling the slightest urge to dash out the door or say goodbye.

But despite his happiness with Jan, he was still uneasy and restless. Despite everyone's insistence that Brown had been the serial rapist, the case against him simply didn't add up. Why would a retired cop now living in Florida suddenly return to Maryland to kill young women? His wife admitted she had recently filed for a divorce, but would that be enough to push him over the edge?

There was also nothing definitely linking Brown with either the Haverdale or Tomkins murder. His whereabouts on the night Haverdale was killed were unknown, although he had been in DC on the day Tomkins was killed. A coincidence?

If he did kill Haverdale and Tomkins, where did he get the boat? And what about the night that Jan was attacked? How did he get there? He was dressed in dark, heavy clothes, so obviously he didn't swim there. They never found a boat or a car. Max suspected that someone had dropped him off—perhaps even hired him to kill Jan.

But why?

And where the hell was Nick through all this? He had conveniently disappeared the very night Jan was attacked. Max had a feeling that something terrible was going on, and Nick was either responsible or, at the very least, involved.

Max distractedly opened up Frannie's file once more. Was Nick the serial rapist and murderer they were looking for? If he was, why had he waited so long after Frannie's murder to kill again?

Max heard the fax machine click on. He hurriedly picked up the fax, excitedly realizing it was what he had been waiting for. Jeff Brown's résumé dated 1975, the year he came to work for the department. He saw what he was looking for halfway down the page.

Suddenly everything fell into place.

53

RUN. OVER THE ROCK, AROUND THE FIRST CURVE—NO TIME TO stop and look for knives. She could hear him behind her, gaining speed. But she was agile and familiar with the path. Unfortunately for her, the full moon shed so much light, one didn't really need to be familiar with the route to maintain speed in the dark. To lose him she would have to veer off the path and wind her way through the brush.

She swung around the second curve and dove into the woods. She didn't even feel the vines scratching her legs and face as she made her way through the thick foliage. She had to wind her way around toward the last curve. She needed to retrieve her gun. It was her only hope.

The brush was thicker now and she used her arms as

a dull machete, slowly realizing the futility of the situation. This hadn't seemed so difficult in her trial runs. She paused for a second, certain that she would feel his hands on her neck.

Nothing.

Had she lost him? Or was he still on the path, waiting for her to come back out?

She started moving again, listening carefully. She circled around, a quiet sense of relief steeping over her as she spotted the tree under which the gun was hidden. She knelt down on her hands and knees, creeping toward the tree.

There was still no sign of him anywhere. Biting her lower lip so hard that it bled, she reached the tree and pulled the rocks away.

The gun was missing.

She dug her fingers into the hard dirt, frantically digging for the gun.

Suddenly she stopped and lifted her head. She heard a deep, throaty laugh as she felt cold steel at the base of her neck. "Lose something?"

The gun slammed against her back, knocking her on the ground. She caught a whiff of . . . what was that? Aftershave lotion. A familiar scent.

"I've caught you," he whispered, yanking her around so she was facing him. She tried to struggle but he was too quick, straddling her with his whole body, making it impossible for her to move.

With his legs wrapped on either side of her, he

calmly set his gun between her breasts and pulled duct tape out of his pocket, ripping off a large piece. He grabbed her wrists and wrenched them over her head, tying them together so tightly it felt as though he was cutting off circulation. Throughout the whole procedure she continued to stare into his eyes, certain that she had met him before. *Think.* Blue eyes. Straight white teeth.

Familiarize yourself, she commanded silently. Rapists often entered a semi-delusional state during the crime. Perhaps if she reminded him of his real life—perhaps a girlfriend or a wife and children, she could snap him out of this.

"Take off your mask," she said calmly. "I want to see your face."

She winced as he yanked her to her feet and pulled her in close. Reacting instinctively, she spit at him.

The force of the blow was almost enough to knock her unconscious. He hit her again across the other side of her face. Something salty in her mouth . . . blood, she realized. Her blood.

Is this what Frannie had felt? The same aching realization that she would soon die?

No! screamed Jan silently. He wasn't going to get both of them.

She opened her eyes and before he could aim his gun, she kicked him. As he reeled backward, she jumped to her feet, her wrists still tied in front of her. He threw himself at her, slamming her into a tree.

He pulled her up by her shirt and held her in front of him. He laughed once more and shook his head. "I said, I've caught you," he whispered, leaning in to kiss her.

Jan heard the click of a gun behind them.

"Not quite," said Nick, stepping out of the woods, his weapon aimed at the rapist. "Let her go, Eddie. It's over."

54

EDDIE? EDDIE WHO? THE SENATOR'S SON?

Ed whipped around, pulling her with him as a shield. "Get away," he hissed.

"I know everything, Eddie. I've been waiting here for you. I called your father. He's on his way."

"You knew?" Jan asked Nick. "You knew who it was?"

"Let her go," Nick said, ignoring her.

With a scream Ed threw her toward Nick. As she slammed into him, Ed took off running. Nick pushed her off and fired into the woods. Ed stumbled, then fell face first on the ground. They watched speechless as he shook for a moment and became still.

Nick dropped the gun to his side.

"You knew all along it was him?" Jan asked quietly, stunned.

Nick didn't answer. He was still staring at Ed's lifeless form.

"Nick——" she pleaded.

"I knew he would come after you," Nick said. "I was trying to protect you."

She shook her head in disbelief. How could he have let a murderer go free? How could he have stood by while he killed other women? "How could you . . ."

He turned back toward her and said, "I tried to tell myself it wasn't him . . ."

The sound of a gunshot rang through the air. Nick's eyes opened wide as he fell into her arms. Ed had taken off his mask and was standing behind them, his gun still aimed at Nick as if he might shoot again.

Within a second she was running back up through the woods. A bullet grazed her shoulder but she didn't feel the pain. She heard Ed behind her, gaining on her. Just when she thought it was over she heard him moan and hit the ground. She glanced behind her just as he started to pick himself up. He was wounded, that was clear. Enough to slow him down and give her a head start.

As she ran she tried to untie the duck tape, catching an end with her teeth and tearing it. It was no use, she realized. And without the use of her hands she would be unable to stop him.

When she could see the roof line of her house she screamed, "Mrs. Fletcher!" She was still screaming as she stepped out of the woods.

But she wasn't fast enough. He grabbed her from behind, causing her to cry out in fear.

At that precise moment, they were bathed in a beam of light. She paused, caught off guard like an animal trapped in the headlights.

And they were headlights, she realized. Hers.

And then she heard it. The roar of a bullet as it blasted in her ear. She rolled down to the ground. *I'm dying*, she thought. *I'm . . .*

She couldn't feel anything. She lay there, very still, waiting to die. But something was wrong. She could move. She hadn't been shot. She was fine. Just fine.

She peeked up.

"No more, Eddie. No more." She heard.

Senator Thurman was perched over the lifeless form of his son.

"Jan?" he said, turning toward her and tucking the gun inside his pants.

"Senator," she whispered. She was confused and disoriented. Had he shot Ed? Had Ed shot himself? She tried to pick herself up, but she fell back down. "Nick—he's been shot."

He lifted her up and said, "Let's untie you."

"Ed," she whispered. "What happened?"

The senator shook his head. "Eddie lost control. Very bad indeed."

"He tried to kill me. . . ." Something in the way the senator was looking at her made her stop. He was not upset. Nor was he surprised. "Nick," she said, nodding behind her. "Nick needs help."

"We'll deal with Nick in a minute," he said. He took

off his leather gloves and bent his head a bit as he motioned for her to hold her wrists out so that he could remove the tape.

"Ed—Eddie," she said, glancing toward his lifeless form, "is he dead?"

"I had no choice, you see," the senator said, busy removing the tape. "I warned him over and over but he simply refused to listen. He lied and lied. Even Nick tried his best with him—"

"So," she said, feeling as if she might throw up. "You both—you knew what he did to my sister?"

"Yes, well, I'm sorry about that."

"You're *sorry* about that?" She wasn't hearing this. She couldn't be.

"Eddie had a problem. As I just said, it was a situation I had to deal with. But my hands were tied, so to speak. It would've broken Betty's heart, you see. She never knew about Eddie."

"But *you* did," she repeated quietly. "You and Nick both knew. Yet you did nothing while he killed Lucy Haverdale. Sarah Tomkins. My sister. . . ."

"No, Jan. Not your sister," the senator said. He finished unwrapping the tape and said, "There you go," as though she should be thanking him for the service.

"Yes, yes he did. . . ."

"Eddie didn't kill your sister," he repeated, his cold grey eyes staring at her intently as he slipped his gloves back on.

How dare he? How dare he stand there and tell her

that his son was not responsible—"She didn't commit suicide!"

"No," he said matter-of-factly, taking the gun out of his pants. "No, she didn't."

She stopped breathing as she recognized the gun. It was a Smith and Wesson, shiny and new, just like the gun she had left under the rock. The gun that was missing.

She heard him say, "I'm afraid I had to deal with your sister."

"That gun," Jan whispered. "Is it, is it mine?"

He nodded and said, "Your sister was making a scene." He held the gun out to her and continued. "She called me, screaming about how Custin wasn't the man who raped her. Begging me for help. My wife . . . she wouldn't have been able to handle it, you see—Eddie's mess. The public humiliation. It would've killed her."

His words broke through her fear. *The senator murdered Frannie. . . .*

"I was furious with Eddie," he continued, tired of waiting for her to take the gun. He put the gun in her hand and curled her fingers around it. "He's always been very irresponsible—Betty wouldn't admit it but he's never been quite right. In any case, I sent him to Europe, hoping that would help him grow up." He shook his head with disgust as he went over to Ed's body and pulled the gun out of his dead son's hand. "He promised to behave. I thought he had turned his life around." He paused for a moment as he opened the cartridge and checked the bullets. "You've met Sarana," he said, chatting as though they were at a cocktail party. "She's a lovely girl." He sighed as he clicked the cartridge back into place. "Yes, well, apparently, she wasn't quite lovely enough."

Jan's mind was working very quickly, assembling all the data as the facts tumbled into place. "Brown was working for you."

"More or less," he said.

"You had him kill Custin. You sent him here to kill me."

"I regretted everything. I really did. But I had no choice. I just wanted to make things right."

"I don't understand," Jan said as calmly as she could, her attention focused on his gloves as her fingers tightened around the trigger of her gun. Did she have any ammunition left? "You came here tonight to save me—right?"

He shook his head sadly as he nodded toward her gun. "I'm afraid I've already used all your bullets, Jan."

She swallowed as she took a step back.

"I'm aware of all the trouble you went to and I thought you deserved an explanation, that's all. Now I want this whole mess to go away," he said, taking another step toward her as he aimed Ed's gun. "I want to grieve for my wife in peace."

"I see," she said, stalling for time. She needed to make a move, to do something. "So you're going to make it look like Ed and I killed each other, right? Like I died in the struggle."

He said, "I'm sorry, Jan. I really am."

"Your wife is dead now, Senator," she said in a loud, clear voice. "You don't have to do this."

There was a loud blast, almost a roar, and the senator fell to the ground, moaning in pain as he grabbed his rear with both hands.

Mrs. Fletcher stepped out of the bushes, her large gun still trained on the senator. She was wearing a purple housecoat and several rollers were dangling from her fine grey hair.

She daintily stepped closer to the senator, all the while smiling proudly as if pleased with her work. Then she glanced at Jan and winked as she said, "Bull's-eye!"

55

FRANNIE, FRANNIE, FRANNIE . . .

Jan didn't even watch as the police carted the senator away.

"It's okay, Jan. Everything's going to be all right," Max said, taking her hand.

The nightmare was over. And Frannie, Lucy Haverdale, Sarah Tomkins, Eddie, and Nick were dead.

"You did it," he was saying proudly. "You got him."

"Nick was killed trying to help me—"

"Nick made his own choices," Max said. "He should've called the police a long time ago."

But he didn't. *I tried to tell myself it wasn't him . . .*

He knew who was responsible. He just loved the senator more than he loved anyone or anything else.

Max glanced at her arm and tenderly ran his finger around the red gash the bullet had made. "We need to get you to the hospital."

"Nick must have been watching my house, waiting for him."

Max nodded sympathetically. "They were all involved. Brown worked security for the senator when he was cop. When Ed raped your sister, the senator just used his connections and whisked his son out of town. I guess they thought since he was married now with kids he had changed his ways."

"Ed's eyes," Jan said remembering. "I know what Frannie felt now."

"You'll be okay," Max said, giving her a squeeze as he helped her to her feet. "I'm going to make sure of it."

Epilogue

October 26

JAN TURNED AROUND TO ADMIRE THE NEAT PILES OF LEAVES THAT were scattered around her yard. She had been raking since eight-thirty that morning. She was certain Mrs. Fletcher would be pleased. Jan's flower beds were neatly carved out and mulched and even the vines were under control . . . almost.

She had worked hard to get her place in shape before she returned to work at the state's attorney's office on Monday. She had an offer to return a couple months ago, but she had waited until she was sure she was ready. The office would be a completely different place than the one she had left only months earlier. Sheila and Dave were gone—they had moved to Chicago where they'd joined a prestigious corporate law firm. Jan had spoken with them yesterday and they both sounded happy and excited about their future. They planned to marry as soon as Sheila's divorce was final.

She was happy for them, but she knew that work wouldn't be the same without her friends. Without Nick.

She still dreamed about him occasionally. The senator had died of a heart attack less than a month after he killed Eddie and so had shed little light on the mysterious and deadly activities, but Nick had left a thick journal in which he detailed his confrontations with Eddie, including those that ended in fisticuffs. Much to her dismay, he also detailed his true feelings for her. Apparently Nick had never been physically attracted to her, much less interested in her romantically. But when the senator's offer of state's attorney failed to distract her from her quest to find her sister's true murderer, Nick had been forced to step in and offer himself as a distraction. Always the diplomat, he had been careful to emphasize that he did, however, *love* Jan and hoped their involvement would persuade Eddie to leave her alone.

The press had demonized Nick. He had betrayed them all, throwing them curve ball after curve ball in an attempt to steer them from the horrible truth. But even though Nick hadn't confessed the truth, he had died trying to save her and she couldn't hate him. She liked to believe that he had somehow underestimated the evil in Ed Thurman. After all, it *was* difficult to believe that someone who seemed so normal, so handsome, well-educated and from such a "good" and famous family could be capable of raping and murdering innocent women. The term sociopath had been bantered about in regard to Nick and the senator, but Ed brought new meaning to the word. He had led a murderous double life for years. Even his own wife claimed to have no knowledge of his deadly past. Edward Thurman had become one for the textbooks, a seemingly upstanding citizen who had cast a wide net of destruction, committing crimes across the ocean with the same ruthless abandon he had in the States. He was suspected of murdering at least a half dozen women in England alone.

"Hey," Max said, stepping behind her and wrapping his arms around her waist. He nodded toward the mulched flower bed and asked, "Is that where you want those bulbs?"

"Yes," she replied.

"What's the matter?" he asked, turning her around to face him. "You look so deep in thought. Remember what I told you. No thinking for at least a year."

She smiled and said, "You got it."

Max pulled her in to him. Secure in his arms, she looked down into the ravine through the half empty trees that framed a picturesque view of the cool water. She could see Max's boat in the distance, bobbing up and down at the mouth of the creek.

As the sun set on a hot, brutal summer, Jan felt a sense of calm she had never experienced before. She looked up at Max, knowing that he would like to take the boat out one last time before the cold weather set in. Maybe now that she had lost that impatient edge, she would even be able to tolerate a few hours at sea. She might even get to like it. With Max by her side, she was sure she would.

Without saying a word, she took Max's hand and led him down toward the water.

LINDA HOWARD

NOW YOU SEE HER

With the scintillating sensuality and high-voltage thrills that distinguish all of her blockbusters of romantic suspense, Linda Howard rips the imagination and touches the heart as only she can, in her sixth dazzling *New York Times* bestseller.

Now available from Pocket Books

**POCKET
BOOKS**

2094